OUR HANDS ARE PALE AS MILK

Our Hands Are Pale As Milk

A NOVEL

SARA KAY RUPNIK

Paperback ISBN: 9781947175747
Library of Congress Control Number: 2025946171

"Falling Leaves" cover art by Sara Kay Rupnik
Cover design by Jacob Arms

Produced in the United States
Published by Serving House Books
Lawrence Landing Company
Raleigh, North Carolina 27609

www.servinghousebooks.com

Serving House Books is a proud member of:

Independent Book Publishers Association
 and

Community of Literary Magazines and Presses

SERVING HOUSE BOOKS

For Nathan and Megan,

there from the start

O Sisters Three,
Come, come to me,
With hands as pale as milk.

  —William Shakespeare,

Midsummer Night's Dream

But no Man moved Me - till the Tide
Went past my simple Shoe -
And past my Apron - and my Belt
And past my Boddice - too –

And made as He would eat me up –

    —Emily Dickinson

Prologue

Our story ends in fire. The funeral pyre on the beach burns so brightly that the witnesses flee from its heat, from the blue-green embers flying heavenward, from the phosphorescence left floating in the sea. The fire is a spectacle, both glorious and nauseating, and we sisters were elsewhere, innocent and unaware.

Our story also begins with fire. We were very young then and ablaze with the idea of passion and romance and the story of a poet who eloped with a schoolgirl. Mary, Fanny and I longed to be carried away from our humdrum lives on Skinner Street and live happily ever after.

"Tell us again, Fanny, how The Poet rescued the beautiful Harriet from her boarding school." Mary lies alongside her mother's grave, staring up through the willows. Her eyes reflect the dreary sky.

Eager to speak, Fanny's pocked face brightens as she bolts upright from opposite the grave. "Certainly." Her hair flies across her face before it settles across her shoulders like a sturdy brown shawl. "The Poet and the fair damsel," she begins, "were in love."

Even though Mary and I know every word she will recite, we never tire of this tale. Fanny is the only sister to know The Poet and his bride, the only one to share meals and stories and laughter in their sparkling company, and while Fanny, The Tragic Sister, is not one to put on airs, she enjoys our attention. She savors the re-telling of experiences that Mary and I do not possess.

"The Poet is expelled from Oxford for his atheist ways," she begins, "and Harriet Westbrook is suffering abandonment at her miserable boarding school."

We listen, here under the willows where our faces take on a greenish cast, where Fanny's story seems more like a fairy tale than ever. Naturally two disenchanted souls would be drawn to one another. Naturally any mortal man would love a beautiful girl. "He leaves London in the dead of night and races into the darkness on a very fast horse." Fanny's eyes widen as her cadence picks up speed.

"What color was the horse?" I ask.

Distracted, Fanny stumbles to a halt. Mary twists on the ground to glare at me. "What does that matter, Jane?"

"A black horse would be invisible on a very dark night."

Fanny starts again. "He rides through the night on a fast, black horse until he comes to Harriet's deplorable school. He dismounts to hide in the hawthorn and toss pebbles at her window."

"How does he know which window is hers?"

Now Mary sits up. "Obviously Harriet told him. They wrote to each other every day."

"The pebbles rouse Harriet, and she appears there in the window above him. He thinks she is an angel looking down from heaven."

Oh, please. I slump against the willow's trunk.

"Then she scampers down the servants' stairway, out the scullery door, and into his arms." Fanny hugs herself. "They race over forested hills and along Scotland's shining lochs and stop only long enough to wed in Edinburgh."

"Would Harriet yet be wearing her dressing gown when they wed?"

"Jane!" Mary hisses. "You know Harriet would be properly dressed."

Of course she would. There is no impropriety in my sisters' minds. Neither Mary nor Fanny think past that moment when Harriet rides off into the night with her arms wrapped around a man who declares he will save her by keeping her for himself. I am more curious than my sisters. I imagine Mary, Fanny, and myself as the ones rescued by a man who desires us madly, and then I wonder. Once his horse halts and we all slide down onto damp English soil, what exactly would any man do to keep a fever burning in our fiery little hearts?

Part One: Jane

The Poet

We three sisters share the same bedroom, but very few confidences. Rather, here in our narrow room overlooking a vermin-filled alley, we are the high priestesses of complaint. We complain about our stilted lives above Father's bookshop on Skinner Street. We complain about Skinner Street and its dearth of culture. We complain about minding the bookshop, even as we secretly crave that duty over household chores. We complain about the favors Mother bestows on Young Will, the prized son and younger brother. We complain about the lavish schooling afforded to our older brother Charles. We complain about the fate of young women who are without means. Mostly we complain about Mother, the one who briskly assigns our duties while tending to The Favorite and fawning over Father. The poor besotted creature.

We sisters do not voice our innermost desires. Not until Fanny is sent away to Wales do Mary and I learn The Poet has broken her heart. Mary assigns blame for this phenomenon to me, the youngest sister. "How could this happen?" She speaks sternly. "I was traveling with the Baxters, while you were here with Fanny all Spring."

True, I tend to ignore Fanny and her fascination with birds and fossils and such. Yet had love bloomed in my presence, would I not have recognized such a wonder? Had our plain, serious sister caught the interest of The Poet and his wife, would I not have been rendered senseless myself? "I was in school," I defend myself to Mary, "and when I was home, Fanny talked unceasingly about *her dear friend Harriet*. Never The Poet. Maybe her kind, sensitive nature led her astray."

"Poor Fanny." Mary sighs. "Since she is gone for the summer, I will sleep her bed. I detest sharing your bed with all your nightly thrashing about."

"I will be lost without you beside me, Sister. My nighttime terrors, those dark woods and monstrous creatures with grasping hands, will overtake me."

"Don't be silly." Mary fluffs her pillow, snapping it up and down like an empty sack. "I will be an arm's length away."

I do not think of myself as silly, although I know better than to argue. Mary is The Sensible Sister and always has her way.

"Jane! Mary!" Mother's voice blasts up the stairwell like a cannon shot. "There are shelves to dust and books to sort and customers waiting. Time is fleeting."

"Yes, ma'am." We descend to the bookshop, me in my girlish, high-necked frock and Mary in her new Tartan plaid. Mary is also The Beautiful Sister. Free of Fanny's unfortunate pock marks or my mysteriously dark complexion, Mary's face could grace an ivory cameo or a portrait by John Opie.

Mary, Fanny, and I are nothing alike. Not one bit. We were three little girls thrown together by the marriage of our practical parents, and unless one counts *step*s and *half*s, we Godwin sisters are not sisters at all.

In the bookstore, Mother is fluttering over Mr. Owen, her best customer. No, fluttering is too dainty a word for Mary Jane Godwin. She is hovering, her tightly corseted bosom propped against the wooden countertop like a cushion along the back of the divan. "Excellent choice, my dear man. Our finest translation of Aesop."

"You have others?" Mr. Owen's head jerks up from his handful of coins.

Mother's smile tightens like a seam above her ruffle of chins. "None to equal this quality, sir."

"Truly?" Mr. Owen's bushy eyebrows knit together.

"Girls." Mother stands to attention and claps her plump hands. "Check the fable and folklore section. The shelf on the left, toward the window." As if we did not know.

"Not to bother, Mrs. Godwin. I shall return at a later time."

Of course he will. Mr. Owen is a fixture in Will Godwin's bookstore.

The bells on the door chime behind him, and my mother beckons to Mary. "I must go out, dear. I expect you and Jane to manage until I return." She arranges her purple silk shawl around her ample self and slips her arm through her market basket. "Mind the dusting," she says as she waves herself out the door.

Mary picks up her Poor Dead Mother's journal, perhaps the only thing in the entire Godwin household we are forbidden to read. I choose to ignore naughtiness rather than to confront Mary. Especially over her own true mother's words. It is far more pleasant to dust and sing. *Lavender's blue, dilly, dilly, lavender's green.* I straighten and re-arrange bookshelves and wish for those carefree days before our parents fancied themselves publishers and booksellers. Then, in our Somer's Town childhood, we sisters had tea parties in a garden of hollyhocks while my mother wormed her way into Will Godwin's heart.

There are no gardens on Skinner Street, no hope of finding hollyhocks. I miss flowers and green growing things. I might even miss Fanny. How could I have guessed she was mad for The Poet, that passionate young man who is also Father's patron? Fanny spoke of him no more fondly than she might speak of a dog she found in the alley. *He is quite lively. His manner is endearing. His coat needs tending.*

I swipe at dust, and when the bells on our door jangle, I edge closer to the entrance, hoping to smell distant blossoms or hear birdsong. There are only shouts of travelers coming and going from Saracen's Head. "Is Will Godwin in?" The customer's voice is strong and high-pitched and elusively familiar. He stands with his back to me, so while I cannot see his face, I notice his clothes are in disarray. As if he has slept in them.

"Mr. Godwin cannot be disturbed, sir." Mary says precisely what Mother has instructed us to say. Even when Father is out of the house, as he is now.

The rumpled young man with unruly brown hair rises to her challenge. "Tell him Percy Shelley is here to see him." He folds his arms and lounges against the countertop. "I shall wait."

Percy Shelley. This is the man, *The Poet,* who broke our sister's heart. He is here before us, and Mary and I are alone. I duck behind the shelf of nature books. *A man of constant motion,* Fanny said of him. *Lovely brown hair. Piercing blue eyes. Eyes that see into your soul.*

Hearing my breath or perhaps the beat of my heart, The Poet swings towards me like a compass needle. His piercing blue eyes are on me before I can give a thought to protecting my soul. Then his handsome face contorts into a smile. "Clarabella! Is that you?"

"No sir, it is not." I step out from behind the bookshelf. "I am Jane. Clairmont," I add, lest he thinks I am a true Godwin.

"Have you forgotten me so quickly, Clarabella?"

Mary eyes him suspiciously. "Her given name is Clara Jane Clairmont. Known to us as Jane."

"She is known to *me* as Clarabella." His voice is teasing. "Surely you remember our walks when you were studying French at Waltham Green?"

"I do, certainly." It is a half-truth. I do recall walking through the gardens with a friend of Father's. I found him so jittery I told Father never to send him again. That young man who frightened me about "unseen creatures" in the flower beds could not be The Poet. Could he? His voice, as high-pitched as a whistle, is quite similar.

"You are also Will Godwin's daughter?" he asks Mary. Observing her golden-haired unlikeness to me or our plain sister Fanny, he sounds doubtful.

"I am. The daughter of Will and Mary Wollstonecraft Godwin." She is smug, keen to claim her famous mother and distance herself from Mary Jane Godwin.

"Mary Wollstonecraft?" The Poet becomes ecstatic. "Your mother was legend for her beauty. I so admire her campaign for the rights of women. I grieve her loss." The perfect sentiment to charm Mary. I wonder if he spoke those same words to Fanny. If his praise of their poor dead mother landed our Fanny with a broken heart.

Although we sisters all pretend to be orphans now and then, Fanny comes the closest. With her Poor Dead Mother and her scoundrel American father, Fanny is The Tragic Sister, gentle and respectful and content to draw chickadees on brown parcel paper. I can imagine her stepping away from her chickadees to greet The Poet when he first came to call on Father. She would offer her able assistance in locating any book in the stacks, while he would notice her long brown hair, blue eyes, and fine figure. He would appreciate Fanny's sincere manner, and she would be captivated by his restless energy, his constant pacing and flapping. Rather like that of a bird.

Now The Poet must be a bit overcome, a bit faint perhaps, to discover Mary is The Beautiful Sister. He shifts his weight from one black boot to the other, and I am about to fetch the stepstool so he may sit down and collect himself when Mother returns. "Mary Jane!" He leaps to hold the door and assist with her overflowing market basket.

"Percy." My mother beams, her larger-than-life presence crowding him into the shelves. "How is dear Harriet?" she asks. "And little Ianthe? You must come to dinner now that the girls are home from school." She catches herself. "Well, aside from Fanny. You have met Jane and Mary?"

"I have." He nods, fixing his blue gaze on Mary as Mother prattles on about Father's writing progress and the dampish weather and the scarcity of customers. Never glancing up, Mary idly turns a page as Mother, her face flushed and moist, at last ceases her chatter and reaches for her fan. Percy loudly clears his throat. "What a fine day for a walk," he begins. "What a sin for these young ladies to be shut away from the fresh healthy air."

"There is no fresh healthy air to be had in Holborn, Percy." Mother unfurls a silken fan printed with Chinamen and waves it under her chins. "And rain is threatening."

"We will stroll only as far as Charterhouse Square, my dear lady."

"I suppose a bit of exercise is good for us all." Mother studies him over the top of her green-tinted glasses. Surely, she realizes The Poet's true interest is my sister, not fresh air. "Naturally Jane will accompany you and Mary."

"Certainly." His blue beam falls on me. "I am delighted for your company, Clarabella." Then, with a sweep of his arm, he ushers us into the late afternoon gloom. Come twilight, purple hues will soften every hard edge of this city, but now, as fate would have it, we are at the hour when the sun cuts through the clouds to give its final blessing. I am so happy to be set free into this golden light that I long to skip.

The Poet also appears to skip. Darting and luminous as a dragonfly, he skitters over the cobblestones and weaves us between throngs of workers and customers and shopkeepers going home for tea. As crowds thin, he offers a passionate discourse on the injustice to mankind, and Mary responds. Her face glows above her tartan plaid, and their voices rise and blend.

I fall behind to observe a red-speckled toadstool under the boxwood. Mary's voice rises clearer and less shrill than The Poet's. "Truly?" she says. "You believe that to be so? Why would I?" Then she laughs. A rare, beautiful sound.

How Fanny would love this toadstool. What a shame she is heartbroken in Wales while The Poet is now with Mary. Fate is cruel. I hurry to catch up to them, but already something has changed. I watch as their sleeves brush and their heads turn toward one another. Their mouths, constantly in motion, are a hand's-width apart. Something as subtle as a clock's tick, something soft and incandescent hangs in the air between them. Is this how love begins? Or how hearts are broken?

We sisters pretend we are orphans because we like the attention that follows such a declaration. We enjoy a tender word, a sympathetic cluck, an occasional sweet or two. Besides, it is easier than explaining our true relationship to one another. "So your mother was the Free Love woman?" a customer might say to Mary or Fanny. "And the three of you are sisters?"

"We were raised together," Mary responds.

"Our father married Jane's mother." Fanny prefers simple detail.

We tell each other that our mothers had exotic tastes in men. With the exception of Will Godwin, who is a bit of a stodgy philosopher. We call ourselves his daughters, because that, too, requires little explanation, although we find much is expected of us. Even as little girls, we were called upon to entertain his literary friends with recitations and songs. To gracefully enter the drawing room in our ruffled, flower-sprigged frocks, to curtsey and charm. The practical Mary Jane Godwin, who well understands our strengths and foibles, bolstered us up on those occasions. "Mary will recite a sonnet. Jane, you may sing, but only *one* verse, and Fanny, you may pass the tray of biscuits."

Now I puzzle over why my perceptive mother appears oblivious to the romance developing under her nose. Every day now The Poet appears in the bookstore to hang around and ogle Mary. She coolly ignores him, while Mother is flattering and effusive. "How is your writing, Percy? Are you making progress on your next collection?"

"My progress is very slow, Mary Jane." He is as disheveled as usual, and he carries a leather satchel over his shoulder. "My stomach is churning to bits."

"Oh, you poor man," Mother soothes. "You must be in a state now that the Shelley household is soon to expand."

Expand? I glance at Mary, who remains as still as a bookend, her head bowed over the store ledger. The Poet tugs nervously at his rumpled linen shirt. His large, blue eyes grow bluer and his shrill voice rises higher. "How are you keeping, Mary?"

"I am well." Her tone is icy.

"How about you, Clarabella, how are you this grand evening?" He turns his blue gaze on me, and I must look away.

"Quite well," I speak heartily to dispel Mary's moodiness.

"Shall we head into the evening?" Now his foot taps. His shoulders twitch. He throws back his head and dust motes sparkle around him.

"Enjoy yourselves," Mother calls. "Some evening you must bring your darling little wife and baby girl along, Percy," she adds in what might be a warning.

Unexpectedly the air is full of blossom scent and birdsong. Petals fall like snow, and when The Poet brushes a spring-green inchworm from my cheek, I fear I will burst into flames. "Fell from the chestnut." He points upward, and suddenly I want to take his hand and hold it fast to where the inchworm clung. Despite his high-pitched voice and his aching intensity over political causes and the peculiarities of his own digestive system, despite the fact that he is married, I worry that I, too, may be a bit in love with The Poet. Such a shocking notion.

At night, in our separate beds, I try to reason with Mary. "You are sixteen, and he is an older man with a young child and pregnant wife."

"That is Mary Jane's nonsense. He is but twenty-two, and he is leaving his wife to prove his devotion to me."

"Yet he remains married."

"Love does not require marriage. That was my mother's greatest belief."

"Your mother married Will."

Mary ignores that bland truth. "Percy loves me," she murmurs as she falls towards sleep. I remain wide awake, wishing for moonlight and worrying. The Poet has taken Fanny from me, and Mary may be next. Mary will leave me alone and I will fall prey to my nightmares.

Tonight, The Poet is less the dashing romantic hero and more the jittery lad I first knew. He frets over his health. He complains about the rights of women and independence for Ireland and the tedium of the British Parliament. "Nothing happens quickly in England," he declares. "Momentous events trickle in drop by drop until we are flooded and awaiting rescue boats." He glances over his shoulder as if looking for his *unseen creatures*. "We shall walk to the pond, where my paper boats, the calm water, and your pleasant company will ease my mind." He tips a vial of laudanum to his lips, a habit I find unsettling.

"To soothe his nerves." Mary reminds me. "To calm his stomach."

Carefully, we lift his delicate little boats from his satchel and arrange them along the grassy shore. Each one is crisply folded from newspaper or old school copybooks or, it appears, letters from his creditors. "How dear," we say of the boats. "How very cunning."

The Poet seems not to hear. "My mind is troubled because my father hates me, and there is naught I can do about it." He sets his first boat afloat without a hitch, and we cheer its launch. At the far side of the pond, small boys gather to welcome its approach. The Poet's eyes are fixed on the water. "My father sent me to suffer at Eton. He will never forgive me for being expelled from Oxford. My father *desires* me to fail."

His mood frightens me. I am tempted to grab Mary and retrace our route to Skinner Street before he knows we are gone, but she is as unruffled as the pond. The Poet sends out two more boats in quick succession. "My wife insists on spending my money, and my words have left me." His face darkens. "My poetry is suffering because of my family."

By *family* he means the beautiful Harriet, of course, and his father and grandfather. Sir Tim and Grandfather Abyss, he mockingly calls them. Perhaps he also despises his mother, who visits him behind Sir Tim's back. Like she is meeting a lover.

Mary bends down to brush a seed pod from his hair. "Your poetry will appear when your head is clear again, Percy. It will never leave you."

His final boat is less perfect than the others, a misshapen scrap of brown parcel paper, and we hold our breath as it wobbles and then capsizes. Oh, my. I long to wade in after it, but Mary holds me back.

"My fate must change course." He continues to hunker by the water, his arms braced against his knees. "I am drowning in debt. My landlord is taking me to court."

Like a mother to a child, Mary lays her small pale hand on The Poet's brown tousled head and murmurs soft assurances while my mind quakes with the image of The Poet being led away in shackles. "What will you do?" I call out to him.

"I have no idea. Secure yet another loan against my family's estate?" He rises to his feet. "Leave my little wife-y?"

"I believed you had left, Percy." Mary steps back from the water.

"Leave-taking is a delicate process." His hands rake through his hair. "A rather long, delicate process in my case."

"You said you left Harriet a fortnight ago."

"Perhaps that was before I was aware of her condition."

"She is expecting a child?"

"She is." He slumps, his fine linen shirt billowing in the sudden breeze across the water.

"Why should Mary Jane Godwin know this before me?" Mary's slender frame grows rigid as a lamppost. Dusk is gathering now. Shadows fall across their faces, and The Poet's shirt glows like a strange moon.

"Mary. I swear I never truly loved Harriet." His voice skips higher, and the little boys across the pond scatter for home. I watch each paper boat slowly fill with water and sink. "She never understood my belief in individual freedoms or my scorn for religion. Worst of all, she never appreciated my poetry, the blood and soul of my being. I saved her from Clapham School, but I never loved her. We were virgins," he adds, as if purity might win Mary's sympathy.

He rants on about Harriet's expensive tastes and her refusal to breastfeed their children and her insistence on reading novels aloud, all of which I find nonsensical. I recall Fanny's fond depiction of Harriet's wit and charm. "He is a madman," I whisper to Mary. "Poor Harriet. Poor little Ianthe and the babe yet to be born."

"Sssh. Say no more, Jane. You know nothing of love."

Mary's words sting like a slap because they are true. I understand nothing about how Fanny's heart was broken or why Mary desires the love of a married man. I stand in silence waiting for the paper boat captain to calm himself and return us to Skinner Street. I wait as the sun slides toward the horizon and our shadows grow long-limbed, and I wonder why in the world The Poet would leave the enchanting Harriet for a sharp-tongued girl like our Mary.

As if to prove how little I know about love, The Poet does indeed leave the lively Harriet and their little daughter, Ianthe. Worse yet, he moves to a flat in nearby Hatton Garden. He pops into the bookshop to see us throughout the day, and I note that leaving Harriet has not improved his disposition or his appearance. Unlike the dashing hero who rescued a damsel from her boarding school, this man is unkempt and raving. "Why must all the women in my life be unfaithful and demanding? And all the men I once counted as friends so unforgiving? How dare they insist I re-pay them when I have nothing?"

He scrambles among the book stacks like the unfortunate fly caught in our window's spider web. I cannot bear to watch either him or the fly, yet Mary remains serene, as if The Poet's troubles with women have naught to do with her. "Marriage is not without its trials, Percy," Mother counsels as she serves him tea and her poppy seed cakes. "You and dear Harriet will weather the storm."

"Some storms wreak too much havoc." He regards the poppy seeds with disgust and returns his cake to the tea tray. "I believe we are past saving, Mary Jane."

Playing the complete innocent, Mary saunters to the display window and repositions a vase of palm fronds without displacing the spider web. The Poet drains his cup and rattles it into his saucer. Again, I wonder why my mother does not notice Mary's long slow glances and The Poet's faltering speech.

Then again, perhaps she does. The Godwins are keen for The Poet's attention, and Mother is flattered to be his confidante. Tonight, we walk eastward until Mary and The Poet are silhouettes that merge together into one rippling shadow. Then the shadows split apart, and Mary stops. "I wish to take you to my mother's grave."

Oh, dear. The grave of Fanny and Mary's mother is sacred ground. "It is growing too dark for the cemetery," I say in alarm.

"We will be quick." She smiles as The Poet grows solemn and quiet, his full, perfect lips folding into a flat line as he takes her hand.

I unhappily trail along. When we come to the gravesite, we grow reverent. Mary kneels to dust her fingers over the stone. "Mother died at age thirty-eight when I was eleven days old."

"An unspeakable tragedy." He chokes a bit. "A great loss to our cause."

"She would have admired you."

"I treasure that knowledge, Mary. I will carry it in my heart."

Oh, for mercy's sake. Mary's claims to her mother's thoughts are fantastical. The poor dead woman has left next to nothing of herself behind. Aside from her grand portrait in Will's study and her books on touring the continent and women's rights. Oh, and her journal, of course. Her private journal, filled with fevered, heartrending entries about her love affair with Fanny's father. Tragic private confessions that were published by Will Godwin when he was down on his luck. When he was crazed by grief. Before The Poet became his patron. Before he married my mother, a woman who believes girls should use their Christian virtues to find themselves as good a man as she has.

I breathe in the cool green air and choke with nostalgia. As girls, we sisters gathered here under the willows. Here we read our books and made up stories featuring ourselves as celestial beings. Mary was the Moon. I was the Sun. Fanny was a distant Star. Here Fanny first told us the heroic tale of Harriet Westbrook's rescue from her ghastly boarding school.

"We will return here tomorrow," Mary says in her calm, holy voice. "Tomorrow I will pledge myself to you, Percy and offer you my sacred gift."

He has the sense to keep quiet then. No further mention of his money woes. Nor his rumbling stomach. No gentle teasing about what gift Mary has in mind. We both comprehend what she is offering to The Poet, and we are struck mute.

The Seduction

I start at her crown and gently, very gently, glide the tortoiseshell hairbrush through Mary's red-gold tresses. The hairbrush belonged to Fanny and Mary's Poor Dead Mother, and I am certain it croons a lullaby only those daughters can hear. "Firm, steady strokes, Jane. Take away all the knots and snarls." Mary raises her chin and her hair ripples down her back like a waterfall.

I brush until sparks fly and loose strands gather in the hairbrush like spun gold, and then I speak. "I cannot go with you tonight, Mary. Please do not ask."

"You must." Mary twists sharply, the hairbrush catches mid-stroke, and she yelps. I drop my hold and the brush clatters to the wooden floor, a thunderbolt that echoes down the stairs and into the bookstore, where Mother is tending to customers. "You promised." Mary holds one fair hand to her head and snatches my wrist with the other. "You gave your vow."

When angry, Mary's face flushes in a blotchy manner that is not at all becoming. What, I wonder, might The Poet think of his beloved now. I do not pull away from her anger. I stand my ground. "I promised to accompany you on evening strolls and jaunts in the park, not to witness your deflowering. You are barely sixteen, and he is a married man with a young child."

"He promises me his heart." She drops my hand to retrieve the hairbrush and presses it to her chest, perhaps in the vicinity of her heart.

"What if you lose your mind like Fanny and are also sent away?

What will I do here without you?"

"I am nothing like Fanny. Not one bit."

"You have the same mother."

"Fanny was the one to fall in love. Percy is not to blame for breaking her heart."

Not to blame. Of the three of us, Fanny is the least fanciful. She is neither theatrical nor easily bored, and she would not fall idly in love for the sake of something to do. Our Fanny was seduced by the words of The Poet. She was so caught up in his passion for nature and mankind that she had to be sent away to recover her wits.

"Fanny is guileless. Tonight is my destiny."

Oh, for the love of God. I have heard more than enough about Mary's destiny, about the comet that heralded her birth and blessed her with brilliance just as it foretold her mother's death. Who knows such things? "In that case," I say, "perhaps I am not *destined* to participate in this bold deed, this *gift,* you plan to offer at your mother's grave. The very thought of your sacrifice makes me queasy."

Mary softens at once, twirling behind me to brush my own hair with the Poor Dead Mother's hairbrush. She whispers apologies. "Oh, please, Jane, you must," she begs as my hair catches and tears. I imagine my tar black strands clinging to the bristles and blending with Mary's gold and Fanny's brown and perhaps even the dead mother's red, but I hear no lullabies from the hairbrush. Even when Mary promises me her newest writing paper and best pen nib if I will be co-conspirator in the seduction of The Poet, I grow sick and anxious. While she selects her least worn undergarments, I lie on my bed with my hands pressed to my stomach.

"Whatever is wrong with you, Jane?" My mother fills our doorway.

"She has a headache." Mary answers for me.

Mother comes into our bedroom and presses her palm to my forehead. Her fingers are cool and soothing against the heat of my face, and I want us all to stay as we are, frozen in place for an eternity or two.

"We are to walk with Percy," Mary says. "The fresh air will cure her."

"Kindly do not go if she has flashing in her eyes, Mary, and do not stay out long." Mother's comforting hand abandons me. "Will and I are dining at Mr. Owen's this evening."

Then she is gone, and Mary is happily humming to herself.

Long before Fanny fell under The Poet's spell, Father read Percy Shelley's letters to us during teatime. We Sisters were too hungry to listen to The Poet's political tirades, even when Father proclaimed him a prized correspondent from a wealthy family. Then The Poet became Father's sponsor. Perhaps The Poet's money will help sustain us, we thought then. Perhaps our meager teas will become more lavish.

Then Father read The Poet's proclamations of free love. We stilled our chewing and looked up from our plates. We allowed The Poet's words to soak through us. Caught in our neighborhood of booksellers and butchers, here where ruffling pages and dying animals are commonplace sounds, we three young girls sought escape. Hopefully in the arms of a handsome suitor. Ah yes, we nodded as we passed the quince jam, this is the romantic poet who writes words of love. The hero who rescued a damsel named Harriet.

"Percy is a man of great depth." Mary echoes Father as we wait for The Poet to appear. "A man given to protecting the poor and downtrodden."

As we are only marginally *poor and downtrodden*, I say nothing in reply, and when The Poet, late and disheveled as usual, arrives for his evening of Destiny, I remain in the periphery of the bookshelves. My black hair and eyes and less-than-ivory skin, apparently inherited from my true mysterious father, allow me to blend into the shadows. *The dark one,* Will Godwin's friends say of me. *The foreign-looking one. The gypsy child,* perhaps they add.

The Poet sees me all the same. "How about you, my Clarabella? How are you this grand evening?"

Although I am mere months younger than Mary, to him I am a child, the youngest sister who will not betray their romance. What a worrisome burden. Mary glares and flounces, and I wonder why, of all evenings, The Poet is paying me any mind. Perhaps he, too, is nervous. Perhaps he is sick at heart to have foolishly encouraged another of Will Godwin's daughters to fall in love with him. Or is he having second thoughts about Mary and her capricious moods?

No, of course not. Soon we are on the street, heading for Destiny. The Poet pirouettes, walking backwards so he can face Mary. "You are lovely," he tells her again and again. "You are a vision to behold." Though he can be charming with his pleasant chatter and his brotherly encouragement – *Your voice is delightful, Clarabella. You must sing for me again.* – there is something frightful in his searing blue stare and high-pitched intensity, in his preoccupation with his health and his feverish dislike for Harriet, his child bride.

St. Pancras Cemetery is a perfect setting for the sacrificial mood of the evening. Mary appears to float through the churchyard gates, her hair hanging to her shoulders as a golden scarf and her face beatific. Like Saint Joan going to the stake. Or St. Pancras himself, who was beheaded at fourteen for professing his love of Christ.

I trail along behind them, but as we near the willows, I find The Poet at my side. "Come, my dear," he says, drawing me toward him. His hand is warm on my elbow as he guides me between rows of headstones. "I thank you for coming tonight, for chaperoning Mary. You are a good sister to her, and I hope you will be a good friend to me." He stops suddenly before a narrow stone bench, all but hidden under an elm. "Clarabella, my darling girl, I ask that you await us here." His eyes flash in the fading light. "For the sake of your sister's modesty."

I turn my head, searching for familiar markers in the fading light. There are none. Here, so close to the gates, I could fall prey to every passer-by in the neighborhood and no one would hear my cries. My heart falls. "No," I tell him. "I am not Clarabella. I am not your *darling girl*, and I refuse to remain here."

His blue, blue gaze locks on mine. I have his attention. I have distracted him from Mary, and I feel faint. His fingers brush my cheek. His palm cups my chin. "I will be here with you in spirit, Jane, and you will be with Mary and me. You are safe in our hearts. I promise you."

I quiver at his touch, and I must clench my jaw to keep from weeping. "I do not want to lose my sister."

His fierce determination melts away. His face softens in sympathy. "Oh, Jane. You understand, do you not, that Mary and you and I are part of a grand design? A wondrous love." Then he kisses me, his lips muting me into silence and obedience. "You are a part of us."

He disappears in the direction of the willows, and I am left here in the stunned silence of the dead to watch the sky darken from pale grey to slate. What has happened? I retrace the burning route of his fingers over my cheek and chin and lips. I recall the sizzle of his words next to my ear and the heat of his kiss, and I am less afraid. With darkness comes the glow of fireflies and the chirp of crickets and the lamplighter on the far side of the cemetery walls. The June bugs bump against the streetlamp's globe with their slow, heavy bodies. How they must envy a firefly's grace and brightness.

I imagine The Poet as a firefly flitting over Mary's body, turning her pale, slug-like skin to a wondrous sheen, bringing roses to her face, and songs to her mouth. I imagine his poetry filling my sister to the brim, and I wait for the spiritual sensation of him to come to me as well.

Nothing happens.

I remain a June bug, dull and clumsy and as abandoned as Fanny in her exile. Slipping from my assigned bench, I walk among the gravestones. Over to the stone wall hung with ivy and back to my shadowy perch under the elm. I refuse to glance toward the willows. Any moment Mary and her Poet will emerge, and yet nothing about them will be the same. The notion of them as changed beings recalls The Poet's *unseen creatures* and frightens me anew. What if The Poet and Mary never return from that exulted land where love has taken them, and I am left to spend the rest of my life bumbling about Skinner Street with my aloof stepfather and meddlesome mother?

Such a life is unimaginable. I am not as beautiful as Mary, nor as tenderhearted as Fanny, but I have spirit aplenty. Here with these departed souls as my witnesses, I vow to cast my June bug carapace into the sweet summer grass. I, too, can become a firefly, flitting unseen through the darkness and glowing whenever and wherever I please. I refuse to be left behind. Then, exhausted by the thought, I sink back on the stone bench to wait.

It is quite dark when The Poet wakes me by singing some made-up song that is too childish to appreciate. "Clara, Clar-a-bella, how is my sister keeping?" The hard bench and the dampness make me stiff and irritable. I creep out from under the elm, and The Poet takes my arm. "It is late, Jane," he says. "Your parents will be waiting."

"They are out to dinner." I stretch. "Where is my sister?" I look past him as a vision, glowing and ghostlike, glides through the darkness. "Mary," I call.

"Shhh." Her face is a glimmering oval. "We must hurry." Her voice is unchanged, and neither is her manner. Perhaps there has been no sacrifice under the willows. But then, when we turn into the alley, The

Poet fiercely grabs hold of her, pressing her spine against the rear wall of the bookstore and murmuring frantically with his head buried in her hair.

"Do not leave me, Mary. Come home with me."

Her voice is muffled. "Not now. Not tonight."

It is like watching a play. Mary slips out from underneath The Poet and leaves him slumped against the wall. "Goodnight, love," she calls as I open the door and draw her inside.

"How do you fare?" I whisper as we tiptoe up the stairs. "Are you well?"

"More than you can imagine."

I cannot comprehend that remark completely, yet it is obvious Mary thinks I am a young, simple girl who will never know what it is to love a man, especially a poet like Percy Bysshe Shelley. I intend to prove her wrong.

3. Lovelorn

I breathe easier when The Poet's feverish presence is not hovering over all of us, but I miss Mary. Since our night in the graveyard, my sister has drawn into herself like a creature living under the sod. She may as well be with Fanny in Wales for all the more she says to me. Today she busies herself with letter-writing, while I lazily dust shelves. Although I am morbidly curious about the precise way men and women come together, I dare not ask what happened in St. Pancras graveyard. I can no longer evoke the wild stirring brought about by The Poet's kiss. That tender man in the cemetery has become a strange and distant being.

My fleeting desire for romance is gone.

I glide my feather duster over *Aesop's Fables* and the Lambs' *Tales of Shakespeare,* and listen to Mr. Owen, who is presently obsessed with brown bats. "Uncannily smart creatures," he claims. "I expect we could learn a lot from them." Mary writes a receipt for his purchase, *The Natural History of Selborne*, and I retreat to the storeroom to tend to Mother's potted pelargonium.

I sing as I fill the watering can. *'Tis Norah, dear Norah, the theme of my song.* Then I turn and find myself face-to-face with Mary. My sister has sought me out!

"Percy is dealing with creditors today." Her voice crackles with worry. "It is a great hardship for him to pay rent for his new flat *and* the house where Harriet lives."

I consider that The Poet's idea of hardship might be difficult for the average man to grasp. "Perhaps we will see him tomorrow."

"I fear it will be longer, Jane. He has gone to Harriet to seek money, and she will keep him away from me for days."

And so it is. When The Poet walks into the bookshop three anxious days later, he is so out-of-character it takes us a moment to place this young father carrying his little daughter. Instead we notice how the child's sweet fingers twine through a lock of his hair, and we think *Mother Goose.* Then we notice the pretty blonde woman. Her heart-shaped face contrasts with her tense manner, her raised chin, and guarded eyes. The strain between her and the father pulls as taut as a rope. This is Harriet.

Mary and I stand like spectators at a fencing match as I recall Fanny's words. *Harriet is kind and beautiful and ever-so-pleasant company when we dine together,* she enthused. *Yet when I said she was a fine lady, Percy said no, not at all, they were ordinary folks. She has a splendid purple frock,* Fanny added, *and she is completely charming when she mocks Percy, mimicking his speech and gestures until my sides are bursting with laughter.*

There is no laughter now. The Poet speaks, his voice rising like the wind. "Harriet, this is Jane Clairmont." His blue eyes sweep from me to Mary. "And this is Mary Wollstonecraft Godwin." I envy how her name sounds like poetry when it comes from his mouth. "You are driving me mad with desire," he says to my sister, "and Harriet is driving me to self-destruction. Kindly speak to her of our future, Mary."

Exactly in that manner, The Poet drops his muddled life at Mary's feet, and she is more than happy to pick it up and smooth it out. "I shall, Percy. Certainly." Mary appears composed, as she always does when she wears black, and her tone is that of a mortuary worker, the one hired to sell coffins to the bereaved. "I am pleased to make your acquaintance, Harriet."

"Percy insisted upon it." Harriet's shoulders rise and straighten under her pale blue frock. She is readying to stand her ground and raise her sword.

"I love Percy," Mary says quietly, "and we desire to be together."

"Quite impossible." At her mother's firm tone, the little girl tucks her blonde head under her father's chin. A chin in need of shaving, I notice. Unless, perhaps, The Poet is growing the beard as a symbol of his misery. "I do not believe in divorce, and I choose to remain his wife."

"We could live together, you understand. You and little Ianthe and Percy and I could live as one family in Percy's Communal of Love."

Mary speaks earnestly, as if this place of Percy's imaginings truly exists and she is happily packing her bags to journey there.

"I dare say you are naïve, Miss Godwin. Too naïve to understand the misery of your husband wanting to share you. You have no idea." Harriet stamps her dainty foot. "See how you like Percy's grand scheme of free love when his friend Hogg comes to live with you. Even as newlyweds, we shared our flat with that man."

So, The Poet's rambling talk of free love is more than political rhetoric, more than fodder for Will Godwin's teatime letters, more than poetic musings? He seriously believes he can love more than one woman, and those women can love more than one man and they will all live together in harmony? And Mary believes it, too? What rubbish.

"Percy's friends are most welcome. We will form a community," Mary repeats, "not a marriage."

"Precisely." Harriet gives one quick nod. "You shall have no marriage as Percy is married to me until death do us part."

I rather admire Harriet's quick, graceful turn and her regal procession out the door. The Poet follows meekly behind. Yes, instead of that wild, charming lad strutting towards us, we now watch a father retreating with his little daughter and pregnant wife. Oh, poor Mary.

The beds in Father's house are as hard as the floor, and to seek a moment of solitude away from my sisters, I often crawl under mine. With Fanny sent away and Mary all but mute, I now have more solitude than not, but out of habit I lie here on the bare wooden floor and stare up at the ticking of the horsehair mattress. My mind holds a jumble of thoughts. I understand The Poet's power. I recall how his words fell down on me like mist from the stars and how every bit of me responded in a sick-sweet rapture. I was in ecstasy as I waited for The Poet in St. Pancras. Then I was in misery. Why would Mary and Fanny or myself claim misery as an acceptable state in exchange for a few secret moments of passion? And why would we ever consider sharing him? I blow an errant goose feather away from my face. Why is love beyond our control?

"Jane." Mary's voice rises out of the stairwell. "Come mind the shop. I must unpack Father's delivery."

I slither out from under the bed, shaking my skirts free of dust as I descend to the bookstore. Mother is at the printer's, and Father is in his study, attempting to write a novel. Our brothers Charles and Young Will are spending their summers in the country, but in separate households of friends and relations.

While Mary unpacks cartons in the workroom, I carry on a one-sided discussion with Mr. Owen. "The Amazon River has thousands of species of fish. Did you know that, Jane? And it is home to the largest snake in the world. The anaconda is so enormous it can eat a goat."

I am amused by how quickly Mr. Owen switches his reading topics. From bats to snakes in less than a week. Such an odd little man. The bells on the shop door announce a visitor, and when I raise my eyes, there is The Poet. He is clean-shaven, and his hair is flattened into waves rather than stirred into a maelstrom. I brace myself. *Please, no outbursts on my watch. Please, dear God, allow Mary to remain in the workroom.*

His eyes flash blue, but he remains subdued. "I seek a word with Will, Jane. Is he in?"

"He is. I shall fetch him." I worry about leaving The Poet unattended, and then I consider Mr. Owen. "Tell us, Percy," I ask, "what do you know of the Amazon?"

"The river or the jungle? Both are quite impressive, I believe." He wrinkles his brow, searching his knowledge, and Mr. Own takes over from there.

"It is, by far, the grandest river in the world," he begins.

I move quickly up the stairs to Father's study and knock gently, bracing myself for his door to swing open and reveal the commanding portrait of Mary and Fanny's Poor Dead Mother. The woman in that portrait frightens me. Her beauty reveals none of her bad luck in choosing thoughtless lovers, yet she strikes me as inconsolable. Lamenting the fact she married the sedate Will Godwin, perhaps, or that she finds herself dead and replaced by Mary Jane. I am certain the woman in the portrait watches me, and I avoid dusting Father's study. Not that he minds in the slightest. Father detests being disturbed from his own deep thoughts.

Conscious of The Poet waiting, I knock louder and hum "Greensleeves" to assure Father it is me, cheerful Jane, rather than moody Mary.

"Silence!" He growls like a dog. "I require complete and utter silence."

"Percy Shelley has come to call, Father."

"One moment." Now more grumble, less growl.

Once again, I find myself wishing for Fanny. While I have little interest in Fanny's tiresome preoccupations with rocks and such, she is calm and honest, a useful person to have around. Mother claims Fanny and The Poet exchanged letters before she was sent away and that his poetic words turned her head. Which is understandable. Naturally Fanny would hang on The Poet's every word, and he would lend a sympathetic ear. Likely she confessed to missing her Poor Dead Mother, the wise, beautiful woman they both admired. Likely she complained about my own headstrong, boisterous mother. She would welcome freedom from the Godwin household, Fanny likely told The Poet.

Yes, our Fanny is guileless and eager to please. I imagine that while The Poet spoke to Fanny of free love communes, she was showing him her treasures: a nuthatch nest or a seashell or the fossils sent by her old maiden aunts. Our dear Fanny would have taken The Poet's every kind word straight into her heart.

I listen to Father tap his pen nib against the ink well and worry over Mr. Owen immersing The Poet in the Amazon River. Then another thought comes to mind. Not only would Fanny have taken The Poet's pipedream of a love commune to heart, she would have asked Father's permission go along. And Will Godwin would have called her *foolish*. He, too, has broken his daughter's heart.

The study door swings open to reveal a rather agreeable countenance. Father swipes at his ruddy cheeks and balding head. He smooths his sideburns into place. "Yes, yes, daughter, I am sorted and eager." Likely he calls me *daughter* because my name slips his mind. He pats my shoulder with his ink-stained fingers. "Let us not keep Shelley waiting." From over his shoulder, the beautiful dead wife stares down at me. I turn away at once.

Father joins the men's discussion of jungle animals, and I retreat to the workroom to assist Mary. I dare not mention The Poet, and I dare not ask about Harriet, and so I say nothing. Mary's hands, so pale and pretty, gently unwrap brown paper, and her bright head tilts in anticipation of each new book title. She is most beautiful when she is pensive, I decide, while Harriet's beauty burst forth with every stamp of her foot, every rise of her voice. In contrast, any beauty I possess is more like a raindrop or a snowflake, briefly lustrous and then gone.

An outburst in the shop pulls us from our reveries, and we regard one other in surprise. "The rowdy boys," Mary says, "are loitering again. Father shall dismiss them."

"Unacceptable." Father roars from beyond the workroom. "Beyond the law of human decency."

I return an unwrapped book to the crate and edge closer to the door.

"Are you telling me you have been with my daughter, sir?"

Oh, dear. The ruckus has nothing to do with the rowdy boys.

"I love her." The Poet is loud and hoarse.

"Oh, for God's sake, you have a family. Do not speak to me of love. This is seduction and depravity and abusing the trust of my family."

"We are destined to be together." His voice is heart-piercing, and when Mary flies through the door to join him, I follow on her heels.

The men resemble pieces on a chessboard. Father, a rook with red face and labored breathing, stands facing the ashen and defiant knight. Mary, always the queen, at once aligns herself beside him, while I am the pawn standing to one side and waiting to be moved. Mr. Owen has fled.

"I wish to be with him, Father."

"That is absurd. Percy has an obligation to his family and if you continue this infatuation with him, you are as much to blame for their unfortunate state as he is. Do you hear me, Mary?" Then Father turns to me. "Go upstairs, Jane. Take your sister with you."

"Mary, my love," The Poet keens. "Do not desert me."

Mary's golden head bows like a daffodil in the rain. She is caught in a web. Caught between Will Godwin, her true father, and Percy Bysshe Shelley, her true love. When I take hold of her hand, she does not resist.

"Mary, I beg you." The Poet calls.

Breathless with envy, I drag Mary away. Oh, to have both a father and a sweetheart to love me so fiercely. No wonder poor Fanny is beside herself.

We roil into the heart of summer when the oppressive air is broken by torrential storms. Winds gust over the cobblestones and set papers and twine and leaves twirling. Rain pelts the shop window, and Mother scrambles to move her display of botany and bird books from the leaky casement. The spider's web, I notice, is gone.

"How perfect," Mary says of the weather. "If only we had lightning to match my jagged heart."

Oh, mercy. If melodrama could kill us, we would all be dead. After the confrontation in the bookstore, Mary is forbidden to venture into the shop or outside the walls. In protest, she shuns us all by moving upstairs to the schoolroom. Mother is left to offer comfort and ease. "Not to worry, dear husband, she shall return when the heat rises to boiling in those upper quarters."

Tucked away in Wales, our Fanny is completely unprepared for the ongoing saga on Skinner Street. "Percy loves *Mary*?" she asks in a flurry of letters. Her disbelief is audible, traveling the distance from her bucolic sanctuary to our grey clamoring city. "But what of Harriet? She and Percy are perfectly suited."

Fanny mails pages about her time spent with Harriet and Percy and how attentive they were to her. How she and Harriet laughed together for hours. Obviously, the woman Mary and I met is not the same gleeful girl Fanny knew, and I ponder how one person can be so many. The lad I met at Waltham Green is nothing like the passionate man in St. Pancras graveyard, nor the one in the bookstore with Harriet and little Ianthe. I doubt Fanny would know this man at all.

Percy praised her for running Father's bookstore, Fanny writes, and he begged her to come live with him and Harriet. *I was first, Jane. I was part of his plan long before Mary.*

I consider Fanny's distress at being replaced by a younger sister and how that applies to me, the youngest of the sisters. Not that The Poet is a desirable suitor. No indeed. Madmen hold no attraction for me, especially now that our family is in tatters. Father is furious and threatening to dissolve his relationship with The Poet. Mother is furious and bemoaning the fate of Harriet and her poor, unborn child. I am furious and complaining about my increased work load while Mary plays the lovesick recluse, shut off from the world like a nun in a cloister. Fanny is furious to be exiled to the countryside.

Then Father pays a series of calls to salvage the good Godwin name. The Poet apologizes for taking liberties with his daughter, and Mother forces Mary to write a formal apology to Harriet. "Percy was an unfortunate choice for you, Mary," she admonishes. "You could have completely jeopardized your father's business arrangement."

By which she means The Poet's continuing financial support. We all breathe easier.

As for The Poet, he may be apologetic, but he is not contrite. He does not run home to Harriet, but hovers around the bookstore as if his mere presence will wear Father down. "My love for Mary is written in the stars," he declares again and again. "We belong together for all of time." Ah yes, Destiny once again. Before he drags his forlorn self to his flat in Hatton Garden, The Poet hands me a book with a letter for Mary hidden inside. I am now go-between for star-crossed lovers.

"Was he here?" Mary flies down upon me when she hears my footsteps on the stairs. "You gave him my message?"

"I did." I am prepared to answer Mary's questions about The Poet. I memorize how he looks and what he says, yet Mary wrenches the book from me and soars upward to her roost without another query. All she desires to know is there in Percy's own hand, and my starring role is reduced to one of stand-in.

In fact, The Poet looks quite awful. He spends his days writing lovelorn poems, shoving them into empty laudanum bottles, and hurling them into the Fleet River. He is unshaven and unwashed and in need of more mothering than even Mother can offer. "You must collect yourself, Percy," she tells him. "You must do the proper thing and return to your family. Taking on lovers, especially one as young and as clever as Mary, will be your undoing."

"I cannot live without her. I cannot go on."

"You can, and you shall. The spirit is stronger than you know."

I do not doubt my mother's strength of spirit, yet it is easy to believe The Poet is dying from love. The romantic suffering of Percy Bysshe Shelley enthralls me. For true love, one must suffer. Oh, if only Mother had kept her hold on my true father, said to be Swiss, my true brother Charles and I could be rowing on glassy lakes and hiking verdant mountains, breathing the pure bright air unknown to Skinner Street and its stench of leather tanning and carpet making. As it is, the air beyond the magnificent, curved display window at 41 Skinner makes us retch.

"Blood," The Poet observes with a sensitive sniff. "It smells like blood."

For the son of a nobleman to be living in our Holborn neighborhood of shopkeepers, laborers, petty criminals, and liberals feeds my ideal of romantic devotion. I, too, crave a love who will twist in agony from desiring me. Though tempted to read the messages hidden in books sent to Mary, I do not. Although I notice his dedication of *Queen Mab* to Harriet is crossed out and re-dedicated to Mary. Sometimes, my thankless sister opens one of the books of old verse or Welsh folk songs and allows me to read ballads about people dying from broken hearts. Mostly she rips open his letters and closes the door in my face. *Bang.*

I imagine those letters contain the most wondrous words ever written, and that too makes me envious. I grow so envious that when The Poet fails to come into the shop with his usual message for Mary, I am somewhat pleased. *He is finished with Mary,* I tell myself. *He has returned to his true wife Harriet.* I fantasize a bit about such a homecoming. I imagine tears and passionate embraces as I pretend to listen to Mr. Owen's re-telling of "The Fox and the Grapes."

At last, Fanny will return home, and we will once again become our ordinary girlhood selves with lessons in singing and drawing and Italian. We will once again entertain at gatherings. Mary will recite and I will sing and Fanny will serve tea. All will be as it was before Percy Bysshe Shelley.

The bells on the door clang rather than chime, and Mr. Owen abruptly sidesteps as a gentleman in his shirtsleeves, lunges toward the counter. "Send Godwin at once. His friend Shelley needs assistance." Then he shouts. "Now, miss. Run and fetch him, for the love of God."

It turns into a long grim day for all of us. Mother quietly creeps about the kitchen to make endless cups of tea and broth. Mary remains in the shop because it is closest to the street and any news that might arrive. "I am to blame." Her voice clogs with remorse. "If we were together, Percy would not be suffering."

At last Father returns, and our hearts catch in their throats. Sternly shaking his oversized head, he flips the placard in the window to *Closed* and gathers us around the dining table. Here in this dark room made darker by the mahogany sideboard and heavy crimson drapes, I feel very alone. Even as I light the lamp, I sense an imbalance, a loss. My brother Charles should be here now. As should Young Will and Fanny. Most especially Fanny.

"Percy will recover," Father begins, and then immediately raises his voice above our thankful murmurings. "When his landlord found him, he was unconscious. An empty vial of laudanum was at his side." He pounds the table with his fist as he looks from Mary, who is on the verge of collapse, to me. "If you girls knew his intentions, you should have come to us at once."

"We knew nothing," I say with indignation. "Percy always carries a vial of laudanum. Surely it was an accident."

"Your own dear mother also became distraught when Fanny's father left her," Father tells Mary. "She, too, made an attempt on her life by jumping from Putney Bridge. I understand your anguish, daughter, and here is my wish for you. Do not give Percy false hope. Be of strong heart and return Percy to his family. Be of courage and grant us all peace."

Clutching her handkerchief, Mary rises to her feet without a word and wafts away, leaving me alone with the parents.

"As for you, Jane." Mother shakes her finger. "You are not to involve yourself in this predicament."

"If Percy has no encouragement to stay, he will give up this foolishness." Father speaks firmly. "If he comes into the shop, you are to fetch me or your mother, not Mary. You are to ignore his presence."

"You do understand," Mother adds, "releasing Percy will be a blessing?"

No, not precisely. The notion of relinquishing someone you love is beyond my comprehension. If I were the one to love The Poet as Mary does, I would completely ignore such advice. Especially since he is a married man and not Mary's to give away in the first place. No, if I were Mary, I would hold on and give love some time. I would risk a broken heart rather than to have no love at all.

But I am not Mary. I return to the room we shared before Mary vacated it for higher ground. Here in our girlhood bedroom with its painted bedsteads, smooth white coverlets, and pillow slips embroidered with forget-me-nots, I admire my sister's neatness, her fondness for keeping order. How like Mary, even in a fit of despair, to make her bed and tidy her books and papers before she moved upstairs to escape us.

A new awareness hits with the force of a slammed book. Unlike me or Fanny, Mary is not impulsive, not easily influenced, not childish in the least. For wise, sensible Mary, love is not a whim likely to fly out of her mind with the change of her frock or a turn in the weather. Mary truly loves Percy Bysshe Shelley, and he is lost without her.

How very shocking to discover that *happiness* and *love* are not synonymous after all. Love stitches people together and creates misery when all they want is resolve. I am dismayed by the hopelessness of it all.

4. The Runaways

I wait, here in the shade of a chestnut tree outside The Poet's flat. When at last I see him approach, I am shaken by his appearance. Head bent and hands in his pockets, he is thin and agitated. His head bounces with each footfall, and when he catches sight of me, he stops still, jerking back like he has been shot through the heart. He raises his arms, his white sleeves flapping like gull wings as flies towards me. His embrace catches me up, swinging me off my feet like a child.

"Thank you for coming, my dear Clarabella."

"You are most welcome." Back on my feet, my head spins. It takes me a moment to bring his gaunt face into focus. "You are well?"

"Shipshape. How is my beloved Mary?"

"She awaits you."

"Splendid." His eyes burn blue as ever. "We insist you accompany us on our journey. We refuse to leave you, to abandon you to Skinner Street."

"Truly?"

"*Absolument*, as Mary Jane would say." He laughs to quote my mother and then describes all there is to see in the world. My heart thumps at the prospect of mountains, waterfalls, olive groves, and fields of sunflowers. Rapturously, he speaks of France and Italy, of Switzerland, the native land of my supposed father, and I am wild to go along. My teeth ache with yearning, and yet I am fearful. The Poet and his extremely sensitive nature worry me. I fear going with him. I fear *not* going with him. I fear remaining here without Mary. I fear leaving Fanny, who is expected home in a fortnight.

"You will be with Mary and me," he persists. "We will be our own family."

Like his kiss in the graveyard, his words make me weak, make me want to say *Why bother with Mary at all?* Yet I know better. "What does Mary say about me coming along?"

He takes my hand, and I allow his blue gaze to pull me in. "Mary will be delighted. You are sisters after all. You belong together. You belong with me."

Which tells me Mary knows nothing of his plan. I am tempted to elaborate on how Mary and I share no blood. Not one drop. Yet since I am tempted by his version of sisterhood, I say nothing.

He kisses my cheek and releases me. "See you in the morrow, Jane."

"You are coming with us?" Mary is cross and suspicious, hardly the happy, generous sister The Poet imagines her to be.

"He insists I should accompany you."

"Percy is generous to a fault." She glances up from the worktable where she is making lists on scraps of Father's paper. Lists of what to take and what to leave. Lists of places she wants to see and places she wants to avoid. Perhaps lists of why I should stay right here on Skinner Street. "Did he say why we should trouble ourselves with you?"

"He said the more, the merrier." I do not have the nerve to tell her that he imagines me as part of his family. Living with Harriet the wife in a love commune is something Mary might consider as Harriet was first in The Poet's heart. Living under the same roof with her lover and her younger sister is unthinkable.

"You understand you must not allow our parents to suspect a thing. We must carry on as usual." Mary is so brittle from worry, I fear she might snap in half. She has returned to our bedroom to make her escape route easier. She has carefully packed her valise and secreted it under her bed. She has fretted over every detail, and now I am a last-minute jostle to her precise planning.

"If you do not want me along, I shall stay here," I say to be contrary. "I will bide my time until I am able to travel wherever I please. Fanny and I could travel together once she returns."

"No, no, if Percy wants you along, you must come. By all means."

Mary changes tact at once. "Remember, we must be careful. We must be very careful."

She turns her fussy attention to what I should pack. As if we have so many possessions, we require a caravan of coaches. "I am to mind the store now, Mary. You pack for me. I grant you permission to search through all my possessions. Kindly do not forget my books."

It is good to have Mary in charge. She is a planner, careful and precise, and I am a dreamer, overly imaginative and easily distracted. Today, when my imagination makes me tremble with equal parts of fear and exhilaration, when I must be vigilant without appearing to have a care in the world, it is soothing to tend the store. It is good to be distracted by a university lad in search of Shakespeare's comedies. It is good not to dwell on the fact that my whole life is about to change.

Before dawn, as we tie our black bonnets and wrap our black shawls over our black dresses, I experience a twist of dread. "Are you certain?" I ask Mary once again. If Fanny were here, she would be the sister to ask that question. The sister to intercede. The sister to go in place of me. Unlike Mary's heavenly comet, my fate is determined by Fanny's absence.

"It is past five o'clock, Jane. We must depart."

We slip down the back stairway into the workroom and then into the muck of the alley. One of Fanny's mongrel dogs greets us, his cold nose butting against my palm, and I am seized by worry. Fanny has named every alley cur, and I have done my best to toss them scraps while she remains in Wales. Should they starve because of my desertion, poor Fanny will discover their carcasses stacked here upon her return.

The alleyway is dark. Once around the corner, we find the streetlights have burned low, making us invisible as we stumble across cobblestones to Hatton Garden and The Poet's hired chaise. He appears from the shadows to load our bags and help us clamber aboard. "Oh, at last!" Mary's relief brings a smile.

We are all in high spirits, although I suspect The Poet may have had help from the chemist to elevate his mood. He talks without ceasing as we settle in for our journey. "Ah, Newgate Prison." He points out looming shapes. "The Old Bailey gallows." He chokes as we pass foul-smelling warehouses. "I shall not miss the stink of London Town."

We travel through the awakening city and into the damp grass smell of countryside. We are on our way at last! The sun rises before us and the carriage races forward and The Poet's voice croons on and on. He describes the Continent, where the rich coexist with the poor, the beautiful youth mix with their wise elders, and artists and statesmen find common ground. Despite my great excitement, our journey is long, and I drowse during The Poet's day-long travelogue, a vibrant lullaby of colors and shapes and lights and shadows.

Abruptly, like a rock smashing into the sea, I am dropped into wakefulness when the carriage stops. It is dusk, and in the fading light, every bit of whiteness glows before me. The wondrous expanse of ocean is dotted with white-capped waves. The lovely white cliffs and wisps of fog magically hover over every growing thing like white canvas sails. Oh, it is heavenly. Many small boats are anchored in the harbor, and I see The Poet and the coachman conversing with sailors on the dock. "We are in good hands," I say, turning to assure Mary.

"Yes." Her face is as white as the landscape, and she speaks without opening her eyes.

"The carriage's motion made you ill?"

She nods without speaking.

I study The Poet's approach. His stride is quick and sure, yet his hands comb through his hair. Never a good sign.

The coachman unloads our bags as The Poet opens the carriage door. "Every ship to Calais was booked in advance," he says as eases us to the ground. First me. Then Mary, who requires more care. "Fortunately, I have secured the services of Captain Davis and his fine boat, The Miranda. We will have a spot of tea and be on our way within the hour."

Mary is unsteady, unable to stand upright without The Poet's support. I worry that no amount of tea will revive her within an hour. I worry about the chop of the sea. And then I see that The Miranda is an open boat. "May we not wait until morning, Percy? Could we stay at an inn until Mary is recovered and another boat, a true vessel, can be found?"

With one arm pinning Mary to his side, he pivots to face me. His eyes, his voice, all his being is fierce. "May I remind you that this journey is not an elopement? I am a married man with a child and an expectant wife. You have cast your fate with me, and we must stay on course before Will Godwin discovers you and Mary missing and comes after us. I am in danger now, Jane, and there is no turning back."

We are pea green from seasickness by the time we arrive in Calais, and we go straight to our beds at the Deissen Inn. Especially Mary, the poor thing. She is beyond desperate, despite having The Poet to cradle her in his arms, her head on his chest, all through the night. As for me, caught up in the glory of our adventure, I sat apart from the lovers on The Miranda. I watched for stars while the water poured over the sides and the chill wind blew right through me. I never felt so alive. This, I told myself all night long, is the beginning of my story.

Mary remains pale and sickly throughout the next day, yet The Poet kisses her full on the mouth. "Come, my ladies, let us stroll along the harbor as the sun sets."

Mary lies back on the bed and closes her eyes. "Take Jane," she says as she turns toward the wall.

And so he does. He ushers me down the stairs and out the door all the while chattering about the sights to be seen, the food to be tasted, the wine to be drunk. "I have never felt better," he proclaims as we mix into the people strolling along the waterfront. "Leaving England far behind me has immensely improved my health and my state of mind."

"Yes," I say, "it has." Even so, I observe him glancing towards the wharf like that long ago lad who feared unseen creatures.

"I do love the sea," he offers as explanation. "The scent of salt and the slap of waves against the dock. The perfect blend of blue between water and sky." He spins me through the jostle of merchants and tourists, exclaiming how he also loves Calais's bustling streets filled with strangers speaking in other tongues. "Isn't it bewitching?"

We are on the street leading toward the harbor when my mother looms before us. At least it is a woman who resembles Mary Jane Godwin. She could be a vision, a harbinger of our future abroad. Then she cries out to me. "Oh, dear Jane! I have found you."

Percy takes my elbow to steer me away, but I stand rooted in disbelief. Witness to a phenomenon. My true mother has traveled miles to find me because she loves me as well as she does Will Godwin. "Oh, my daughter." Her embrace squeezes air from my lungs. "I was beside myself with worry. I feared I would never see your dear face again."

When she pulls back to clearly see my *dear face again*, tears stream down her own fleshy cheeks. Her mouth quivers, much as it does when she is angry, and I understand that she is quaking from exhaustion. From the shock of waking yesterday morning to find her only daughter gone. My heart breaks for her. "I am sorry, Mother. Truly sorry to have caused you grief."

"Indeed, you have. In being a confidante to your sister, you made a grievous error in judgment." That quickly, Mother pushes her emotion aside, and I have a flash of memory: my mother pronouncing the same poor judgment on Mary for loving Percy. I falter, unsure what to say next.

The Poet, to his credit, has remained quiet and steadfast at my side. Now he steps forward, his voice high with indignation. Or intimidation. "Your daughter freely chose to accompany us on this journey, Mary Jane."

"Perhaps she did, although I blame you for Jane's poor decision-making. Mary is a strong-willed, badly spoiled child, yet she is Will's responsibility. Jane is mine. You understand I could have you arrested for kidnapping, Percy?"

"She acted of her own free will," he says again, not floundering exactly, but less forceful.

"Be that as it may, she is a child, and she is journeying home with me in the morrow."

I believe her. I have experienced my brilliant adventure, and my place is with my mother who loves me after all. My mother loves me deeply enough to leave Will to survive on his limited household skills and search for me. Here against the surreal backdrop of Calais vendors, foreign tongues, and sea smells, I am relieved to be found. To be spared from Mary's petulant stares and biting tongue, and the nighttime murmurs and rustlings she and The Poet make in their adjoining room. I tell myself I will learn to find comfort living an ordinary life on Skinner Street.

Mother and I share my room next to The Poet and Mary's, and before I fall into the sweet slumber of a beloved child who was lost and then found and returned to her own dear mother, I wonder what she must think of their murmurings and sighs. "Oh, my precious, whatever would I do without you?" Their words trickle into my dreams, and I want to believe they were spoken by my mother.

In the morning as Mother and I leave for the dock, The Poet waylays us in the street. "Kindly allow me to speak to Jane."

"By all means." Her composure recovered, Mother returns to her old self. As if she is dealing with a demanding customer in the bookstore.

The Poet draws me away, his hand a hot vise on my arm. "Listen to me, darling girl." His eyes are as blinding as the sun. "I wish for you to remain here with me." Even in my dazed state of mind, I notice he does not mention Mary.

"How is that possible?" My vision of a new life with The Poet and Mary has turned too dreamlike to be true. How senseless, how childish, of me to think otherwise.

"It is your decision, Jane, but please know I want you to remain here. I vow to protect you, to nurture you, to educate you in the ways of the world. I will give your heart ease."

If I was not in love with The Poet before, I might be now. Awestruck, I watch him reason with Mother, always prey to his charms. "I vow to care for your daughter, Mary Jane. Not only will I feed and clothe her being, I will feed her mind and soul with beauty. I will teach her the language of music and poetry and nature. I will attend to her as well as you yourself would. Perhaps better! Jane and Mary and I will be together as we were in England, and once our traveling days are past, we will return. Jane will return to you as a well-educated young woman."

"What of your wife, Percy, what shall become of her? What of poor little Ianthe and your child yet-to-be born?"

"I have all our best interests at heart, Mary Jane." His eyes flash blue as they do when he speaks of the poor and downtrodden. His curls swirl over his forehead as he trembles with intensity. "Set your mind at rest, dear woman."

Somehow, I have become the source of his passion.

An eternity passes as he and Mother haggle. Cooking smells make me dizzy, and the sun, hot and bright, shifts in the sky. Then, at long last, the boat whistle sounds. My mother holds me tightly. "You will always have a place with me, dear daughter." Then, she walks away, her blue skirt flapping like a flag of surrender.

Only when I begin to weep like an abandoned child does The Poet draw me close and soothe me with claims of victory. "I have freed you at last, my girl. I have freed you to be with me."

5. France

Mary and I are not the youngest runaways in Paris, although we probably look like we are. Here where the young women wear stylish French frocks, we are noticeable for our simple black dresses. Truly. Give us pith helmets, and we could pass as missionaries bound for the tropics. I blame Mother's puritanical streak for dressing us as she does.

The Poet does not notice, despite the fact his own clothes are of the highest quality, rumpled or not. No, he is fixated on our finances, or, more precisely, our lack of finances. Although he has managed to obtain sixty pounds through his English bankers, he claims such funds will barely keep us alive. He claims they will not cover our transport to Switzerland, the land I most want to see. I harbor the daydream that a fine Swiss gentleman will emerge from his roadside chalet and recognize me as his long-lost daughter. My black ringlets and dark eyes will mark me as his own true child, and we will have a touching, heartfelt reunion with the Alps as a glorious backdrop. Alas, now we may be too penniless for the Alps.

The Poet is never short on schemes, especially in a state of poverty. "We shall walk to Switzerland," he now declares. "Mary is recovering, and we are fit and hardy from walking all over London town."

It is an idea born of desperation, and since my French is superior to both The Poet's and Mary's, he takes me along to hire a donkey. "Tell the monsieur we need a beast of burden," he says as we approach the stables. "Tell him we are serious travelers with limited funds, but require a strong, young donkey."

"You are free to speak for yourself," I remind The Poet. "I will gladly correct your French as you proceed." I imagine once the stable boy sees his English customers, the price will increase at once. I imagine Fanny would burst from laughter at the scene of a romantic poet and a runaway girl bartering for a donkey. Except, of course, Fanny would prefer to be the girl with the donkey.

No sooner do we walk out of lovely, civilized Paris, than we find ourselves in a countryside ravaged by war. Surrounded by torn landscape and destroyed villages, our donkey collapses into the dirt and we have to drag him to the nearest burned-out village to trade him for a mule. More money spent on a lost cause. Perhaps it is good Fanny was left behind. Traveling through these once-pretty villages, we witness the truly poor and desperate. Starving shoeless children and women falling to their knees to beg for coins. Men bearing knives and threatening attitudes. "So much for your revolution, Percy," Mary says before she begins to retch.

We are along an overgrown country lane, and Mary, bent from the waist, is partially hidden by a stand of pines. The Poet's arm encircles her shoulders as he removes her bonnet and catches her bright hair away from her ghostly face. His actions are gentle and compassionate, yet in the day's receding light, he looks wide-eyed and far younger than his twenty-two years. He looks like a small boy awakened from a nightmare and not certain the reality is any better than his dream. How very strange to discover that Percy Bysshe Shelley, our protector and savior, our leader in a new consecrated life, is not The Poet after all, but merely a mortal man.

We are fortunate not to sleep in the open air. Not yet, anyway. Percy is skilled at wheedling our way into respectable inns, a gift I find astonishing. The Poet takes it for granted. As if he believes his noble heritage will never fail to provide for his needs. When he injured his leg leaping a stile yesterday, he spent the last of his coins to hire a carriage. Or, I wonder, was he was simply tired of walking!

There are some nights I wonder if I might prefer for us to sleep under the stars. I detest sleeping alone, and when I awake to the sound of rats scampering and imagine the terror of their little paws scrabbling over me, I run screaming into my sister's room. Like a small child, I crawl into bed with Mary and Percy to seek comfort. Only there in their warm fold, do I sleep my soundest.

On evenings when Mary is exhausted, Percy and I sit together outside our inn and talk well into the night. "Ah, Clarabella, we have been in France a month." He props his sprained leg on the porch balustrade. "Perhaps I no longer have to worry that someone in authority will find us and throw me in prison.

After everything we have seen in this ravaged countryside, I am certain the French have little interest in searching for three English runaways. To divert Percy away from his fixation on being arrested, I say the first thing that comes to mind. "I believe Mary is with child."

His face loses expression. "Christ, I should have guessed as much." A deep sigh, then a lighter tone. "Well, it shall be loved, this child of Mary's and mine." All the same, he appears distressed. Perhaps he is thinking of Harriet and her unborn child. Or perhaps not. He tugs on his hair so hard, his head tilts backward and exposes his throat, so pale and tender that I am tempted to kiss his Adam's apple. The thought, both delicious and perverse, frightens me. Why would I harbor such a strange desire?

Fortunately, Percy quickly rights himself. "Mary is not thinking of leaving, is she? You are not thinking of contacting Will and Mary Jane?"

"Certainly not."

"You swear you never sent word to your mother when we traveled along the road to Dover?"

"No. I swear. A hundred times no."

"Then how did Mary Jane find us? Does she possess the gift of second sight?"

"She would like to think so."

I believe Mary left a letter for Will when we ran away, and then Mother found it and took off after us. Not that I will share my speculation with Percy. Not now anyway. "You saved me, Percy," I say as darkness begins to fall. "You risked going to prison for me. I am not a little girl who runs home because she misses her mother."

"No." His sideways look makes me quiver again. "You are not a little girl." He takes my hand so I can help him hobble into the garden. Here we lie in the grass to look for shooting stars. We are inches apart, and I sense the warmth rolling from his body toward mine. If he were not so preoccupied by thoughts of Mary, I would sing to him. A love song. A lullaby. Alas, this is not a night for singing. Beside me, Percy squirms. "I cannot decide what to do."

"About Mary?"

"About Harriet. Perhaps it would be good if she and Ianthe were here with us. If we were all in this adventure together. Should I write and ask her to come along, Jane? She could bring some currency to tide us over."

I discern a spark in the upper right section of sky, yet such a small flash is too quick to be a star. I say nothing.

"Naturally Mary is receptive to the idea. If Harriet and my daughter were to meet us in Switzerland, would you accept and welcome them?"

His question is beyond my consideration. If the wise, gentle Mary gives her blessing, there is little reason to ask for mine, yet this is Percy's concept of equality. Loving Mary, worrying about Harriet, and being considerate of me. Compassion without common sense. Where in our travel accommodations does he imagine we might fit another body? Harriet in bed with Percy and Mary? Little Ianthe with me? I want none of it. Most days I do not even want Mary with us.

How very like Percy Shelley to be lying in a field of French starlight and yet dreaming of his mythical love commune.

From my adjoining chamber, I hear everything that passes between Mary and Percy. Everything. I learn more than I ever wanted to know about the habits of men with women. Not only do I learn what it means when Percy moans and sobs, I learn by the sound of his breathing how long it will be before he moans and sobs. I could set my watch by it. If I had a watch. We have pawned all our jewelry, including Mary's gold confirmation earrings, my silver cross, and both our bracelets, for the sake of food and lodging and transportation. Percy's watch was the only piece of great value.

I also endure Percy and Mary talking together in bed, which is far worse than their lovemaking. I endure their disagreements and their endearments. She is his Maie or Dormouse or Pecksie, and he is her Elf. Their discussions about politics and poetry always lead them into proclamations of love and fate and how they are destined to be together, how each is the other's half, on and on ad nauseam. I prefer the days when Mary is too queasy to speak.

"I adore this line, Percy." Mary loudly turns pages as she prettily recites verse about wildflowers. The same verse, I am fairly certain, that Percy originally wrote for Harriet. Wouldn't Mary know that? Their intensity moves on to other topics, and I lie there in my lonely room listening to their exulted talk about Percy's Communal of Love. How he and Mary will fill the place, wherever that place might be, with music and books for the orphans they will adopt from all over the world. How Mary will teach the children to read and write, and I will teach them French and music. How our songs and poems and stories will ring across the fields. A part of me is sorry Harriet is not coming to live with us after all. If anyone can offer perception into the workings of Percy's mind, it is Harriet, his child bride.

"We could adopt the precious girl I saw on the street yesterday." Excitement rises in Percy's voice. "An urchin with eyes like saucers. You would adore her, Mary."

"Everyone would be welcome," Mary responds. "Every child would know our love."

"Love will rule." His voice grows. "We will educate the poor and the downtrodden, and love will guide everything we do. Every board and nail of our home. Every stalk of corn we grow and every loaf of bread we bake." These are the promises of The Poet, a son of wealth who has never nailed or grown or baked. Such an Exotic.

"Our life shall be sweet, my love," Mary coos.

Listening from the darkness of my room, I recognize that she is placating rather than agreeing with his plan. Mary believes Percy's Communal of Love is born from an absence of love in his childhood. *It is his fantasy, Jane*, she tells me. *We must nurture our fantasies.*

Perhaps. Fantasy is difficult for me to nurture when I am hungry, and we are always hungry on this journey. Percy's talk of baking causes me to salivate over my own fantasy of slathering black currant jam over thick-crusted bread.

"Harriet shall join us eventually," Percy says to my sister. "Harriet and Ianthe and the new baby. You and Jane and our new baby. Maybe Fanny and my dear friend Hogg. Such a beautiful life we shall have, Mary."

Hogg. The dreaded name. Mary seems not to hear it. "Fanny is unwell, and Harriet refuses to join us. You must accept that, my love. You read her letter yourself."

"Given time, Harriet will come around."

I have not read Harriet's letter, yet I can always read *about* Harriet in Percy's journal. Which is Mary's fault. Little Miss Efficiency forgot to pack my journal, forgot to pack all but one of my books, and then she claimed *Adeline Mowbray* as hers anyway. "Calm yourself." Percy admonished me when I threw a tantrum. "You can write in the back of my journal. See?" He flipped his leather-bound volume from head to toe and opened it before me. "A blank slate for your words alone, dear Jane."

He says nothing about his words or my eyes, so I become his most faithful reader, a voyeur of his intimate moments with Mary. *She moans when I kiss her belly, my Mary who never moans. The touch of my tongue brings her ecstasy.* Sometimes I believe Percy Shelley is writing solely for my benefit, that through his journal he is making love to me.

Aside from our lame donkey and our lame leader, I am enthralled by our journey. Mary and I have survived our haphazard childhoods and escaped Skinner Street and are traveling together into foreign territory. In my mind nothing could be better than these endless forests and meadows, these hills and vales. Here in these cloud-reflecting lakes and streams, we shed our clothes to bathe in the icy depths. Of course, it is Percy and I who bathe. Genteel Mary remains with the carriage.

"Oh, what pleasure you forbid yourself," Percy calls to her. "No other water could be so pure. The tears of the gods." When he splashes me from beyond the boulder, I scream and swim away. We behave like playful children. Innocent brother and sister encounters. Yet in those fleeting moments between being clothed and unclothed, I sense his eyes lingering on me, and I do not insist he look away.

When we cross into Switzerland, land of my ancestry, I am feverish with anticipation. Mary and Percy are less enthused. They declare the landscape cold and unappealing, nothing at all like the setting of William Tell. Again, Percy finds himself without funds. "Harriet has sorely disappointed me," he says with a tragic air. "She is forcing our return to England."

How is that possible? In this beautiful countryside of sweet-smelling pines and firs, our lungs must be filled to overflowing with all the fresh pure air Percy is keen on. It strikes me that he is giving up entirely too easily. To my way of thinking, only a quitter would turn back now. Not that I call Percy a quitter.

Now all my efforts divert from climbing over rough terrain to plotting how to stay in Percy's good graces when we return to England. I do not want to leave Percy and Mary to return to Skinner Street. I am no longer the girl I was a month ago, and I cannot bear to live under Will and Mary Jane Godwin's roof again.

My one consolation in leaving France is that we return by a different route. A water route through Germany and Holland. Instead of teetering on a rocky precipice, we now have long, languorous days to read and write as we glide along. Some days I am so hopeful I burst into song, which always pleases Percy. On other days, I despair. I convince myself I am doomed to live the rest of my life with Fanny. Together we will grow old running the bookstore. We will become the spinster sisters of Skinner Street. On those days I cannot bear to open either a book or my mouth. Instead, I sit silently watching the glory of Europe slip away.

6. Homecoming

Mary and I wait in agony here on Chapel Street, outside the home of Harriet's parents. After two miserable hours of sitting in this stifling carriage, I am shaking with fury. Mary is asleep, her head propped on my shoulder, while opposite us, the boatman glowers. He, too, has had enough of waiting for the great Percy Shelley. The *penniless* Percy Shelley.

Up until we docked at Gravesend this morning, I did not consider *penniless* a literal term. I believed Percy was being overly poetic during our journey, and there was no good reason at all why we should abandon our travel plans. Then, today, at the bottom of the gangplank, our good Captain was waiting. "A word with you, Sir?" he says to Percy.

Mary and I stood discreetly to the side, but we are neither deaf nor slow-witted, and the Captain's message was clear. He wants paid for our travel, and he will send his boatman, Elliott, along to collect what we owe. Thus, despite Percy's best efforts, despite his polished words and charming manners, we sit in a smelly carriage while Percy is with Harriet. I cannot bear to think what they are saying or what they are doing for hours on end. Elliott shifts and the carriage rocks. "I be stretching my legs, miss," he says as lets himself out.

Who can blame him? I, too, would prefer to walk than to sit here feeling sorry for myself, yet that is precisely what I do. It is hard to admit defeat, to realize that the stuff of dreams is no more than smoke and fog. Our lovely adventure has become a foolish undertaking, and we are exhausted and bedraggled. I stare out the smeared carriage window at the London gloom. Gray rain clouds are set like boulders into sooty skies.

If I were a braver girl, I would have stayed in Amsterdam, where I fell in love with the canals and the tall narrow houses. I envisioned myself living there on a canal boat with the sound of water lapping me to sleep and then awakening in the morning to find my day's provisions mere steps away. The always fanciful Percy played along. "We shall live like great sea serpents," he said. "Swimming away to warmer climes when we are bored with our routine or with the Dutch and their practical natures."

Perhaps I would have fared better with the practical Dutch, I tell myself now. I slip out from under Mary's weight and lay her along the length of the carriage seat. I ease myself onto the cobblestones. "Elliott," I call to the disgruntled boatman, "kindly knock on the Westbrooks' door and tell Percy Shelley his time is up. Tell him he must pay up now or go to debtor's prison." What manner of man visits his estranged wife while his new love and her sister wait outside on the street with the debt collector?

Now settled here at 56 Margaret Street in Cavendish Square, Percy, Mary, and I find we have become lost, shameful souls. Will Godwin has disowned Mary, and, despite her last whispered vow to me in France, Mother will not allow me to return home unless I sever ties with Percy and Mary. Our Fanny is forbidden to contact us. "So much for good Christian folk," Percy says. Although I think my mother is the only Godwin proclaiming to be Christian.

Percy's friends Peacock, Hookham, and Hogg are gentlemen of the finest degree. Keats, Wordsworth, Lamb, Southey, Coleridge, and the like are the smart literary set Percy speaks of with endless rapture. All of them are most displeased with him for leaving his pregnant wife and innocent child for two less literary, less sophisticated girls such as Mary and myself. We are home wreckers. Fallen women. The dregs of society. We pray none of them realize Mary herself is with child.

To add to our woes, Percy goes away for days at a stretch to avoid arrest for unpaid debts. "My creditors are tracking me like hounds after a hare," he claims during his brief visits to Margaret Street. "I have no shelter to call my own." He paces and mutters, much as he did that summer evening he sank his armada of paper boats. "Harriet is lost to me. The woman I longed to keep as a friend, as a sister to my soul, has nothing but contempt for me. She insists my struggle for money is a myth of my own making. Does she not remember my mercy and kindness to her?"

Mercy and kindness? I study Mary's cameo-like profile. Not a ripple of worry creases her face, yet surely she must quake inwardly. How can anyone, even Mary herself, believe Percy treats Harriet with kindness and mercy? Should my husband leave me and my daughter and unborn child to claim another as his true love, I would be far less gracious than Harriet. I would make daily visits to Skinner Street and give the Godwins a piece of my mind. I would track down Mary and deliver dire warnings. I would be relentless in my revenge. Fortunately, Harriet is a kinder woman than I, and here in Cavendish Square, we are difficult to find.

"Are you moping again, Jane?" Mary's golden eyebrow rises as if she is reading my thoughts. "You know I cannot bear your moods."

"You are one to talk, dear sister." Annoyed, I watch Percy stuff his valise with half-written poems and balled-up clothing. How is it that less than three years after our dashing hero rode through the starry night to save the beautiful Harriet Westbrook, they are now enemies? Surely Mary worries over the fate of her own love story.

"I sense my health failing, my lungs filling with rot." Percy coughs violently, spewing phlegm across his shirt front. "If sent to debtor's prison, I shall die." At the thought of his own death, he grows weepy and embraces us as if for the last time. "Send me your love," he calls on his way out the door.

Percy is always a bit theatrical, yet the feverishness of his farewell causes me to squirm. We are all suffering, I want to shout. There are days when Mary and I become so hungry, we claim we would sell our souls for a loaf of bread. Percy's days, on the other hand, are spent with stockbrokers and lawyers trying to coax money from his father's account or convince Harriet to sign settlements. Also, there is an air of intrigue and mystery hanging over his comings and goings.

"He could be in training as a royal spy," I suggest.

"No spy could be as loquacious as Percy."

Since Mary prefers hard truth over my whimsical speculations on Percy's whereabouts, we pry the sealing wax from Harriet's letters and read them for ourselves. I approach each one gingerly, as if uncovering a cobra, while Mary dives right in.

I promise you, dear Bysshe, Harriet writes, *I have nothing in my heart save the concern of your children, of* **our** *children. I sought out lawyers solely for their advice, not to prosecute you. Say what you will of Mistress Mary, I am the woman to whom you first promised love. I am the one you married. Keeping you as my "true friend" means nothing to me now. Take care, dear one. Remember to protect yourself from the cold as autumn approaches. Wear your flannels. Keep your head dry. Affectionately yours, HWS.*

After every reading, Mary fumes. "I am his love, not his *mistress.*"

"She could have called you worse. Why these endearments to Percy?"

"She loves him still."

Yes, indeed she does. What, I wonder, might Percy say in his letters to Harriet? Carefully, we hold the candle flame to the wax and reseal her love inside the parchment. If only sealing wax could protect us from her hold on Percy.

As often as he is able, Percy sends for Mary to meet him in quiet inns or parks or street corners, perhaps a graveyard or two, and I am left to fend for myself. Here, during long evenings alone in the empty flat, I miss Fanny. I miss my mother.

I imagine Mother presiding over tea in her flowing crimson dress. Her head held high and her chin jutting ever so slightly as she passes Fanny's biscuits to Will. Fanny worriedly fussing with the tablecloth, awaiting her father's judgment. Maintaining a proper attitude will save face for the Godwins, Mother thinks as she slices the bread and lectures Fanny and Young Will on the penalties of love before marriage.

Mary and I are ostracized from Skinner Street for casting Will and Mary Jane in the scandal of Percy leaving his pregnant wife. None of the Godwins, not even Fanny, know Mary is also pregnant. Another scandal entirely. "So if I reject Percy, as our parents wish, and come home with a bastard child, I would be welcomed?" Mary is scornful.

"Mother could pretend the child was her own. That she and Will adopted it out of the goodness of their hearts."

"I would rather Harriet raise my child than your mother."

"Is that so?" I say tartly. "Where would you be without my mother?"

My mother always claims, with an air of humility, that she married Will Godwin because Fanny and Mary were in need of a mother, while my brother Charles claims we were in need of a roof over our heads and Will's roof was the closest-by. I have a few vivid images of that time when our families came together. I remember meeting those little Godwin girls with their big eyes and their little storybooks. *The Butterfly's Ball. The Grasshopper's Feast.* I remember my mother having tea parties for us under the hollyhocks. I remember her lemon tarts. I remember thinking that the lives of Fanny and Mary were one continuous tea party.

"You are a blessed man," my mother said to Will, "to have such lovely daughters."

"I thank you for your attention to Fanny and Mary, Mrs. Clairmont," Will responded. "They miss a mother's touch."

Mary says nothing more to me now, and that is for the best. I must not upset Mary. I must not lose favor with Percy. I must be very tactful, or I will find myself back on Skinner Street, which will be no tea party at all.

Sometimes, when Percy has been gone for days and we are hungry and I have endured enough of Mary's superior, suffering attitude, I lose my composure. "I am free to leave you at any moment." I remind her. "Mother and Father would welcome me home, and I could be warm and well-fed and in far less dour company than yours." I rise to my feet, as if to leave. "I have chosen to be a good sister rather than a good daughter, and if you want to remain here alone waiting for Percy to reappear, simply say the word and I will be gone, Mary. I will be gone by the chime of the hour!"

Mary gives me her full attention, her head snapping so quickly that one of her tortoiseshell combs clatters to the floor. "You would renounce me and Percy as immoral influences for the sake of your mother's fine cooking? You would prefer to tend to Father's shop and listen to Fanny whine about being left behind? Is that truly what you want, Jane?"

Immediately I fear for her safety. What if she injures her unborn child? What if Percy returns to find her collapsed? "Oh Mary, forgive me." I kneel by her chair. "Please forget what I said."

"Mary Jane and Father are traitors to my poor dead mother. Thinking they must protect Fanny and our brothers from my influence. Bah!" A loosened hank of golden hair falls across her face. "Why has my father rejected my mother's theories on free love and the right of women to choose their partners? What hypocrisy!"

Percy would be proud, I think as I pick up Mary's comb and help re-pin her lovely hair. Mary is truly her mother's daughter, while I am the daughter who knows to stay with Mary and wait for Percy because my only hope of a future lies with him. I am no different than my mother, who knew her only hope of a future lay with Will Godwin. So much for the equal rights of women.

Eventually Percy returns, and Mary reverts to her calm, caring self in his presence, but her words cling to me like a fine layer of dust. Irony is rich, I tell myself on these evenings I am alone and missing my mother. Our wishes never to return to Skinner Street have been granted, and yet look where we are now.

The realization that Mary and I are shut off from the world seeps into us like the autumnal drafts through the walls of our little flat. We do our best to keep up with our studies, our reading, our journals, yet without Percy, it is a dull existence. Without food, we are too weary to function. Then, on those rare occasions when Percy is home, we are on the move. Like many of London's smart literary set, we flee from flat to flat, scraping to keep body and soul together as Percy borrows on his debts and slips past landlords. Apparently this is what artistic people do, even artistic people who come from wealth.

We live for Sundays, when the bailiff is off-duty, and Percy comes home to fill our dismal little lives with his exuberance. Gaily, we walk on Hampstead Heath and sail paper boats in Primrose Hill pond. We laugh and sing, and if Mary is feeling poorly, Percy and I walk alone. He claims I distract him from his worries, that I remind him of his dreams for a new society. "All men deserve the freedoms of the wealthy. Poverty should not be a barrier to raising a family."

"Women also deserve freedoms, Percy. Women should not endure poverty because they are without husbands or brothers or fathers."

"Indeed!" Percy declares, his eyes flashing blue sparks. "Oppression of women is beyond the pale." Then, almost at once, he begins to harp on Harriet's selfishness or his fears for his health. "Tell me, Jane." He halts mid-path to tug on his eyelid. "Do the whites of my eyes show signs of yellow?" Such an Exotic.

When Percy is in residence on Sundays, I resent the amount of time he spends in bed with Mary. I hear it all, exactly as I did on our travels. *Oh, Elf. Dear Maie. Pecksie. Dormouse.* All those hours of murmuring and reciting poetry and then stealthily speaking in low tones about the difficulties of two women sharing the same household wear on me. When Percy is with us, Mary and I bicker over the smallest of things. A piece of fruit. A waste of ink. A misplaced thimble. We drive Percy to his wits' end.

On evenings when Mary is feeling robust, she is the one to walk with Percy, and I remain behind. Then I sit by the window overlooking the dusky street below and give my imagination free reign. I pretend to wait for my own lover, and while I have grown used to overhearing, and thus imagining, the lovemaking of Percy Bysshe Shelley, the lover who currently takes shape in my imagination is that of Lord George Gordon Byron. Lord Byron. LB. Albee, as I like to think of him.

Mary and Percy and I are devoted to Lord Byron's poetry. Like Percy, Albee is a man of passion. Unlike Percy, he has neither wife nor child nor lack of funds, and he is said to have many lovers. Young women, mature women, married women, beautiful women, talented women, plain women. He seems not at all particular about who he loves. I, too, could be one of Albee's women. Perhaps I, too, have sufficient talent and beauty to charm a poet.

Once Percy is gone again, Mary and I continue to bicker and then fall into longer spells of quiet, each of us immersed in her own mind. In one of these quiet, self-contained moments, I begin a secret correspondence with Fanny. She is the one to fetch and sort the mail for the shop, so I have hope my letters will not be discovered by Will or my mother. *It is lonely here with so little company, dear Fanny. Percy is on the road, traveling to visit his family in Sussex, and Mary is feeling poorly. An autumn chill, I imagine.*

I envision Fanny smoothing her brown hair and wiping her rough cheeks as she reads my words. Poor Fanny. It will take an act of courage for her to reply to me. Yet I wait. I bicker with Mary over the last of our writing paper, over the spilled cream in the larder, and the color of the sky at night, and I pray for Fanny to respond.

When she does, weeks later, her words are triumphant. She hid her letter under her drawings, she explains, and then slipped it in with posts sent from the bookstore. *I am hurt and angry to find you and Mary gone from our home,* she laments. *I returned from Wales for the dear company of my sisters.*

It is more likely that Fanny returned for the dear company of Percy and Harriet, and she must be both horrified and envious to discover Mary and I are now living with him. Yet she is pleased to take on the role of missionary. To offer her services. To be needed. *I shall do my best, dear Jane, to come to your side. To bring news of the neighborhood to you and Mary.* While I doubt Fanny has the courage to disobey Will Godwin, she might not mind going behind my mother's broad back. A subtle little revenge for being sent from Skinner Street in the first place.

On a blustery night in late November, a messenger comes to our door in Church Terrace seeking Percy. Percy, easily flustered under the best of circumstances, scrambles about, gathering up his warmest coat and his satchel of papers and clothing. "I must leave, Mary." Ringlets spring away from his head in a dusty cloud. "Now. At once. Harriet has given birth to my son, and I must go to them."

And just that quickly, he is gone. Out into the dark of the night. I shut the door against the wind and turn to Mary. She is pale and eerily calm. "We may never see him again, Jane. Now that he has an heir, he may return to Harriet forever."

I, too, am worried. When he writes, as he does faithfully, Percy's tone is a bit too witty, a bit too fun-loving as he merrily describes the lavish hospitality of his many friends and their fine homes. Such news causes Mary to grow sulky and irrational. "I fear he is living with Harriet," she says again and again. "I fear for our future."

"If Percy is with Harriet," I say to reassure us both, "it is to cajole her into signing their deed of separation."

"She will take him to court rather than agree to separate." Mary wraps her shawl tighter. "She is determined to make us all suffer."

"Percy will borrow funds from his Grandfather Abyss and Sir Tim."

"You realize Sir Tim will not recognize my child when it is born? Percy and Harriet married twice, once in Scotland and once in England to make certain their son would the rightful Shelley heir."

I have nothing to say about heirs, so I address a more immediate need. "What say you pawn Percy's microscope so we might buy food? I refuse to starve while waiting for his return."

The color bleeds out of our landscape in early winter— no grass green, blue sky, yellow sun days for us. We fear any messenger might bring bad news, and when a plain, purposeful-looking woman knocks at 5 Church Terrace, we cower behind our tattered curtains. "Looks like a woman to hand out tracts and save souls," Mary whispers. "Send her away."

I brace myself, opening the door so suddenly the good Christian woman screams in fright. Then Mary also screams, and at last I recognize that our saver of souls is none other than Fanny. How could I not know her when she looks precisely the same?

"Oh, sister," we cry, "we thought you would never come. Come in, come in." We tug on her arms and help her with her parasol and urge her into our best chair, the blue cushioned one that Percy himself favors. "Oh, it has been an eternity, dear Fanny. How well you look. How good of you to come."

Pleased with her reception, Fanny smiles her pure, broad smile. "Father shall disown me if he finds out I am here," she says with a flash of boldness, "yet I dare say Mary Jane would rejoice if I were to stay away forever."

"No!" Mary and I laugh. "Mary Jane would miss you minding the store."

We grow giddy from the familiarity of being together again under the same roof. After our many months apart, we are relieved to discover we are the same sisters we have always been. At least I think we are.

Fanny gazes around. "Oh, my. You are living in close quarters."

"Cheek to jowl." It is something Mother would say. "Come, sit, and we shall serve you tea in our single solitary good teacup."

As pleased as Fanny is to see us, she remains a nervous soul. "I must not tarry long," she says between sips of tea. When we urge her to tell us all she knows, to share tales from Skinner Street, she describes the usual humdrum visitors to the bookstore. Mr. Owen and his latest obsession with the harpsichord. The porter's recent gastric problems. The students disassembling Mary Jane's book displays.

Oh, good grief. We are politely attentive, yet for first time since our return to London, I am feeling less remorseful about our banishment. Mary yawns outright.

"Are you well?" Fanny is a natural worrier.

"We are weary," I say. "It has been a long summer and an unsettling autumn."

Fanny is overly careful when she is preoccupied. I recall that trait now as she fusses with her empty teacup, twisting it this way and that as she returns it to its saucer. "I was sorry not to go with you this summer, dear sisters. France is the country of my birth, you know."

I did not know this, but I suppose Mary must. "We departed quite suddenly, Fanny," she says. "On a moment's notice."

"You could have sent word. I could have arranged travel to Dover and met you in Calais." With each word, she raises our good teacup and then plunks it against the saucer, like she is beating a drum. "I would have done anything to join you, Mary. If only you had asked."

"More tea, Fanny?" I stand to take her cup away, but she keeps it in her grasp.

"You know you hurt more than *my* feelings when you left." Fanny grows bolder. "Mary Jane is angry all the time now. Father is ashamed to tell his customers his esteemed patron ran off with his daughter. As for you, Jane." She turns to me and her broad forehead reddens. "Your brother Charles had to summon me home to mind the store while Mary Jane went after you. Young Will is so sick of it all that he, too, tried running away. You girls caused the dominoes to fall, one after another. You two have caused nothing but ruin."

"Oh, Fanny, that is enough." I snap at her. "If you had been with us, do you think there would have fewer *fallen dominos*? Consider yourself lucky to remain in Will's good graces. Unlike ourselves." Mostly I am angry that Fanny does not cast one bit of blame on Percy, and if she expects me to ask her forgiveness, she will be sorely disappointed.

"Our summer abroad is long over, Fanny." Mary is dismissive, yet Fanny remains the proverbial dog holding fast to her bone. Or should I say teacup?

"Had I been home instead of with my cousins," Fanny persists, "Percy would have taken me with you. He is the dearest, most compassionate man I know."

At the mention of Percy's name, Mary buries her head in her hands. Falling in love and running away and being with child are in collusion to throw our calmest, wisest sister into a muddle. "Oh, sister." Fanny rises from her seat, dropping the teacup as she bends to pat Mary's shoulders. "Please forgive me. Is Percy causing you distress? Is he having money troubles again? I can spare some pounds to sustain you." Fanny, ever helpful and steadfast, reaches into the bodice of her navy blue frock.

Mary tearfully waves her away. "No need, Fanny. We shall be fine."

Fanny bows her head, and I imagine she is contemplating the events of our respective summers and reviewing Mary's unseemly outburst. She raises her face in wonder, and we know she has fitted the pieces together. "You are with child. You are carrying Percy's child."

Mary offers no response, and Fanny's envy over not being chosen by Percy evaporates. It is as visible to me as the steam rising from our kettle. Whatever her fate with the Godwins, Fanny is thinking, she is not ruined for life. "Oh, Mary. I am so sorry to find you in this wretched state." She kneels to stroke Mary's hair as the fire crackles in the grate and shadows fall across the floor.

"We shall be fine, Fanny," I say.

She glances my way. "Your mother is grief-stricken, you know. She hates that I am there in the house instead of you. She blames Mary and Percy for corrupting you."

I laugh at my mother's indignation, but Mary is not amused. "Why do you not defend us, Fanny? Why do you not tell Mary Jane that she will never, ever, replace our true mother in Father's heart?"

Poor Fanny is too startled to respond, so I help her to her feet and ease her out the door to stand in the fading light. "Do not despair, dear sister. Mary's condition causes her to brood."

"I see." She blinks rapidly, her eyes as soft and brown as mushroom caps. "Yes. I must hurry now to catch my coach." She re-ties her best bonnet, grey and white as a nuthatch, but too large for her head. "I was hoping to see Percy before I left."

Oh, dear. She yet loves Percy. "Perhaps next time. Thank you for calling on us, Fanny. Thank you for your bravery."

"Come home with me, Jane. Your mother would give anything to see you again."

I hand Fanny her gloves. "Mother wants to see the daughter she imagines. A good, clever daughter. Not me. I am no longer her little girl."

"I am old, too, I guess." Finger by finger, she eases on the gloves. "We do not belong anywhere, do we? Because of Percy. He stirred us up so much that we cannot steady ourselves. We will never be content with anyone else."

We linger on the cobbles to speak about the likelihood of Percy's Communal of Love ever coming to fruition, and how living in the countryside and raising forlorn children could be the very thing we leftover sisters need. "It is possible," we say, yet our voices lack confidence, and a sudden chill gust blows our words away.

While a letter from Fanny cheers me, one from Percy transforms Mary. Healed by the mere words of a wandering poet, she grows pink-cheeked and chatty as she hands me a pound note. "He sends his love from Sussex and money for food until he arrives, most likely within the week. Sir Tim is in generous mood, it appears."

Percy's father is always generous when Percy spends time with his legal wife, although I refrain from reminding Mary of that fact. "Perhaps Sir Tim's generosity will allow us to purchase a new book," I suggest, "and some writing supplies." Of late, Mary and I have been writing stories to entertain one another. Hers feature motherless children, while mine involve complicated romances.

"Writing paper would be a treasure," she cheerfully agrees. Then like a queen bestowing a title, she hands me a folded square of parchment, my own missive from Percy.

I will be home soon, my darling Clarabella, and we shall go hopping around the town like rabbits.

Carefully, I re-fold Percy's words and close my hand around it to discern his touch, to decipher his words. *We,* he writes. Does *we* include Mary? Or is *we* merely Percy and me? I wonder what Mary might think, yet she is thankfully preoccupied with her own correspondence.

"From Hogg." Mary hands me a letter. "Percy claims he is infatuated with me."

Dearest Mary, the apple of Percy's jaded eye, pray let me pledge my undying gratitude for making my best friend, always a heartless, thoughtless ass, such a happy, happy man. If only you could do the same for poor, lowly me. In love and anticipation, TJ Hogg.

What might this mean? I glance at Mary for an explanation, and she shrugs. "He is quite the character, don't you think?"

"A character, all right." I keep my tone light, even as I recall Harriet's tone of disgust that day she came to the bookstore. *See how you like Percy's grand scheme for free love when his friend Hogg comes to call.*

Then I worry for Mary. And perhaps for myself as well.

7. The Seduction Redux

Nothing about Percy's entrances are ever quiet. There is the staccato beat of his boot heels against the stairs followed by the thump, thump, thump of whatever parcels he drags behind him. Our door bursts open by the force of his shoulder against the latch. "Mary," he cries as every one of his burdens fall to floor. "Mary, my love, I am home." Graceful as a dancer, he leaps over his various parcels, over his leather pouch and his battered valise, to sweep her into his arms and then dance her around the floor. "Oh, my darling, it seems like years since I've gazed upon your lovely face."

Tonight Percy's entrance is precisely the same except after he throws himself on Mary, I hear a heavier, slower tread on the stairway. In the doorway appears a tall, well-kept man, his face glowing with cold. He bows his balding head towards me. "You must be one of the Godwin sisters." He has a pleasant voice with a calmer, lower pitch than Percy's, and his clothes, unlike Percy's, are without wrinkles and spots.

"I am Jane."

"I am Percy's mate Hogg." He smiles. "And I've brought sausages for our supper."

Thomas Jefferson Hogg. Mary's ardent admirer is not a handsome man, but neither is he the swine-like man of my imaginings. "Please come in. Allow me to take your coat."

"Gladly." His manner is jolly, rather like a good-humored cleric. He smiles again as Percy fuses himself to Mary in their usual welcome-home waltz. As she steps back, he steps forward, leaving no space between their bodies. "So this is your harem, Shelley?" Hogg jokes.

"The keepers of my flame." Percy buries his face in Mary's neck.

"I understand you are a poet?" I say to shift Hogg's eyes away from them.

"A novelist of sorts." He speaks with a humble air. "With a small law practice on the side."

I find his humility suspicious and would question him more closely, except I am interrupted by Percy. "Ah, my dear girl." He wraps me in an embrace more reserved than Mary's. "Are you ready for an evening on the town?"

"Certainly." After months of being shut away from the world, I desire attention, and during our days apart, Percy's company has become more desirable to me. His eyes fasten on me like a blue beam, and my breath falters.

Hogg swoops in on Mary. "A pleasure to meet one of Percy's friends," she says graciously.

"His best friend." Hogg corrects her. "His oldest friend. We were tossed out of Oxford together, you know." Oh yes, this is Percy's conspirator in distributing atheist tracks. So much for my cleric image. Yet I enjoy his wry tone and his thoughtfulness in bringing us our supper. "For the love of God, Shelley, try a sausage," Hogg insists. "Lack of meat will render your brain useless."

"Meat-eating leads to war, my friend." Percy, pale and possibly anemic, cannot be persuaded to give up his vegetables. He compromises by drinking wine with his oldest friend and soon a pleasing pinkness rises in his cheeks.

Their tongues well-oiled, the men continue some previous literary debate on the merits of Wordsworth and Byron. "Wordsworth is as steady and dependable as dust," Hogg declares, "and who needs to worry about making a living from poetry when you are a Lord?"

There is little need for small talk from starving girls like Mary and me. After our fruit stand and street vendor dining experiences with Percy, the penniless vegetarian, Hogg's modest meal is a luxury. The sausages are crisp-skinned and flavorful. The fish is fresh and flaky. The claret is sublime. Mary, now mellow, smiles at me from across the table. I sigh in contentment as the men reminisce about the days of their youth, a topic far more fascinating than the usual politics.

"Do you remember, Hogg, how you fell into a well while chasing your mother's maidservant?" Percy leans forward, planting his elbows on the table, and I notice how the candlelight and the ample food and our good company ease his worried appearance. Without creases about his mouth and eyes, he appears to be no older than Mary.

"How about the time," Hogg responds, "when you claimed an old man was living in your attic in order to frighten your mother and sisters?"

"A lark I kept going for months." Percy nods. "Do you recall the wallpaper covered in grapes and vines that was in the flat we shared? I yet have dreams of those grotesque vines."

"Yes, of course, 15 Poland Street. Such sophisticated lads we were." Hogg wipes his mouth with his fist. "Until your father came after us, ranting like a madman about my evil influence on you."

"Evil indeed!" Percy sneers in delight.

Hogg turns to Mary. "Then Sir Tim writes to *my* father who insists I must return home to York because Shelley's influence will corrupt *me*. Such rubbish." He offers Percy more wine. "I heard tales of *Mad Shelley* long before I met him. My favorite was the one where he skewered a bully's hand to the tabletop with a fork. Now there's a good chap, I thought to myself."

I hang on every word. Hogg's stories are like rare artifacts, bones or buttons or crockery shards that reveal clues to their owner. Also, for the first time in months Mary and I are not hungry or fretful or hiding from the bailiff, and we laugh riotously. As if we had not a care in the world.

Then Hogg makes a misstep. "How are your children keeping?" he asks. A question rooted in goodwill, but Percy's mood dampens at once.

"They thrive in my absence." His head slumps over his chest. "I gave my best last try with Harriet. My marriage is dead."

"I'm sorry to hear that," Hogg says. "I enjoyed Harriet's company in the early days."

"You two had a lot in common since Father detested you as much as he did her." Now Percy fidgets, his fingers tapping the table and his shoulders beginning to twitch. "He blamed you, as I recall, for me marrying the daughter of an innkeeper."

"It seems but a moment ago that the two of you eloped, so happy and excited to catch the mail coach from the Bull and Mouth Tavern and then journey on to Edinburgh."

A *mail coach?* A *tavern?* I glance at Mary. What about the elopement of our girlhood fantasy, the story of Percy astride the very fast horse? Mary's placid face reveals nothing. "Of course Shelley was short of funds," Hogg continues, "so when the coach stopped in York, I met him and lent him some pounds. He was as frantic as a rooster awaiting a fox. *We will live on love after this is gone,* he told me." Hogg laughs good-naturedly.

Percy is not laughing. "Harriet is despicable. She spreads the rumor that Godwin sold his daughters to me." He struggles to keep his voice from rising. "That I paid 800 pounds for Mary and 700 for Jane." His youthful sheen fades into weariness. "Such spitefulness. Harriet has gone from being my helpmate in campaigning for reform in Ireland to a common English wife. A matron of privilege." He deflates completely over his plate of potatoes and parsnips. "Harriet was my best friend when I rescued her from Clapham School, but there was never passion between us." His head jerks towards Mary. "You understand my passion, Mary."

Mary looks doubtful. Passion is likely the last thing on her mind at this juncture.

"I am convinced Harriet had lovers," Percy adds darkly. "I shall support her offspring, yet I wash my hands of her."

To speak of little Ianthe and the infant Charles as if he has no blood claim to them makes me queasy, and I put down my spoon. For all his talk of adopting children, I wonder if he even likes them. I glance up from my empty plate and understand our delicious meal is over. "Mary is weary," Percy insists as he helps her to her feet. "We should postpone our plans for the evening."

"It shall be my pleasure to stay here with Mary." Hogg speaks quietly. "You two go about your evening."

Percy hesitates. "I did promise Jane a night on the town. Do you mind, Mary?"

Mary's cheeks grow unusually pink, and her eyes are unusually bright. I wait for her to tell Percy precisely how much she minds him leaving her again so quickly. "Not at all," she says. "Go on, enjoy yourselves."

This moment strikes me as odd. Like it has happened before, or maybe happened without me. Or is Mary keeping Hogg's company as revenge for Percy's long absence? I wave at Mary, abandoned to Hogg, and she lifts a lily-white hand in response.

Once on the street, Percy's spirits revive quickly. As we did in France, he and I walk off into the night arm-in-arm. I know so little about the city after dark that we could be walking directly into the Thames, yet I do not care. Percy has recovered his good humor and is telling tales, poking fun at his father and pointing out houses of people he once counted as friends. Then he pulls me under a lamppost and kisses me so hard, so fast, that I have no time to imagine where his wine-flavored kiss might lead. I gasp for air, and he holds my face between his hands. "This night is ours, thanks to my dear friend, Hogg."

"Hogg," I repeat. My senses swirl, leaping from Percy's kiss to Harriet's warning of Hogg. I blink. Even in the dim lamplight, I sense Percy's eyes are fixed on mine.

"Hogg has taken a room at an inn, but he is with Mary, and I am here with you."

Eventually it becomes clear that Percy wants me to go to Hogg's lodging, where there will be no Hogg, only Percy himself. And then what? Does it matter? Percy is the man to save me from Skinner Street and show me the world, the man who has clothed and fed me for months. How can I refuse him *anything* he asks? I feel faint.

Apparently, a great deal of subterfuge is required to smuggle a girl into an inn, especially one favored by university lads and the clergy. We avoid the lobby. No longer the lad frightened by unseen creatures, Percy bravely leads me down a vile alleyway reeking of rotting fish and spilled ale and then up a rickety stairway. My stomach, already churning, lurches into my throat, and I stumble.

"Ah, dear girl, we are almost there. I thank you for your trust and your courage." He kisses my cheek before leading me into a corridor so dark that being seen is of no consequence. Then I panic.

Flee, my mind screams. *Quick. Down that black stairwell and through the rotting alleyway. Now! Run!* Instead, I willingly allow Percy to draw me inside a room. I stand quaking as he lights the nearest lamp, which illuminates next to nothing. His face hangs there in darkness like a slice of moon before he takes me in his arms and kisses me again and again. *Oh, my.* As he had earlier with Mary, he walks me backwards across the room. Then I am sinking, my head thrown back to find Percy looming above me as he falls across the length of me.

For all his compassionate speeches and tender verses, the poet Shelley is a force of single-minded determination. His hand are cold on my skin, yet my laces and stays and layers of broadcloth and muslin and swansdown offer no resistance to his skilled fingers. *Oh, mother of God, have mercy.* I pray aloud as great swathes of my flesh are quickly revealed to him. *Oh. Take care with me, please,* I whisper.

"You are lovely, dear Jane. You are a beauty." If it were not for Percy's new voice, a voice that is soft and silky rather than shrill and strident, I would flee right now. I would gather my clothes around me and run down the dark hallway and into the night. Were it not for his warm, tender voice coaxing me through every twist and turn and thrust I would call out for my mother. I would die from sheer terror. "Oh, my dear girl," Percy croons again and again. "Oh my lovely child."

My body is breaking apart. I *am* dying. *Oh, Mother*, I call out. I am breaking into so many pieces there will be nothing left of me for my mother to mourn. "Oh, Percy," I cry. "Kindly cease."

He does not appear to hear me, yet when he rises from the bed, he becomes himself once again. "I love you, my dear girl," he proclaims in his usual voice. He dabs my tender places with his fine linen shirt and kisses me gently. My belly. My breasts. My forehead. My mouth. "You are mine, Clarabella. I am your first lover, and you shall always be mine."

I am his. As Mary is his? I glance around this dim room, so starkly plain and utilitarian. So much less thrilling than a gravesite under the willows. So completely unromantic. I wonder if Mary knows I am here and what that might mean. Does Percy imagine the Godwin girls will happily become interchangeable? "Claire," I say as Percy returns to the bed. My voice echoes from the corners of this bare room. "My name shall be Claire now."

Part Two: Claire

8. Bad Sister

Mary is in bed and asleep when we return to our flat, and Hogg is thankfully gone. I am numb with worry, with shock perhaps, and Percy, having eased his evening with laudanum, is asleep on his feet. "Goodnight, my dear," he whispers as he blows out the lamps.

There in the darkness I sense his retreat. I imagine him pulling off his breeches and sliding under the coverlet next to the sleeping Mary, his arms wrapping around her, his heavy breath on her face, his hands cupping the mound of their unborn child, while I stand waiting, wanting for something more. My bed is in the alcove, a windowless recess along the drafty rear wall, and yet tonight I am warm and aching. My blood burns under my skin like a demon chorus. *What will become of Mary?* I wake from fitful sleep. *By all that is holy, what have I done?*

When morning breaks, I sense that Mary knows everything. I stand before her in my wrapper and shawl, certain that every one of Percy's touches is etched upon my face. Surely the print of his lips and the curved swoop of his thumbprint are as visible as throbbing red burns.

"Percy is sleeping," she whispers as she lights the fire and fills the kettle. Thankfully, her eyes avoid mine, and that discretion saves me from confession. I am certain my eyes carry the blaze of Percy's passion for me, and I am strangely disappointed not to shout *Percy loves me too! The three of us are bound together for all of time.*

Of course I cannot confess. By loving us both, Percy has cleverly torn our sisterhood apart. How foolish for me to think otherwise. I stand here shivering on these cold stones and watch Mary's golden head delicately bend over the teacups. I fight to find words, any words. "How was your evening with Hogg?" I say at last. "Do you believe he is infatuated with you?"

"Oh, Hogg is Percy's doing." She directs the teapot's steam away from her face. "You know, his Communal of Love?"

"Pure fantasy, is it not?"

"Percy believes we are all free to love whomever we choose."

"Surely you would not *choose* Hogg, would you?" I grow faint at the thought. "He knows you are with child?"

Mary smiles at my outrage. "Nothing untoward occurred, Jane. I assured Hogg that I respect Percy's belief in free love, although for now my mind is set on my child's birth."

I nod in agreement and then, off-handedly add. "By the by, I prefer to be known as Claire now."

Mary's eyes flicker across my face as if ascertaining what she already knows. She says nothing, yet I sense her slipping away. In this instant, we fall farther apart than ever. We are now destined to set up boundaries. To challenge one another. To become competitors for Percy's heart. What a sorry day for the Godwin sisters.

With Percy gone off again, our only diversion is Thomas Jefferson Hogg, who behaves as a perfect gentleman. Who could have imagined? He comes to call every evening and entertains us with stories of his college days, when Percy and he were misfits and pranksters. "More attention-seekers than atheists," he says with a smile.

"Such a lovely man," Mary and I tell one another. "Such a good friend for Percy."

We are especially in need of company right now as Mary is too self-conscious of her pregnancy to venture out, and left alone together, Mary and I grow temperamental. We bicker daily, and Fanny casts further gloom upon us with her terse reports from Skinner Street. *Mary Jane sold everything you left behind. Will weeps when he has too much drink and refuses to speak Mary's name.*

Then, precisely when we feel we can bear no more, Percy lands on our doorstep like a ray of sunshine and dispels our gloom. "Oh, my darlings, I have sorely missed you." His embrace holds Mary in place as he murmurs into her ear, words too soft, too loving, perhaps, for me to hear. Then he lifts me into the air until my feet swing like a bell's clapper. "At last," he shouts, "I am home, and all is well."

"Truly, Percy?" Mary asks. "All is well?"

"I am here, Mary. We are together. What could be finer?"

Percy never directly answers Mary's questions, and I am clever enough not to ask directly. Soon enough, the truth about his debts and his children and Harriet will emerge in dribs and drabs. I agree with Percy; why spoil the moment at hand?

He bustles about he always does, rebuilding the fire until its flames leap and spark and our faces glow. He exclaims over us. "Oh, Mary, what a beautiful mother you shall be. What a beautiful child we shall have. Tell me, Claire, how is your reading of *The Empire of the Nairs*? Are you keeping up with your French and Italian?"

He settles beside us with a glass of port and relates what he knows of the smart literary set. "Hookham tells me Leigh Hunt is writing a lyrical account of the victory over Napoleon. Imagine writing in the suffocating dankness of a prison cell? It is unthinkable."

"The poor man," Mary says. "I am grateful you have escaped such a fate, Percy."

"Hunt also has debts?" I ask.

"Hunt libeled the Prince Regent. So much for free speech in our country." He stretches himself out full-length in front of the fire. "Peacock claims Lord Byron is to marry Lady Annabella Millbanke. All subject to change, I dare say."

I notice the secondhand nature of Percy's news. He knows neither Hunt nor Byron, and he cannot mention Will Godwin for Mary's sake. For Mary to be disowned while Percy is welcomed into the Godwin home comes as a hard truth. Men of title, even those in debt, are honored, while we penniless women are disgraced. Oh, the fodder for Percy's poems.

Sensing our dejection, Percy calls out with exaggerated cheer. "Clarabella, favor us with a song! Something ghoulish to match this dreary season looming at the end of the year. How about Barbara Allen?"

I am eager to sing on any occasion, yet Percy's cheerful elder brother façade confuses me. Does he not recall our evening together? Why then his insistence that I read about the Nairs and their free love between many people, including brothers and sisters? How dare he ignore me!

I allow my hand to brush his when I serve the bread. I force his eyes to meet mine over the tea table. Only then does his voice fall into a lower register and set the blue flame flickering in his gaze. Only then does he encourage me to stay awake and listen as he reads aloud long into the night. Mary sleeps in her quiet bed while Percy and I frighten ourselves with tales of ghoulies and ghosties and unseen creatures. "I miss you, Clarabella," he whispers before he slips away to Mary. "I miss your tender touch and your merry laugh. I miss the warmth of you under me."

I am pleased that he desires me, and for the time being, it is enough. His words of longing make it easy to remain the patient, kindly sister and keep my distance from Percy. I tell myself that once his latest poetry is published, once his debts are settled, once his marriage to Harriet is ended and Mary's child is born, we will all live together in a real house with a full larder. Percy and Mary and I will become our own family at last.

On Christmas Day, Mary and I grow homesick, while Percy mopes around the flat with every complaint imaginable. His aching head and riotous bowels, his congested lungs and feverish brow all conspire to make him sulky and difficult to bear. Mary and I sigh. We miss Fanny and Charles and Young Will. Especially Young Will.

"Do you remember when we taught him to read, Mary?"

She laughs. "Never was there a more stubborn pupil. I doubt he yet can write a legible sentence."

"I hope he continues to believe in Father Christmas."

We labor to put our families out of our minds as we wish each other good cheer and eat our inferior versions of Mother's mince pie and plum pudding. In his own attempt at celebration, Percy has sherry with his usual vegetables, and then immediately grows tearful thinking of little Ianthe and the infant Charles. "I worry for them," he says as he spears a cabbage leaf. "I worry that woman will turn them against me. They are my heart and soul, Mary."

Mary turns pale. "Then go to them, Percy. I shall not keep you from your children."

When he rises from his chair, we hold our breath. He bursts out the door and then flies back in again. He opens his book of Emerson's essays and then slams it shut. When at last, he meanders off to bed, Mary and I exhale in relief.

"I welcome the day my own child is born," Mary says. "The day I share a child with Percy cannot come soon enough."

Again, I worry about what will become of me once her baby is born. Despite Percy's one evening of apparent pleasure in my company, despite his whispers conveying his desire for me, I count for little when compared to the woman bearing his child. Despite all the allure I imagine between Percy and myself, I remain merely the stepsister of Mary Wollstonecraft's daughter. The girl with no literary legacy. With no legacy of any sort.

Ever the optimists, by New Year's Eve we three rise from our gloom and become hopeful for a fresh start. Returned to his old ebullient self, Percy splurges on oysters and wine. "We are young," he begins, raising his cup. "We are courageous in the face of adversity. We have climbed mountains and traversed worn-torn France. We have survived cold and hunger and one lame donkey. We are strong and resilient souls."

"Here, here." Mary and I cheer him on.

"Very soon," he promises, "we shall move to a larger flat. Soon my latest book of poems will be published. Soon, although not too soon, we shall have a new child to bless our home! Here's to an auspicious 1815!"

"To 1815." The wine is strong and rich. It warms my throat and my mind grows loose while Percy twirls around the room like a young boy. Once Mary retreats to bed, I tell myself, I shall be alone with him. We will drink more wine and I will slide him into my narrow alcove bed and allow him to plant kisses all over me. Unlike last time, I will open to his touch and not cry out. I will respect my sister by keeping my silence.

Percy stops twirling. He goes to Mary and carefully draws her up from her chair so they may sway together, a dance in slow motion. "Sing for us, Claire," he calls to me.

"For auld lang syne, my dear." My voice does not waver, although the song inevitably makes me sad. "For auld lang syne." I watch as their lumbering dance takes them toward the bedroom, and my voice cracks.

"Goodnight, Claire," Mary calls as she disappears from sight.

"I'll take a cup of kindness then." Not missing a note, I step across the room and take Percy's hand. "For auld lang syne." I press his cold fingers to my warm mouth.

He winces. Then, he turns away. "Goodnight, Claire."

I stand there watching the fire die and worry what new misery 1815 might bring. I go to sleep in my cold little bed, and sometime before dawn I awaken to the sound of Percy stirring the ashes in the grate. I hear him settle at his writing desk and the sound of pages turning. He is writing a poem, his first of the year. I curl myself tighter under my coverlet and tell myself it is a good omen. Percy is always happy when he is writing.

In the first days of the new year, Percy becomes so completely devoted to his new poetry that he is too preoccupied to move us into a larger flat. Mary is unperturbed. She is content to have Percy home, to have Hogg coming to call, to be desired by two brilliant men. She is so filled with good humor, she insists I walk with her. "Only a short distance, Claire. I want to feel the crisp snap of the cold on my face. I want to feel alive."

I am happy to humor her. I must endear myself to her before the baby arrives and she is tempted to send me packing. We wrap our heads in woolen scarves and set off into the bright day. I slow my usual pace to match hers as we imagine the house of our dreams. "Spacious," we say in unison. The wind brings tears to our eyes.

"Space aplenty for our books."

"And Percy's writing desk."

"A sunny little garden for the baby to play." Mary wraps her scarf tighter. "Can you imagine me a mother? By Springtime, I shall have a child. It does not seem possible."

I agree. In less than a year's time, our lives have turned and gathered speed. If we were better sisters, we might also confess our fears. I face abandonment, and Mary faces death. She must constantly think of her own mother, who died so soon after Mary's birth. She must worry that she, too, could die and leave her infant in another woman's care. In my care. The thought brings me to tears. I take Mary's hand, wanting to say I would care for her orphaned child as if it were my very own. Yet I am the daughter of Mary's stepmother, and we both know how badly that arrangement turned out. And in truth, while I am somewhat fond of children, I would not know what to do with an infant.

We return to our latest quarters on Nelson Square with wind-reddened faces and frozen fingers, only to find Percy pacing with his bottle of laudanum. "What is wrong?" Mary cries out.

Percy's eyes grow larger when his mind is racing, and right now his eyes are as endless and blue as the cloudless sky. "My grandfather is dead. He died last week, I have learned, and his will is to be read in Sussex in two days' time." Mary and I watch in silence as he tracks back and forth across our creaking floorboards. His pattern creates a rhythm of step and creak, step and creak. "The weather is unpredictable at best. I have no money to hire a carriage." Finally he ceases. "Dammit, Mary, what shall I do?"

"Considering the distance and the season, no one would expect you to attend."

"You are right, yes." He drains the last of his bottle. "Will you accompany me?"

"If that is your wish." Mary agrees, although surely she must loathe the notion of setting off on a winter's journey in her condition. She readies her warmest clothes and gloves to wear with her spencer jacket and her long, hooded cloak. Both of them black, of course. I watch her preparations with compassion, wondering if Percy is compelled to travel to Sussex because he expects Grandfather Abyss to leave him an inheritance or because he wishes to make peace with Sir Tim and the estranged Shelley family.

The next morning barely dawns. Our windows are coated with ice, and wind blows through every crevice with its cold breath. Mary is wracked with fatigue and unable to rise. "Please go in my place, Claire." Her voice is calm, but her eyes are dark with worry. She does not trust me, and rightfully so.

"Oh, I could not," I say to appear less eager than I am.

Percy leaves no room for debate. "You must accompany me, Claire."

I rejoice over my unexpected gift. I am happy to travel, happy to don Mary's spencer and cloak and gloves, all of which are superior to my own, and climb into the chaise with Percy. I will do anything to be alone with Percy. Even if it involves a long, miserable coach ride and boring legal matters.

We set off in good spirits. Percy is stocked with his writing materials and enough laudanum to soothe an entire grieving family, while I carry only my valise of fresh undergarments, a mourning-worthy dress, my book, *The Empire of the Nairs,* and my journal. "I thank you for your company, Claire." He gives me his somber blue look.

"You are welcome, kind sir," I say to make him smile.

We are not far into the countryside when the puddles on the road turn to ice-covered ponds. The farther we travel, the heavier the ice shower becomes. Limbs snap off trees and litter our route. The coachman travels at a snail's pace, inching around the obstacles.

"Shall we stop at an inn?"

"No time to sleep, darling girl. No money for an inn."

A few times we pull off the road for other coaches to pass. At one point, we step out and push, only to crawl back into the coach chilled and damp. Percy sips his laudanum and falls into fitful slumber. It is a torturous journey, and night is coming on. I think of Mary, warm by the fire, and am grateful she stayed behind.

By the time we arrive in Horsham, I am weary and disheveled and would gladly sell *The Nairs* for a room at an inn and a chance to tidy myself before meeting the Shelleys. Percy, however, is impatient, wild with worry at the prospect at facing Sir Tim. "Better to swallow my medicine now," he says, "before I lose courage."

As often as Mary and I have heard about the Shelley family's wealth and how Percy must fight for mere dribbles of his share, I am not prepared to witness what wealth truly means. When the coach turns into the gates of Field Place, a drive as long and wide as a country lane stretches before us. It takes minutes before the gatekeeper's house, a house larger than any I know, comes into view.

I grow weak. I brush at the nap of Mary's black cloak. I run my hands over my hair, tucking loose black curls into place. I should not be here. At last, the grand manor house comes into view. Built of cut stone and slate, Field Place has six enormous windows running above the entrance and six massive chimneys rising from the rooftop. Not to mention the two wings on either side that could well serve as houses entirely by themselves. The grounds extend far beyond our line of vision. Even now, in this dead grey season of winter, they are stately and well-kept. The divide between the noble class and the middle class could never be more obvious than it is in this moment, and I am tempted to ask Percy for a sip from his medicine bottle.

Only a love for the arts, I realize as Percy jumps from the carriage, could ever bind the Shelleys and the Godwins together.

Sadly, I am not a Godwin, and Sir Tim is not a patron of the arts.

An encounter with the people who live behind these massive doors will be no less traumatic than an encounter with a colony of lepers. Except I will be the leper.

"Who will I say I am?" I ask as Percy assists me from the carriage.

"Why yourself, of course." His laugh is brittle.

"Do we knock?" I touch the polished door with the fingertips of my borrowed gloves.

He lifts the heavy latch and propels us inward. "Hello," he calls as we step into the foyer. Patterned rugs from the Orient cover parquet floors. A crystal lamp sparkles from its marble stand, illuminating a curved, ruby-carpeted staircase. There, a gray-haired woman descends so quickly that her black silk dress, similar to the one I have in my valise, rustles. "Bysshe, dear lad, where have ye been?"

Percy scoops her up from the bottom step and playfully swings her off her feet. "Traversing snow, ice, gloom. The usual English winter roads." He sets her on the floor. "Have you missed me?"

"I have, Bysshe. The place is a tomb without ye." Then, maybe thinking better of her word choice, she turns to me. "This is Mary?"

"Claire." I hold out my gloved hand. "Mary's sister."

She takes my hand. "My pleasure, Claire. Such a clever lass to dress for the cold. Cold for three days now." She pronounces three as *tree*.

"Is my father around?" Percy shifts from one foot to the other.

"I shall find him, Bysshe. You remain here."

I find it odd to be left standing in the entryway. Despite Mother's disappointment in me, I imagine myself thundering up the stairs from the book shop to the parlor should I ever return home again. Oh, there would be histrionics to accompany my arrival, yet I cannot envision myself standing among the bookshelves in Will's store and waiting for Mother to sashay forth in her own good time.

Percy continues shifting from side to side. Despite his long brown coat, likely cashmere, and his warm gloves, he shivers. He pulls a spotless handkerchief from his pocket and covers the whole of his face to catch a cough that resembles the call of a goose.

"Your mother was pleased to see you," I say to calm his breathing.

He ceases coughing to cast a blue flash my way. "That was Sybil. Our housekeeper."

Of course, Field Place would have a wing full of servants. My ignorance is boundless. When I imagined myself staying in Sir Tim's home, I worried there would be no room for guests. That I would be relegated to sharing a room with a maiden aunt or a band of small cousins. How laughable.

The man striding through the arched doorway at the end of the foyer is not pleased to see us. Silver-haired and red-faced, he hisses, also rather like a goose. "Where is your common sense, Bysshe? Do you possess so little esteem for our family? For your grandfather's memory?" His eyes, frighteningly like Percy's, flash toward me. "How dare you bring your whores into this house?"

"It is my right to be here, Father."

"As long as you carry on with your bohemian madness, this poetry and free love nonsense, you and your runaway girls are not welcome. Now depart this instant. Leave."

His face aflame, Percy holds up his hands in surrender and backs away. "I shall stay at the Gateway until I speak with the solicitors."

"Every will has conditions, and your grandfather's is no exception."

Thus we are cast back in the cold air with icy pellets stinging our faces. We climb into the coach as damp and chilled and penniless as when we arrived. "That," Percy says to me, "was Sir Tim."

"Would he have been more welcoming to Mary?"

"He thought you were Mary."

I am grateful Mary was spared the indignity of meeting Percy's father, although I am dismayed to be called a *whore*. Does Sir Tim think Percy paid me to come along? Or does his cruel remark have something to do with my appearance, the jet black tendrils curling around my face or my flushed olive skin? When Percy signs us into our rooms at the Gateway Inn, I glimpse myself in the looking glass and am shocked to discover that I look all of twelve years. I look like what I am: a girl in a plain frock wearing her elder sister's coat.

"For the record," Percy says as he leads me away, "you are my sister, Miss Shelley."

No, I am a girl who cannot wait to crawl into a warm bed with her stepsister's lover. Perhaps Sir Tim is justified in his thinking after all.

9. Conditions of Dying

We spend three days at the Gateway waiting for something legal and binding to occur. Grandfather Abyss, who was American-born and then returned to England to make his fortune by marrying heiresses, has not made matters easy for his own heirs. Percy is an heir, that is our good news, yet as Sir Tim hinted, there are conditions. Much as he did in London, Percy spends most of our time in Sussex meeting with lawyers. "I shall never be free of them." He collapses on the bed. "Come, Claire. Come, soothe me. Ease my weary mind." Naturally, I go to him. His days may be spent in law offices, but his nights are devoted to me, and I have grown fond of this pattern.

On the day Percy arranges to meet his mother in the lobby, she does not appear, and he returns to our rooms as troubled and forlorn as a young boy. "I have only Sir Tim to blame." He sits in the straight-backed chair facing the fire. "His whims determine all of our fates."

I worry when he shivers. Percy's constitution is perpetually weak, and when he is feeling poorly, his mood plummets with the sun. "Shall I pour you some sherry? Send for fresh water?"

He shakes his head, and I anxiously wait to hear what body part troubles him now. Are his joints aching or is his chest filling with fluid? Is his stomach roiling or a headache causing him double vision? Percy has many complaints, and I lack Mary's patience in dealing with them. Surprisingly, he leaps from the chair. "We must have a bath, dear girl. I shall order one at once."

A bath? Oh, such a luxury. "Are we celebrating victory, Percy? Or are you spending your inheritance in advance?"

"Progress." He smiles. "We are celebrating progress."

Once the bathtub, such a splendid creation, is delivered to our room and the water poured, steam rises from its copper bed and fills the room with a warm, moist cloud. "We could be in a jungle, Percy! In Mr. Owen's Amazon. What a lovely way to spend a winter day."

He bows from his waist, his hand skimming the deep blue carpet. "Ladies first."

I am happy to shed my sister's winter-worn clothing as Percy watches in appreciation. Happier still for his assistance in easing myself into the tub. "It is heavenly." I sigh. "Far better than a jungle."

"What a pity not to have some paper boats." He squats by my bath and trails his hand through the water.

Knowing he is unable to resist the sight of my slick, honeyed skin, I ignore talk of paper boats. "What do you suppose Mary imagines we are doing here together, Percy?"

"I sent her word of my legal entanglements."

"Did she reply?"

"Mary understands how I am, Claire." His fingers are slippery against my face. "I will say nothing of our time here together, but she will know. Mary and I communicate our passionate natures without words. We respect each other's desires, and I respect that you are sisters."

Since I have heard their nighttime murmurings with my own ears, his claim of silent communication holds no ground for me, and the continuing sister fallacy irks me. I want to say I am no more Mary's sister than I am Harriet's, but why bother? "I am happy to be here with you, Percy."

I lick a water droplet from the tip of his nose, and in return, he kisses my forehead. "Hogg is looking after Mary while we are away, and we are never to discuss what we do here. Is that understood?"

"It is. Completely." I think of Mary sitting in the quiet flat or falling into her empty bed. She must grieve to imagine Percy with me. Hogg or no Hogg, she must be in misery. Then Percy's hands slide over my body like he is sculpting me, shaping me from water, and Mary floats out from my mind.

By our third day together, I cannot imagine myself without Percy. He has become as necessary to me as food, water, and air, and I can no longer imagine looking into Mary's placid face and behaving as though nothing happened between us. I cannot imagine sleeping alone in my own narrow bed. Every beat of my blood is filled with Percy. I touch his face when he stirs to wakefulness. "I do not want to leave," I whisper.

Half asleep, he murmurs agreement. "'Tis a dull journey ahead."

"I want to be with you once we return to London." I know what I am asking. Mary and I have read *Rights of Women*. We have read *The Empire of the Nairs*. Many times.

He rolls towards me and pulls me close. "You shall be with me forever, darling girl, but there are some things we cannot ask of your sister. Now come, we must start our journey." He kisses my cheek and leaps from our bed.

Since Percy despises sulking, I remain silent, even as I question his reasoning. Mary will not share Percy with me because I am her stepsister rather than a complete stranger? We carry too much familiarity of each other, perhaps? Percy and I climb into the coach, and it creaks from the cold. Such a strange, ominous sound. When the wheels crunch over the ice, I think of bones breaking. We travel less than a mile before the snow begins to fall afresh.

Although it takes us less time to travel north than it did to go south, we are away from London longer than expected. It is well past midnight when we arrive home, and the lamp is burning. Mary is awake. What woman could sleep when her lover, the father of her unborn child, has gone off with her sister?

"Mary, dear Mary," Percy calls out as he opens the door. "We are returned."

Mary wafts into the parlor holding her belly. Between the white of her face and the white of her nightgown, she appears as a ghost. Then she speaks, and I know she is real. "I fear the baby is coming."

"Impossible," he replies. "It is far too early."

I know little to nothing about childbirth. Not how endlessly a birthing can grind on or how to care for the mother or how to assist the midwife without simply being in her way. The midwife, a Mrs. Grace Church, does not think much of me and Percy and our road-weary appearance. He with his unkempt hair and a day's growth of beard. Me with my mussy clothes and nervous manner. "Shouldn't you be tending to your studies?" She asks me.

"Not today," I say with spirit.

Percy goes out to the chemist for a refill of laudanum. "Percy," I beg him. "Pray come back soon." Left alone in this silent, sacred hour, I am frightened to death for Mary and the baby and what will happen next. Even when Percy returns in a calmer state and the baby is finally born, I feel detached, like I am floating untethered along the ceiling.

"Father only," says Mrs. Grace Church when I attempt to follow Percy into their bed chamber. This time I believe she is acting on Mary's orders.

"Percy!" I call after him. He is mellow in that moment, too awash in emotion over his new daughter and his precious Mary to respond to me. I am the bad sister, made to wait by myself in the parlor, and heartsick that I have lost my slim hold on the father of Mary's new babe. I make tea to calm my own nerves and grudgingly offer a cup to Grace Church. "Mary is doing well?"

"For a first birth, all went as expected." Grace Church sips loudly. "She is young. She will heal."

I hope she was kinder to Mary.

When Percy emerges from the bedroom, he is aglow with details of their daughter's beauty, her delicate face, her tiny hands. "She is the very image of Mary," he says, "and her name is Clara. What do you think of that?"

I do not know what to think. Even after Mary rouses and allows me to hold my namesake, I am struck mute. Holding Clara is like holding a flower. She looks to be formed from blue-veined white petals, and she weighs nothing. Reverently, I hand her back to Mary. "She is exquisite." It is all I can think to say.

Mary smiles. "I must let Hogg know of Clara's arrival."

"I would not encourage him," I tell her. "Percy plans to return to his writing, and Hogg will be a disruption."

"Very true. Percy needs time and space to think. We are so fortunate that Clara sleeps so well. That she is such a quiet baby."

"Very fortunate," I say, and I mean it.

Braving the wrath of the Godwins, Fanny and my brother Charles stealthily come to call, but at different times. Fanny is awestruck. "A dear, wee baby," she says of Clara. "She resembles Percy." My brother is more sheepish, stealthily handing over a package of baby linens, a gift from Mother that we are forbidden to outwardly acknowledge.

"For women of ill repute, you appear quite wholesome." He teases as he embraces us.

Like Percy, Charles is always in a rush, but unlike Percy, he is always in good humor, and we welcome him like a tonic. "You are a sight for sore eyes, dear brother," we tell him. "How bold you are to keep our company."

"Yes indeed," he says with a wink, "you girls really stirred up a hornet's nest. Mother wanted to call out the guard. Father wanted to send you both to the convent. None of us were ever to speak to you again. Which is quite possibly why I am here today."

"Such a brave man," Mary teases in return. "What will you say to Father?"

"Not a thing. Unless I am found out. Then I will report only that you are quite alive and not living in the street nor completely in the slums."

We laugh with him, feeling hopeful once again. And when I walk him to the door, I study my handsome brother, comparing his fair complexion to my dark one. "Do you believe we share the same father?"

"Likely not." His smile is impish, a slash of white in his ruddy face. "What does it matter?" Then, before he dashes away, he offers me encouragement. "We come from a long history of scraping by, you know."

By scraping by, he is referring to Mother, of course, and her own ability to keep from living on the streets by captivating men of means. Charles' father. My father. Will Godwin. "I suppose we do." I frown.

"Mother has good instincts. She can think on her feet. You are like her in that respect, sister."

I do not want to believe I am anything like my mother, yet I want to believe that I will survive my uncertain future in Percy's household. That Mary will not throw me out on the street. That I will not starve or grow sick from the cold and damp. That I will not have to return to Skinner Street to seek comfort.

Despite all the fragility of our household, Hogg arrives to assist in our move to a larger place, and we are all delighted. Our new quarters overlook a tidy courtyard in Arabella Row, and we now have two bed chambers, both large and airy, with a nook by the window for Clara's cradle. There is even room for a piano, were we able to afford one. Our Mary is beside herself with domesticity. She loves being a mother, she tells Hogg, and looks forward to those many children Percy is planning.

The winter turns rainy. Percy is with his solicitors, and Hogg is tending to his own affairs. The quiet flat becomes too large and the empty spaces too empty. Ours voices echo. "What do you imagine Fanny and Charles will say about the first Godwin grandchild?" Mary asks me as we gaze out on the rain puddles.

What Mary is really asking is if our siblings will say *anything* about her baby. Not acknowledging Clara's existence is too painful to contemplate, and so I take a stab at humor. "I imagine they will speak in code. Charles will be clipped and to-the-point. *The delivery has arrived,* he will tell Mother. Fanny, who can never get to the point under ordinary circumstances, will go on about the weather first and then say, 'oh, Father, a daughter like myself is a blessing. A daughter with soft golden hair and fair skin is a beauty.'"

Mary laughs at my silliness which I take as a good sign. If I can make my sister laugh, she will want me to stay around.

Our contented state of domesticity on Arabella Row lasts for four full days. Mary rises at dawn to feed Clara, the flower baby who never cries, and finds her both silent and dead. Now nothing will ever be the same.

I am filled with contempt for the Godwins. Will is sticking to his principles, or whatever he calls his particular set of perversions, and refuses to call on Mary, his only true daughter, in her time of grief. He will not acknowledge either the birth or the death of his first grandchild, and Mary is crushed by his cruelty. Fanny and my own flesh-and-blood Mother lack the courage to go behind Will's back, so we are shut away here on Arabella Row like plague victims. Mary becomes despondent and recedes away from us by turning herself into a mute, expressionless statue that sits in the window by the empty cradle.

There will be no funeral, no family services, so sensitive, grief-stricken Percy arranges for the burial. I remain with Mary, who is oblivious to my presence. She ignores the cups of tea and feeble words I offer as comfort. "Oh look, the sun is shining," I say in one breath, and "Oh dear sister, I am sorry for your loss" in the next breath. I hum old hymns rather than sing anything too cheerful. I wish for Percy's hasty return from the graveyard. I watch a cloud blot out the sun, and the rain begin again.

Percy is soaked and feverish when he bursts through the door. Yet he throws himself at Mary's feet. Coughing and shivering, he remains there for hours, holding her hand and reassuring her in his anxious, intense manner that she is not to blame. "Please do not torture yourself like this, my love. There will be future babies, I promise you."

Mary does not respond. She will not allow him to carry her to bed when night falls, and he covers her with the black shawl she wore when we left for France. Now an eternity ago. He sleeps at her feet, curling into a ball when I cover him with my own black shawl. I leave them in their tortured sleep and steal off to my bed chamber, which is no warmer than my old alcove.

It is days before Mary rouses from her faraway trance, and even then her face is clouded, like is she wearing a caul. Like she has been reborn. The devoted Percy is elated. He turns to me with a triumphant smile. At last, he is thinking, Mary has borne the highest tide of her grief, and we can be hopeful that she will survive.

In that moment, Mary's head snaps upward. She sees that smile that passes between Percy and me, and I attempt to reassure her. "Thank God, Mary." I rush to her side. "You gave us a fright." I smooth a wisp of golden hair away from her pale face. "What do you like most right now? A cup of tea? A bowl of porridge? We have an apple."

"I would like for you to leave, Claire. I cannot go on living as long as you are here."

10. Prodigal

The single condition for my return to Skinner Street is quite clear. If I dissolve my relationship with Percy Shelley, I will be forgiven. I will be welcomed home. For the sake of Mary's sanity, I agree to a brief visit with the Godwins.

"Please do not go, Claire." Percy watches me tie on my bonnet. "Be patient. Give Mary time. She does not mean what she says now."

"Yes, Percy, she does." I gather up my gloves. "Fanny and I are long overdue for a visit, and I will return by dusk. Do not worry yourself."

As I set off for the carriage stop, I think to look back, to glance up at the window of our flat, and I find Mary there, watching me leave. Hoping, no doubt, that I will never return. Mary never wanted me in her life with Percy, and now I worry Perry may consider himself better off with one less woman in his household and in his debt.

London in winter is a grey landscape of wet streets, dirty snow, and gloomy skies. On Skinner Street, the skies are dingier, and the snow is greyer. Frozen sculptures of dog excrement stand on every corner, especially on our corner where Fanny's strays hover like ghosts of their summer selves. Above the bookshop door, the stone carving of Aesop is outlined in soot. The peeling signboard creaks in the wind. Could any place in the world be drearier?

Inside, I am greeted with the familiar scent of leather and paper and dust. I breathe it in, and, scrapping my original plan to charge up the stairs like my old self, I ring the hand bell on the counter instead. Let Mother come to me. I wait, head cocked for the sound of the door closing at the top of the stairs and then her heavy footfalls.

She appears like a dream, her long purple shawl writhing around her like a collapsed gypsy tent. She stops dead, pressing her palm to her heaving cleavage. "For the love of God, Clara Jane. You could have given me an apoplexy. Why not write ahead to grant me fair warning?"

"I go by Claire now, Mother."

"I understand that." She stretches open her arms and waits, her eyes moist, and I understand that I could depart and come back a thousand times, and Mother will continue to stand here holding onto her high expectations that I will return as the good, proper daughter she desires. It is too late for me.

Even so, I step into her embrace. "Oh, Mother." I breathe in greedily. Ink and candlewax. Lavender and rose water. Despite everything, my mother's scent is an elixir.

"Thank God you are here." She kisses my cheek, my forehead, the tip of my nose. "There, now." She pats my back. "You must sup with us. Fanny made her best soup this morning, and she will be distressed if you do not stay."

"And you, Mother? Do you want me to stay?" I came here to ask this question, yet I quake as she steps backward, studying my face through her tinted glasses.

"Oh, daughter." She wraps her purple shawl around her neck, which puts me in mind of a turtle. "Even though you and Mary have brought disgrace upon our family and poor dear Will can barely hold up his head in the company of his friends, I have *prayed* for this moment of your return. Surely you know that." She ushers me toward the staircase. "I know you are not the one to blame, and you have my forgiveness."

"Who might you blame, Mother?" I follow her upward, observing how her broad behind sways with every step. Mary Jane Godwin has not gone hungry while Mary and I starved.

"I know Percy is responsible for your corruption. I lie awake counting up the favors we bestowed on that lad and his dear little wife and look how he repaid us. Stealing our daughters in the dark of night!"

"It was daybreak."

"Irrelevant, Jane."

"Claire. My name is Claire, and I went with Percy of my own free will."

By the top of the stairs, she is recounting that day in Calais, and her loss of me to Percy. Again I hear about Percy's treachery and Mary's misguided influence on me. Already, I am weary, and only the sight of Fanny rushing toward me saves me from fleeing.

"Are you home to stay, Sister? I have missed you so." Her hands are like butterflies as they brush over my shoulders and along my arms. Her kisses barely graze my cheeks, yet her words are heartfelt and true. "Come, sit at the table, and let me serve you. Oh dear, I should have baked bread today."

I take my old familiar place at the table, while my mother drops heavily into the chair that Mary once occupied. "Men like Percy," she begins again. "Men like Percy, who are brilliant and charming, can also be devious. He took advantage of two young impressionable girls, and now look at the sad state of things. Mary is barred from Will's fine household, and you are estranged from us."

"You are responsible for our estrangement, Mother. And I am your only daughter." Every beat of my blood tells me to rise up and run away. Then I glance into Fanny's wide, worried eyes. For the sake of poor Fanny, the sister left behind on Skinner Street, I stay to eat her soup.

"How is it?" Fanny worries over me, her brows drawn together and her hands aflutter. "Not enough pepper? Too much salted ham? I find pease soup is best in winter, do you not agree?"

"Indeed. It is lovely, Fanny. Well done."

Fanny chatters on. She describes the precise slicing of the onion and the soaking of the peas. The exact sharpness of the knife blade. The correct amount of water and the size of the pot. I listen as best I can, reminding myself that since Mary and Harriet have been cast from Fanny's world, I must remain the composed sister, the sister to bring Fanny news of those she so loves. Yet I cannot mention Mary or Harriet or dear, departed Baby Clara in my mother's presence. My mind sputters. If only I could fashion news of Mary into a code for Fanny to decipher.

My mother continues her lament. "Unlike my dear Will, Percy uses his charm and wit to satisfy his lust rather than better the world."

Mention of Percy sparks Fanny to speak of more than soup-making. "Percy looked well enough on Tuesday when he called as usual." She blushes. "Less frail, I believe he was."

I look up from my bowl. Fanny saw Percy weekly? Our Fanny, the first Godwin sister to fall under Percy's spell, is welcomed home from Wales and permitted to keep Percy's company, while I must choose one or the other? Oh, the hypocrisy!

To calm myself, I let my mind wander. If I were to live here again, I could have my own room as Fanny is now in the old schoolroom. I would have no Mary to fuss after me about making the bed or folding my petticoats, and yet I would be privy to Percy's visits. Could I spirit him up the stairs and into my bed if I lived here under Mother's sharp-eyed vigil? Could I woo him away from Mary? Would I ever be bold enough to try?

"I cannot abide the thought of you ending up in the gutter to die poor and unloved," Mother says as she passes a plate of dried figs.

"Unloved?"

"I shall not live forever, dear daughter. Someday you will suffer the loss of my boundless love."

"More tea, Claire?" Fanny rises from her chair like a plain brown bird pursued by a cat, yet Mother stays on track.

"For me to return from France without you was the greatest disappointment of my life. The basest humiliation."

The very mention of the word *France* sets my mind drifting back to the glory of being carefree in an exotic country where every day brought new lush scenery. A castle ruin. An ice cold lake. A sparkling canal. Oh, what I would have missed if I had stayed on Skinner Street and remained a good and proper daughter. I eat my soup in silence. I watch the shadows gather as I listen to Mother's lectures and Fanny's tiresome conversation, and I realize I have no choices after all. To spare myself from utter boredom, I shall return to Arabella Row and take my chances with Mary. I will hang on there until I am forced out.

Winter drags on, and Percy pursues employment for me as a teacher or as a companion to wealthy old ladies. He beseeches friends to take me in. To no avail. Thankfully we have some relief in Hogg, Mary's ardent admirer. He continues to call, to squire her to the zoo, to discuss poetry, to flatter her unceasingly, even as Mary remains in her state of grief and worry. She frets about Harriet's hold on Percy and Percy's hold on me, and when they argue, our spacious accommodations fill with the same misery as our little flat on Church Terrace.

"I cannot simply toss Claire out on the street." Percy's voice rises like a storm.

"Yes, Percy. You can do exactly that." Mary's tone is desperate, and we fear she teeters so close to the edge of madness that she will topple.

"I have a plan." Percy says with a new vigor. "We shall have ourselves a little holiday, Mary. Spring is a lovely time for an excursion in the countryside. Can you promise to hold on until my funds are available?"

Although I question the veracity of Percy's *funds*, it is a splendid plan, and to improve Mary's state of mind until the end of April, I stay out of sight for hours on end. I run errands. I shop for Percy's fresh fruit and vegetables in the market. While Mary takes her daily walk, I undertake Percy's daily laundry. The man detests dirt, yet he owns few clothes, and for someone who aligns himself with the poor and downtrodden, he is more fussy than not.

On fine days, I carry my journal to the park and write until the sun hides behind clouds and my fingers grew too stiff with cold to function. And on days when the weather is unsuitable, I stay in my bed. I light the lamp and lie with my books and papers surrounding me. It is rather pleasant, like being on an island, and it is the only place in the flat where I can remain out of Mary's sight.

This is how we pass our days until Percy and Mary leave for their holiday at Salt Hill. "We shall return in a few days, Claire." My sister is gracious now that she is about to be alone with Percy, although he risks her collapse with a good-bye kiss to my forehead.

As they ride away, I unwrap the package of pounds Percy left for my expenses. It is quite a lot, and I do not believe Percy has truly received his inheritance. What if he and Mary are gone for good and this is his parting gift to me?

Now alone, I take long walks and, always hungry, spend large sums of Percy's money on food. Then I return to the flat and sit alone at the table to consume bread and cheese and potted meat, a perfect golden orange, a handful of raisins, dates dusted in sugar. Evenings are the worst time to be lonely, and to avoid thinking about Percy and Mary on their romantic holiday, I gaze at the empty space under the window where Clara's cradle once stood. Then I feel less sorry for myself.

In the morning, sick from my gluttony of the night before, I eat dry toast and drank cups of tea, which is Mother's remedy for most anything. Then I return to my bed and contemplate how to survive without begging Will Godwin to take me in. If there is a God, which Mother believes and Percy does not, I hope he has a plan for me. One that includes accommodations.

When Mary and Percy return with their fresh air exuberance and bright freckled faces, I swing open the door to breathe in their scent of sunshine and lovemaking and frighten my sister.

"Claire! I believed you gone." She flies at Percy like an angry robin. "You promised me."

Percy's eyes are a glorious contrast to his golden skin. "Soon, my dear." He addresses me, not Mary, and his words do not sound like a threat.

"You had a pleasant time?" I watch Mary fuss with her valise. Her vim and vigor have returned, yet her stiff, choppy motions reveal her fury.

"You shall not remain here. Do not fool yourself into thinking you can change Percy's mind."

Percy steps around her to reach me. "You managed by yourself?" He squeezes my shoulders in sympathy. "Your turn will come, Claire. Soon, a holiday for you as well."

In May, the air turns soft against our faces, and we are drunk with the scent of blossoms. We comb petals from our hair and shade our eyes from the sun. At last Percy receives some bit of settlement from Grandfather Abyss's estate, and he promises to take me to Devon. I view this journey as my chance to shine. Alone with Percy, I shall convince him of what he will miss if I am gone. If he chooses Mary over me.

I plan my role as the carefree, spirited sister. *Oh dear Percy,* I will say, *how very thoughtful. What a splendid day. Shall we stop for a stroll?* I have always considered becoming an actress.

Unfortunately, Percy is preoccupied and oblivious to my charms. He hurries us along in his usual impassioned, quick-stepping, agitated manner. "I am concerned," he says to start out our journey, "about the sorry state of the nation."

Oh, mercy.

From there he goes on to worry about the Prince Regent and the starving children and a war that supposedly lies around the corner. He is concerned for Mary, naturally, and, as always, his own health. "I have abscesses on my lungs, Claire," he tells me as we ride out of the city. "Quite possibly, I am dying."

I have learned not to overreact to Percy's bouts of hypochondria. "Oh, dear Percy," I say. "You must rest now that your finances are in order. You must recover your strength for Mary's sake." I give him a confident pat on his arm. "Let us enjoy this lovely countryside." I smile my brightest smile. "Let us live every moment."

"Do you ever miss your mother?" His voice is a low hum.

I point to the nearest meadow. "Notice the Rose of Sharon," I say to distract him. "Isn't it stunning?"

"You understand that Mary Jane was wounded that day in Calais." He leans across the seat to take my hand, but his fingertips are disconcertingly smooth and unaccustomedly slippery. "You would be welcomed home now, Claire."

I retract my hand. "What do you know of Fanny nowadays?" It is a test of honesty, a chance for him to confess that he visits the Godwins more often than Mary knows. "She speaks so highly of you in her letters."

"I see Fanny on occasion. She is quite well."

"You see her when you call on Father?" Be honest with me, I want to say. Tell me your secrets. Tell me you love me. Tell me you cannot live without me.

His eyes, so strangely dark in this carriage, flit about as I wait for him to speak. "I have spoken to Will Godwin on your behalf."

The sunlight flashes past in sickening streaks, and I begin to babble. About the chance of rain. About the works of Chaucer. About Fanny's gift for drawing. My tongue stumbles over my words. My eyes water. "A year ago, we spent every evening like tonight walking away from Skinner Street. Do you remember those nights when we skipped over the cobblestones? You with your paper boats and Mary in her tartan dress and me floating along like the good sister I was. How could a year have changed us so completely?"

"Will and Mary Jane will both welcome you home now."

"Oh, Percy." My face stings. "You truly wish for me to leave? Is that what you are saying? Is that what you most desire?"

"Losing you is the last thing I desire."

I know by the change in his voice that I am doomed. When Percy speaks normally, his tone is as high and piercing as a blue jay's call. Whether discussing the weather or Parliament or the complexity of his debts, it all sounds oddly affirmative, and when Percy speaks about what is lost, like his father's respect or his marriage to Harriet, his voice falls into a flat plane. Not merely solemn, but barren. Even now, as he proclaims he never wants me to leave, his voice holds no inflection, no spark of promise.

"Please, Percy, I beg you."

"Devon is stunning, Claire. You will see."

I no longer want to see the beauty of Devon. The horse picks up his pace, speeding us along moss-covered stonewalls. Sunlight flashes across my face in wavering patterns. *I am the sister being sent away.* I turn away from Percy and vomit on the carriage floor.

11. Woodbine Cottage

There may be beautiful Devonshire scenery along our way to Lynmouth, but I do not see it. Instead I sit with my elbows braced on my knees and my head bent over the empty feed pail at my feet. I try to ignore Percy's voice droning above my head like a cacophony of gnats. "You are suffering from nerves," it whines. "Take a draught of my laudanum."

I refuse to respond. Hunched over in misery, my hair curtaining my face, I contemplate how I have fallen victim to the unhappy history of the Godwin women. Into a bubbling pool of high expectations that the men we love will return our love and never abandon us. Even my own mother has no notion of what became of either Charles' father or my own. "He was believed to be Swiss, dear," she says of the man who conceived me. As if that is all I will ever care to know.

At least Mother never tried to kill herself as the first Mrs. Godwin did when Fanny's father left. I quell another rise of nausea as the carriage rounds a bend. Percy grasps my shoulders to steady me. I shrug him off and think of Fanny, the first sister to fall under Percy's spell and promise to follow him everywhere. Had she been the sister to run away with Percy and Mary, would she be the one on her way to Lynmouth today? Having survived Wales, perhaps Fanny would make a better outcast than I.

I raise my head from the bucket, but the scent of lilacs and apple blossoms makes my head spin. I lie along the carriage seat and close my eyes against the green and flowering countryside. Percy places a clammy hand along my cheek. "Any better?"

"Do not touch me." I hiss at him, and when he withdraws, the loss of his touch becomes an ache.

I am in misery when at last the carriage stops. I climb down to solid ground and take stock of my future. Percy holds on to me for fear I shall faint and once again begins his flowery description of the moors and the gorge and the sea. The moon and the stars and the sky. "Harriet and I honeymooned here for a month, and it was delightful."

I moan, hoping he will cease talking.

"You must see this, Claire," he insists as he gingerly walks me to the edge of the cliff. "Lynmouth Bay. Is it not breathtaking to have the sparkle of water before you every day when you rise?"

It is breathtaking. Even feeling as poorly as I do in this moment, the sight of water spread out before me promises peace and calm. For the first time since we returned from France, I have a slight flicker of hope. Perhaps I am like my mother. Perhaps I can turn my own fate here in Devon and survive as well or better as she has. Quickly, before Percy says more than I can bear, I tell him to leave. "Please, Percy. Do not spend the night. Go now while I am standing on my own and feeling stronger. Go before Mary worries herself to death."

Speechless, he stands before me with his eyes reflecting the sea and the sun catching in his hair, and I immediately want to take back every word I said. Quickly, before I do something I will regret, I walk away. The coachman has opened the cottage and unloaded my bags and stands waiting for Percy's orders to stay or to go. "He shall be leaving at once," I say, and the driver nods in agreement.

Rose-covered Woodbine Cottage has the storybook setting where I might have imagined myself living. Back when I was a dreamy, romantic schoolgirl. The fact that Percy and Harriet spent their honeymoon here is hardly a good omen, and to avoid falling into madness, I force myself to banish thoughts of them so young and in love in this place. Ah, the dear souls.

There is beauty everywhere. The moors rise up behind the cottage like a wall carved from emerald. Within a stone's throw is Glen Lyn Gorge and East Lynn River. Surely I will not be as wretched as I was with Mary nor as wretched as I would be on Skinner Street. *Oh, please God.*

I breathe in the sea air and the scent of roses all day as I take up my books and my writing and my needlework. I spend hours walking. Up the hills and down the hills and along the paths overlooking the bay. Since a lone girl is suspect in any English village, I send for supplies from Barnstaple, as Percy has instructed me, and I encounter only Mrs. Blackmore, the landlady who comes to collect the rent, and the nameless old lacemaker at the end of the road. Neither woman says more than *good day, miss,* although I imagine they have quite a lot to say outside my presence.

Yes, Woodbine Cottage in Lynmouth is the very sort of place where I could live a solitary life. Here I can write and sing and read all the day long, and I am surrounded by nature. What could be better? Except. The reality of living in solitude, no matter how beautiful, is not romantic at all. I grow desperately lonely.

Mornings are the worst. The sunlight shines onto the water and bounces into my eyes. Even the sky is too bright. The light sickens me. I write Percy long, pleading letters. *When shall I see you again? I am sick to death without you.*

His responses take weeks to arrive. He is working on new poetry, he reports. *I am giving into my muse, dear Claire.* Then, almost as a postscript, he adds *I miss you, my fierce, beautiful comet. Soon, very soon, we will collide.* In Percy's world, *soon* could mean any old time at all, although *collide* must mean a purely physical connection. Which is but a fraction of what I miss.

I also faithfully write to Mary to tell her how blessed I am to be in a calm, quiet place. *It is quite lovely,* I add, *here in this cottage where Percy and Harriet once stayed.* It is my own paltry jab of revenge.

Mostly I write to Fanny, the only one who truly understands what it is to be left behind, to be shut out of Percy's spinning orbit. I describe the flowers and the trees and the rocky outcroppings she would greatly admire. I add a few mentions of bracken and fungi, and then find myself writing *being young and alone is almost too much for me to bear. At seventeen, I have grown old.* The words appear on the page before I can stop them, and rather than scratch them out or start over, I let them be.

Being in exile gives me many hours to contemplate life. Too many hours, I must say. This summer only recalls last summer as I tick off the passing of days. A year ago today, I tell myself, you were an excitable girl acting as lookout in St. Pancras Cemetery. A year ago today you left Skinner Street in Percy's chaise bound for Dover. A year ago today you landed free and happy in France only to have Mother find you. A year ago today you and Mary and Percy began your trek to Switzerland. And on and on. Oh, it pains me to think about our last wondrous summer.

I take some satisfaction from walking through the Lynmouth churchyard precisely as the sun slides downward over the stones. That slant of light and sudden shadows causes me a delicious shiver, as if the dead are calling me. It recalls the hours that Mary, Fanny, and I spent with our books at the grave of Mary's mother. We were pleased to be in each other's company then. We were certain nothing would change us.

I contemplate our lost sisterhood as I trudge around the countryside, and I wonder if our girlhood time at St. Pancras ever crossed Mary's mind when we went there with Percy. Strange how the mind plays tricks, tamping down some memories and having others rise and bloom when you least expect them. Like my old fantasies of Lord Byron. Such a complete and utter waste of time. The man is now married, although some in Percy's smart literary crowd gossip that the union will not last, and I have no means to meet him even if he were free. But, ah, he is a splendid poet, whose words warm my heart long into the night.

I exist in solitude for six weeks before Percy comes to call.

He is lovely, this Percy who comes to me and stitches me to his side in our vine-covered cottage. I listen to his tales about the forests and lakes of Great Windsor Park, which he visited on his way to see me. "The light there is lovely, Claire. A painter's delight and a poet's challenge." As always when he is passionate about something, the heat rises from him. His warmth passes through our garments and into me. The scent of his skin, rather like watercress and hyssop, makes me weak. I study the thrilling shape of his hands, hands that are as eloquent as his words. They rise with the inflection of his voice. They comb through his sun-streaked hair. They clasp together to emphasize some point. I fold my own hands to keep from touching him.

"How is dear Mary?" I think to ask.

He is slow to answer. Instead he makes a wary, sideways, blue assessment, as if determining how much news of Mary I can actually endure. Those eyes, more than his words, could kill me. Then he speaks, and his blue light shifts away. "She is quite well," he says. "She is quite content at the moment."

I suppose Mary's contentment stems from my absence, but I will not play a martyr. "How are Ianthe and baby Charles? Do you see them?"

"Harriet and I do our best to avoid one another. Sir Tim sends her a monthly allowance, and Grandfather's inheritance took care of my debts. I made good on my promises to Will Godwin. I have funds to pay for your cottage, Claire. I am in good standing."

"What about me?" I tease. "Perhaps I want compensation for my captivity."

"Captivity?" He looks uncertain. "What compensation do you desire?"

"I desire you, of course."

Percy rubs those perfectly-shaped fingers over his fine face. "Mary does not know I am here," he confesses at last.

"Where does she imagine you are?"

"In London." He draws me to him, and his mouth is warm and pliant. Then he falls back on my bed while wrapping me so tightly to him that our bones grind together. "This is how I want to die," he whispers. "With us joined together for all of eternity. What other heaven could there be?"

Indeed. I fear for Mary and where in Percy's heaven she might be. Yet not for long. Percy is with me. No, not until he rises from the bed at daybreak, do I catch hold of his hand and force myself to ask "how soon will you leave me?"

"Not until you wish me gone."

I am doubtful, yet I drowse with the sharp, sweet scent of Percy's hair upon my pillow. *You taste of the sea*, he whispered last night. *Of salt brine and sunshine.* Then Percy's morning words, words as quick and easy as a wave, ebb into my brain. *I shall stay as many days, as many weeks, as I please.* Percy has left Mary to come to me. He had chosen me at last. I listen to the gulls diving toward the sea and think of Mary, now the one left alone. I hope with all my heart that Hogg remains eager to call on her.

Here in Devon in July, the very heart of summer, everything is glorious. The sun. The rain. The calm sea. The tempest. My new life with Percy settles down upon us with ease. He rises early to write or walk alone in the moors, contemplative acts which make him happiest, and when he returns to me, he bears gifts of wild strawberries or hazelnuts or a perfect green fern. We spend our afternoons reading and our evenings at the river's edge sailing paper boats or skipping stones. Not once does he speak about the state of his bowels or the tightness in his lungs or an eruption of pink spots on his neck. Out from under his debts, he is less troubled, but I give myself credit, too. Among the Godwin sisters, I am the sun.

At nightfall, Percy lights a bonfire, and we sit before it, telling stories we remember from our childhoods. Mostly stories with morals about good and evil. Percy and I change the endings to suit this life we are creating together. Our hare beats the tortoise, and our grasshopper survives his winter in as fine a fettle as the ant. Icarus flies into the heavens with nary a glance at his reflection, while Reynard the Fox has his comeuppance.

"Our grapes are always sweet," Percy declares with complete little boy solemnity, and I laugh until my breath is gone. Tipsy with mirth, I collapse on the ground. Percy lies beside me, and we float there under the night sky with only the gleam of the watchful fireflies and the sparking embers to guide us together, to remind us we are real and whole and in love. He kisses me and clasps my face between his palms. "You are my muse, Claire. The poems I write now will be a revelation. They will live beyond us. These poems will be my epitaph."

A chill night breeze from Lynmouth Bay blows over us, and there, throbbing between us, is a shudder, a quickness, an awareness of life. "Percy." I grip his hands with mine and will him to listen with me. "I believe I am with child."

Percy and I behave as if we invented the act of procreation for the sole pleasure of the rest of the world. We are giddy to the point of fantasy. This site of my exile is now the place of dreams, the perfect place to raise our child.

"Have you spoken to Mrs. Blackmore about staying on here in our dear cottage? Can you not envision the picnics and berry picking and all the fine walking we shall enjoy with our child, Percy?"

"Certainly. An infant will not inconvenience us in the slightest. We will keep up our daily routine, and when winter comes and we tire of English weather and narrow-mindedness, we can travel abroad with the baby. Nothing will change between us."

I believe every word. I believe him wholeheartedly until Mary's letters start pouring in, a new one every day. Now I am no longer certain of anything.

Dear Claire -- I have regrettable news. Percy is gone, and I cannot find him in his usual haunts. I am greatly concerned. I called on Hogg and Peacock and his other dear friends. I called on Harriet. I am so distressed, I even sent word to Father. Should Percy come to you, kindly tell him to return home. Your dearest sister, Mary

I hide the first letter. I tell myself I do not want to alarm Percy with Mary's hysterical tone. She is obviously well and safe. Why disrupt his peace and quiet?

Her next letter is worse.

Dear Claire-- I am becoming desperate. I cannot bear for one more loss to befall me this year. Promise you will send Percy home when you see him. I beg you. I am not at all myself without him. Your fretful sister, Mary

And then:

Dear Claire -- This is my retribution, is it not? This agony of knowing Percy is ignoring me is exactly the fate Harriet suffered a year ago when you and Percy and I so merrily sailed off together. I was so smugly self-righteous, blaming her for what we ourselves caused. Why are young girls like us so easily replaced? Tell Percy to come home, and I shall be my loving self again. Your despairing sister, Mary

The days are growing shorter, but today the sun shines brightly. It is warm in the sun and cool in the shade, a day too perfect for secrets. I look out at Percy reading under the fig tree and decide to give him Mary's letters. Not because I am a good girl or a caring sister or a genuinely kindhearted human being – I am none of those compared to Mary or Fanny. I will give Percy the letters, because I am weary of being caught in the middle, and I am confident he will remain with me. Our days at Woodbine Cottage have proven his devotion.

He does not look up as I approach. He is engrossed, as he often is, in a letter from his great literary friend Thomas Peacock. So I set Mary's letters there by his elbow and sit on the wall overlooking the sparkle of Lynmouth Bay. Percy is a fast reader, but he tends to ponder every sentence, so I wait, counting the months until I will become a mother. March, perhaps?

When Percy walks towards me with the letters in his hand, his eyes are as damp and blue as the sea, and I am frightened. I step away from the blue, away from the wall and the cliff tumbling below it. I walk toward the cottage and its history of doomed romance. "Leave if you must," I say before he can speak. "Return to dreary Mary and her mournful moods, but I am keeping our child."

"We cannot do that to Mary." He reaches for me, but I am too quick to catch.

"You adore children." I scream at him. "You want a commune filled with children."

Percy, too, is quick. Quick and supple and strong. He overtakes me from behind, wrapping his arms across my chest and hunching his body along my spine. His breath is heavy on my neck. "Peacock writes that Mary, too, is with child. If you have a fine healthy child and she not does, it will kill her. If you keep this child, Claire, your sister will die from grief."

"Then so be it, Percy. Let Destiny have her way."

Part Three: Albee

12. Spring, 1816

March in London is a roll of the dice. When it begins to snow, we may receive a blizzard, and when the snow turns to rain, the streets are likely to flood and then coat with mud. When I am finally summoned to Piccadilly Terrace for an audience with the great Lord Byron, I do not quite trust the sunlight streaming through the clouds. I am more confident in gloom. All the same, I skirt the handfuls of people, mostly journalists and young women, who gather in front of Number 13 to wait patiently for a glimpse of the famous poet. They have my pity. Lord Byron is diminutive, not easy to search out in a crowd, and yet once, quite by accident, I saw him for myself in Drury Lane. His deformed foot makes him immediately noticeable.

To gather my confidence today, I mentally recreate that brief glimpse of him. First comes his sweeping, off-kilter stride. Then his handsome face, his aristocratic bearing. *Ah, Lord Byron*, the people whisper as he passes by. Once the dust settles behind him, onlookers offer more vulgar observations of his life. *It is said that he and his sister Augusta Leigh are lovers. That Byron has fathered her daughter. Is it any wonder he threatens to leave England forever?*

I make my way to the door, stepping around a scruffy man selling poems and slipping through a gaggle of awestruck girls. I am not deterred by lurid stories claiming Augusta and Lord Byron are lovers or by the large number of women he is said to have loved and callously dismissed in his bachelor days. Not at all. I know what it is to love a poet, a man whose mind floats beyond the physical and into the ethereal even when I am in his grasp. I raise the brass knocker and let it fall with a resounding peal. "I have an appointment," I say to the indignant girls and the man with muddied scraps of parchment in his grizzled hands. "I am expected," I say to the manservant who answers the door.

Quite tall and crisp in his blue and white uniform, he ticks off my name on his rather long list and ushers me into a foyer filled with others who await an audience with the great Lord Byron. I take the nearest chair, a claret red velvet, and perch on its edge with my manuscript on my lap. I close my eyes and give myself a silent lecture: you are here today as a writer, and you will speak as an intelligent woman, not a stammering girl. You will proceed with deliberate steps, rather than wild romping. You will not give your heart away at the first tender word. Your sister may have a fine poet in Percy, but if you are clever, you will have a greater poet in Albee. The best known poet in all of England.

My eyes snap open. It is all well to tell myself these things, but Albee is due to leave England within the month, and time presses around me like a garrote. I glance at my competition: several men in stiff collars and two young women in fur-trimmed shawls. Their eyes shift from my parcel to my face, judging and dismissing me in some way I cannot discern. Perhaps they find me too young or too eager to be of any consequence. The men glance away, preoccupied with their hats which they balance on their knees while their fingers nervously caress the brims. The women are of more concern. One, paler and blonder than Mary, is as buxom and matronly as Mother, while the other is slight, all but swallowed up by her lavish feathered hat. I wear no feathers, no fur, not one bit of adornment, yet I am hopeful that my teal blue dress, not new, but well-cut with its empire waist and Juliet sleeves, flatters me.

The wall clock ticks on behind my head. The patch of sunshine on the parquet floor disappears, and the room grows chill. The buxom woman tightens her shawl around her shoulders while the smaller one fidgets, fixing me with a steady look. I do not blink. I am good at waiting. I waited for Mary and Percy in the St. Pancras graveyard. I waited through my exile in Lynmouth. I waited for every stolen moment with Percy, for his every touch, his every word. I will wait as long as necessary to see Albee.

Slowly, one by one, the men are ushered into the room at the far end of the foyer and never seen again. Either they leave by another route or they are gathered together in a salon, one riotous party with Albee at its center. Next is the young woman with the over-sized hat. Then the matronly woman. She glances at me over her broad shoulder. A look that says *I shall be with him now, girlie, you may as well go home.*

I long to say *he is saving the best for last*, even as I grow anxious. I have memorized down to the last syllable what I plan to say, yet it is impossible to prepare for what Lord Byron himself might say. I expect him to be cocksure and charming. I expect him to behave as if his duties for the Drury Lane Theatre are merely a lark, a means for the dissolute poet to present a proper front.

At last, the tall crisp manservant ushers me into a disappointingly meager room, rather like an extension of the foyer, with another door by which to exit. I had hoped for a grand salon with a piano at its center. Instead, there is a smallish writing table, and sitting behind it, with his head propped in his hands, is the great Lord Byron. He rises upon my entrance. "Miss Clairmont," the manservant announces.

"Thank you, Fletcher." His curly head dips his dismissal, and his graceful hand motions toward a straight-backed chair. He is all business. "Miss Clairmont, kindly tell me of your interest in Drury Lane Theatre." Even smaller in stature than I recall, Albee is a dim star compared to his poetic heroes. Yet he is quite handsome in a cool, self-contained manner.

"I have a novella, of sorts." I am careful to make eye contact although his eyes, distant and grey, reveal nothing. "I believe it could be adapted into a play." My manuscript is, in fact, the end result of all the writing done during those long winter months after we returned from France. Those cold, bitter days when Percy roamed the city in search of funds while Mary and I bickered. Those days after Clara's death when I shut myself in my room to stay out of my sister's sight. Those painful, beautiful weeks in Woodbine Cottage before Percy came to save me. Briefly. "It has strong dramatic elements," I add. "Somewhat based on my life." I smile up at him. "I believe you know my stepfather, William Godwin."

"Not well. Although I respect Godwin. Despite his recent difficulties." His voice, lower-pitched than Percy's, carries a pleasant hint of Scotland.

"England drives good men abroad with her insular ways."

While Percy's being beckons like the glow of lamplight, Albee's essence dares approach. I am his last appointment of the day, and it is evident he is eager for me to be on my way. His face sags with exhaustion, and I take pity on him. "I thank you for your time, my Lord. For your kind attention."

"Yes, Miss Clairmont, I am happy to read your novella and make a recommendation." He rises to dismiss me, and my heart stumbles. The great Lord Byron is offering me the vague promise of Drury Lane Theatre, but nothing of himself, the man and the poet.

I, too, rise to my feet and place my manuscript in his slender hand. "I am very fond of your poetry, Lord Byron. I greatly admire *Lara* and *Childe Harold's Pilgrimage*." Heat rises in my face, but I carry on. "I beg you, sir, kindly allow me to perform my finest talent."

His eyes reveal the merest flicker of interest. "By all means." He remains standing, slumped a bit to one side with his arm braced against the table for support.

I, too, am exhausted by the realization that my last chance to be captivating is now upon me. When I open my mouth, my chin trembles and my voice quavers, but I do not falter as I sing the very stanzas Albee himself has written. I pour every sweet note of my voice into his words, praying for them to enter his famously hard heart and crack it wide open.

Albee's song hangs in the air as I curtsey. Then, steadying my breath, I dare to glance his way. Perhaps his countenance lifts in an expression of enchantment. Perhaps his eyes are brighter. Perhaps he appears less fatigued. It is hard to say.

Quickly, before the spell is broken, I speak boldly. "May I call on you again, Lord Byron? Would I be welcomed and not made to wait in your chilly foyer?"

His laugh is quick and rich and deep. So unlike Percy's shrill bursts of mirth, it is a laugh I could easily love.

Never again do I wait in the foyer at Piccadilly Terrace. Unlike the childish Jane with Percy, I am now the clever Claire, quick-witted and confident. Albee finds me amusing, and I dare say he is fascinated by the gossip featuring Percy and Mary and me. Likely he feels kinship with the poet made infamous for leaving his beautiful wife and running away with two young maidens.

"You are here to tap into my mind, Miss Clairmont?" He asks when I call again. "You are here to absorb my vision? My poetry? Perhaps my soul?"

"If such a thing were possible, dear sir," I reply, "I would become a sponge to soak up your poetry. I would become a sea creature for the sake of your very soul."

"Even a tarnished soul such as my own?"

"I am quite familiar with the chore of polishing blackness from silver. Would the same process apply to your soul?"

"You believe polishing my soul would be a *chore*?"

I frown as if in serious contemplation and give him a moment to notice the luster of my hair and face, the snap of my dark eyes. "Yes, sir," I say at last, "I believe it would. A mighty chore."

"Aha." He regards me with his derisive sneer.

"Tell me, Lord Byron, would the same amount of labor also apply to your heart?"

"No indeed, no labor at all." He lifts his regal cleft chin. "I have no heart."

Albee is cynical on most matters, yet I hold my own in discussing the aftermath of the French Revolution, which, I remind him, I have witnessed firsthand. He says little about my travels abroad and less still about Shelley the poet, and yet my history with Percy must hang there before him like a glittering orb, tantalizing and so close at hand.

He offers comments on my novella. "I question why your heroine would suffer such boredom at the hands of her family. She is bright and somewhat talented. Why not make her own way in the world?"

"Because she is a woman of limited means."

"Perhaps she should break the mold."

"Ah yes, but my fiction is not fantasy."

"What a pity."

Our meetings are spirited, but predictably, maddeningly, civil. Always Fletcher admits me without comment and then brings in tea and biscuits. Always I sing for Albee. Always I send him a note of appreciation sealed with the elegant stamp which Percy once gave me.

Albee's departure date draws near, and I grow impatient. Quickly, before Albee abandons me in England, I must set my own words upon his heart. From the echoing spaces of Arabella Row, I send Albee my most important letter. *I promise you my complete devotion, my abiding love, dear Albee. With every beat of my heart, I am yours, unreservedly yours. I ask nothing in return beyond your silence and mercy.*

Seducing Lord Byron is my mission, and I am moving steadily in that direction. If Mary can claim a comet as her fate, I shall claim a poet. Then I look around this familiar flat on Arabella Row, and I am consumed with doubt. I am weakened by loss. So much loss. I have to lie down.

I cannot yet bear to think about the loss Percy forced upon me. I cannot think about him, safely returned to Mary and now living in Surrey, without weeping. Since my exile in Lynmouth, I have stayed in motion. I travel with my brother Charles. I visit Mother and Fanny. I call on Mary and Percy and their new son, Will. I am the good sister. I have borne my loss well. Or so it would seem.

I glance at the empty place under the window where Clara's cradle once stood, and rail at Fate. Had I loved an ordinary man, a man without privilege or wealth or title, I, too, would have a child. A fine healthy son, I imagine. My downfall was taking a lover from the class of people who know their way around the medical profession. Those who happen to have a running tab at the chemist's shop, for instance.

Impatient to sear myself into Albee's heart, I make the arrangements for our tryst. Naturally, he offers no resistance. As his own carriage is the size of a mountain, and equally conspicuous, he hires a chaise to collect me from Arabella Row. I wear yellow, the color of madness. I want to shine against the London streets like a brightly blooming daffodil.

"Ah, the lovely Claire. How are you, my dear?" he asks as the coachman assists me aboard.

"I am well. And yourself, Lord Byron?"

"Enchanted, Miss Clairmont. Enchanted by your glowing presence."

Oh indeed, Albee is in a fine mood as we set off for our night at a country inn. Alone in the small space of a carriage that smells reassuringly of old leather and newly-turned sod, he swivels to face me, propping his lame leg on the seat between us. In that moment I long to touch him, to swear my love, to promise eternal faithfulness, but his cool appraisal makes me mute. He draws a silver flask from his coat pocket and tips it to his mouth.

Then as the city clamor and stench falls behind us like a malevolent cloud, he begins to recite. *He caught me in his silken net, and shut me in his golden cage. Then, laughing, sports and plays with me.* Albee's rich voice swells above the thrum of the carriage wheels. *He loves to sit and hear me sing; then stretches out my golden wing, and mocks my loss of liberty.* I already know Albee's reputation for playing with women's hearts, and his mockery for those unfortunates who fall in love with him. So is his recital of William Blake merely a warning or something more sinister?

"Please do not trouble yourself, Albee. I have no desire to be caught."

"My sentiments entirely." He raises his flask in salute. "May God have mercy on us all."

By the time Albee and I undergo the subterfuge of booking into the inn as man and wife, we have lost what camaraderie we shared on the carriage ride. Albee is tipsy, and his limp more pronounced. "The precipice awaits," he says upon seeing the bed. He tosses his coat and hat onto the settee.

"We need not jump." I tease, priding myself on my wit. "We can back away from the edge and frolic in the meadow for a spell."

Albee feigns alarm. "My dear girl, I have paid a fortune in my lifetime for *frolicking*. From you, I expect the sublime."

"With no threat to your fortune, may I assure you." My confidence is ebbing. What can I offer a man of Albee's experience? Precious little.

He unbuttons his waistcoat and loosens his cravat before tossing himself onto the bed. He moans as he elevates his leg, resting his boot heel against the footboard. "Sing for me, Claire. Sing for me and ease my pain."

I know Albee's story as well as my own. He, too, was abandoned by his father and it fell to his mother to raise him single-handedly. He was a small lame boy who hated to be left alone, and when his mother died, he hated her for leaving him behind. I have no song for this unfortunate son. As I slide off his boots and work my fingers over his misshapen foot, I croon the same wordless melodies Mother once sang to soothe me. He watches me through half-lidded eyes, and then he is asleep.

So much for our night of romance. I observe him in his slumber. His fine features and tossed curls invite my touch, and I am drawn to the openness of his face. In repose, at least, he drops his haughty façade.

My throat is parched. Gently I reposition his foot on the coverlet and round the bed to reach the water pitcher. His hand shoots out to grasp my wrist, and with surprising strength, he draws me down until my face rests against his. "What else might you have to offer me, dear Claire?"

He smells of whiskey, yet he is quite alert. There behind those half-lidded eyes, he is wide awake and waiting to pounce. "Only myself."

"Allow me to witness this *self* of which you speak." He frees my wrist. "Kindly reveal to me what you have so generously promised." He props himself up on his elbows and taunts me with a nod. An invitation. A dare.

If there was ever a time to change my mind, it is now. This is the moment to take my dignity and my songs and my intense longing for the great Lord Byron and flee. Yet I was never a girl to run the other way. Albee watches me, testing my devotion. Whether I do as he asks or not, he plans to enjoy the moment at hand.

My pale yellow gown with a twisting vine embroidered along its hem is the very opposite of the prim black silk I wore the day I ran away with Mary and Percy. Or the dark blue I wore when Percy took me to Hogg's rented room. For that complete lack of similarity, I am grateful. I untie the golden ribbon encircling my bodice, and the frock drops from my shoulders like a swath of moonlight.

Under the gown, I remain my mother's daughter. My petticoat is stiff and unyielding with its boned hem and well-placed tucks, and while my corset lacks boning, linen stays are laced under my breasts. Amused, Albee whistles a jaunty tune and folds his hands under his head to watch me loosen ties and hooks. He laughs joyously as my corset falls away to reveal a plain muslin chemise. A garment much like a young girl would wear.

"You must come to me now. Come to me, dear." He rolls onto his side and kneads the coverlet like a cat, a gesture I find both seductive and depraved. I am suddenly unwilling to surrender what little control I possess. I want to give myself freely rather than let myself be taken, so I pull off the chemise and step naked over the clouds of cloth gathered at my feet. I leave my stockings in place as one last touch of modesty.

"You are so young." Albee shakes his head. "So young and glorious." He opens his arms and pulls me to him with a sigh.

His movements are light and graceful as he draws me onto bed, snuffs out the lamp, and sheds his waistcoat and breeches. I remember hearing he was a swimmer in his youth, a very fast swimmer, and now he is atop me in one quick splash. His hands are smaller and swifter than Percy's, yet, like Percy, his back —under my hands, under his linen shirt -- is bony and supple, and when he dives into me, there is a strength and ease that Percy never possessed. Albee is as smooth and gliding as a seal, and if I hang on, I believe I too can swim. I can reach the far shoreline and turn back around again. With Albee, I can stay afloat forever.

Yet Albee is not Percy. He offers no sweet murmurings, no tuneless hum next to my ear, no tender ministrations nor easy conversation afterward. "At least I did not have to concern myself with your virginity," he says as he collapses onto his pillow and falls into slumber.

I could be any girl here with Albee tonight. To him, lovers are indistinguishable. We are mere distractions, amusements, releases. I lie still and listen to his deep satisfied breaths while that truth presses down on me. Percy is all heart; Albee has none.

By morning I am determined to become more than a lover. While Albee sleeps, I tiptoe around the room, tidying up as Fletcher would. Folding his clothes, rinsing out his empty flask. Simple domestic chores he is unlikely to notice or appreciate. Yet, here I am, happily humming like a housemaid and waiting for him to waken and find me being a dutiful companion.

When he awakes, he is in pain. The slightest movement of his lame leg causes him to grimace and moan, and when his eyes open to slits, he flings his forearm across his forehead to block out the daylight. When I pull the drapes tighter, he recognizes my presence. "Morning is not for the faint-of-heart." He grits his teeth. "Morning lays too much of us bare."

I know not to speak. Obviously, Albee's view of the world is nothing like Percy's. Percy is chirpy in the morning. Nothing cheers him more than wandering off alone in the countryside to encounter every creature and every growing thing. On those rare occasions when I was permitted to tag along, I grew accustomed to him cooing over a wren's nest or eating dew-laden gooseberries. Now I sit quietly on a dainty brocade chair as Albee struggles to bring himself to wakefulness.

"Oh, Christ." He inches upward into a sitting position, and finally, squinting, looks my way. "Find us some tea and call for the carriage, will you, dear girl?"

It could be worse, I tell myself. He could order me to leave. He could disparage our night together. He could call by the wrong name rather than no name at all. He is broken by his lost wife and daughter, I tell myself. He is broken by his tormented childhood. He is a broken man, and I can be as quiet and sympathetic as I can be glib. I can be whatever Lord Byron desires.

13. Plotting a Course

Albee at rest is a different man from the one in motion. His face softens. All his sharp bony surfaces dissolve. His curls loosen. His mouth grows less scornful and his eyes less wary and his tongue less cruel. Although pain is his constant torment, we have our moments of quiet. He comes to me on Arabella Row and slouches on the divan drinking port and re-reading *Waverly*, while I sit in the tattered chair that Percy once favored. I take up my needlework, and Albee, his head propped against his palm, nods in contentment. Such a picture of domestic bliss.

"No pistols and pundits to rouse you tonight?" I tease.

"Such men bore me. England bores me. My own thoughts are my best company these days."

"Man cannot exist alone." I look up from my stitches.

He rises slowly and limps to the window to raise the sash. "I find my dogs and birds and beautiful beasts to be fine companions."

Oh yes, his menagerie of exotic creatures. "What shall become of them when you leave England?" The air from the window is cool on my neck.

"I'm having crates built." He stands there looking out on the night, and I imagine I hear the sound of boards being nailed in place.

Later, he takes me to bed and swims into me again, but his desire is matter-of-fact. The gift, once given, can never be returned, I imagine my mother saying, and Albee's mind is elsewhere. He is fixed on Europe. I am but a temporary diversion, and that knowledge is driving me mad.

To completely seduce Albee, I must tempt him with something rare and beautiful and brilliant. Something beyond his mortal reach. What better than Mary Godwin? Surely the brilliant, beautiful daughter of free love advocates and also the lover of the rebellious poet Percy Shelley can lure Albee into my life.

As Mary and I are better together when Percy is absent, I call on her in their old Marchmont flat. She is staying there with baby William while Percy is in Sussex attempting to wrestle more of his inheritance away from Sir Tim. "I do not like to be in the countryside alone," she tells me. "Especially when our little Willmouse is so young."

I glance at the baby, so alert and bright-eyed, so unlike the listless Clara. "Willmouse, say hello to your Aunty Claire." I run my finger over his soft cheek. "His nickname suits him."

Mary smiles as she smooths the baby's gown. "He will be a clever lad, we think."

We sit by the window to catch the late morning sunshine. I try not to twitch with nerves as Mary speaks of babies and their constitutions and the necessity for the fresh air they experience in Surrey, there on the edge of Great Windsor Park. I wait for her to pause. "I imagine you miss outings in London," I say with a sympathetic tone. "The smart literary crowd. How would you like an introduction to Lord Byron while you are here in the city?"

"You have the acquaintance of Lord Byron?" Mary tucks sweet Willmouse into his cradle. "How is that possible, Claire?" She regards me with suspicion.

"From Drury Lane Theatre." I speak airily, as if I am a fixture at the Drury. "He was kind enough to read my novella and make suggestions. He would likely read your novel as well."

"Lord Byron?" Again, the disbelief.

"I vow you shall find him a complete gentleman," I assure her. "He admires Percy and Will and the writing of your own dear mother. He is curious, I would say." Mary blanches at *curious*, so I begin again. "Lord Byron is an honorable member of society, Mary, and you will receive his utmost respect. His other proclivities and his ne'er-do-well reputation do not interfere with his civic duties."

Mary does not ask why I am so knowledgeable of Lord Byron's private behaviors. No doubt she thinks a man like Albee would never find me desirable. Albee, on the other hand, needs no reassuring about Mary. He knows all about the Godwins, and in his own aloof manner, Albee is intrigued by Mary.

"Kindly do not keep my sister waiting in your chilly hall, dear Albee," I chide him. "She is a charming woman, as you will see. Witty and beautiful and ever her mother's daughter. I would not be surprised if you fell in love with her."

"Highly unlikely." He grimaces.

No, Albee is not the sort to fall in love at a moment's notice. Or to fall in love at all. Rather, as predicted, he is the perfect gentleman with Mary. Each comes away admiring the other and exclaiming over the power of the written word. "She may ascribe to Godwin's theories, yet she is her own woman," Albee reports. "I enjoyed her company."

"What a lovely encounter, Claire." Mary is flushed and livelier than she has been since Willmouse's birth. "The afternoon was over before it began."

Yet their meeting does little to help my own cause. Even with the prospect of new, like-minded friends to entertain him in London, Albee officially books his departure from England. A single fare. Every day I grow more downhearted, more the desperate sort of woman all men despise. Especially Albee.

"I believe I have loved you all my life." I wince to hear myself speak. "I believe we are fated to be together."

"You are talking rubbish, Claire, and I do not believe in fate, as you well know." His scorn is palpable. "I am off on an adventure, a manly pursuit that holds no place for women and their romantic notions."

I am undaunted. "To my way of thinking, romance is quite an adventure, my dear man. Did I tell you the Shelleys are likewise traveling to the Continent this summer? Would it not be an adventure for two renowned English poets to meet in Geneva?"

"I take it you will once again be with Shelley?" Oh, the scorn. If only he knew that I am inventing this journey, calling forth imaginary details with every word I speak.

"My father is Swiss. I welcome any chance to visit my ancestral land."

"Shelley is a decent poet." Not an affirmation precisely, but perhaps my scheme is taking root in his mind.

When next I visit Percy and Mary, I ease into my proposal by reminiscing about our adventure of two years ago. I set them laughing about the lame donkey and the pawned jewelry and the obnoxious American on our canal boat, and then when the laughter ceases and we are lost in our memories, I speak as if the idea is only now entering my mind. "We should return to the Continent! We could spend our entire summer in Europe!" I caress Willmouse's tiny foot, so pinkly perfect, and force myself to speak calmly, to not burst with emotion. "It is my dream to return to that lovely land," I say to Mary. "Willmouse is a good traveler, is he not?"

In turn, Mary glances towards Percy. He stands with his back to us, intent on gazing out the window with one hand atop his head and fingers threaded through his mane. Silence is never Percy's immediate reaction to any proposal, yet his silence tells me more than words. He is bored. Like Albee, Percy is bored with the pretense of English society. He is bored with his quiet life in Great Windsor Park with only Mary and Willmouse to hear his theories on love and equality and respond to his poems with contented cooing. He, too, desires a change of scene.

"Willmouse is an excellent traveler." Mary speaks as a proud mother. "Yet I worry about the dangers of traveling so far. The unreliable boats. The endless sea."

"I understand Lord Byron is leaving England forever," I say in an off-hand manner. "For Italy or Greece. Traveling the Rhine Valley to Switzerland, I believe. Can you envisage two great poets converging on Geneva at the start of the summer season?"

Even as I speak, I find myself recalling our previous summer, the summer none of us ever mentions. Although Mary is skilled at keeping unpleasant thoughts to herself, she must know Percy was contemplating a future with me there in Lynmouth. That Willmouse is what brought him back to her. No wonder she is reluctant to comment.

"Oh, Mary." Percy can no longer stay still. He spins away from the window to expand on the grandeurs of Europe and the petty-mindedness of England. "I am exhausted from defending our honor. As if our love counts for nothing. As if our lack of marriage vows makes us immoral, evil monsters. I say immorality is in the souls of those fine English folks who despise us. You too, deserve better, Claire, and you will be a valuable helpmate for your sister."

I suspect Percy spent the entire last year describing me as a *valuable helpmate*. He teased Mary, I imagine, assuring her that he and I are no more than brother and sister. And now as she murmurs assent to my plan, Mary wants to be seen as a benevolent soul.

"Splendid!" Percy leaps into a jig. "I will have my funds before we depart. We will hire carriages and spare our feet — not to mention lame donkeys. We will finish the journey we began two years ago, and this time we will sojourn for as long as we please." Perhaps Percy also imagines himself an expatriate, but he is hardly in Albee's league. Unlike Percy, Albee has shed himself of encumbrances like a wife and a child and has only to concern himself with transporting his mammoth coach and menagerie of dogs and birds and such.

"Would you consider allowing Fanny to join us?" I ask Mary. Fanny and I have a cordial relationship now, but she knows nothing of my time with Percy last summer. Nothing of Albee this spring. Even though I fear Fanny capable of looking into my soul and shivering, I despair of leaving her behind yet again.

"I will consider it," Mary says. "The last time Fanny stayed with us, her presence wore thin on Percy."

It is easy to imagine Fanny shadowing Mary, commenting on her thinness and worrying over Willmouse. Comparing him, perhaps, to the poor dead Clara. "Fanny is fretful," I agree, "yet given the chance to join us, she would be on her best behavior."

I sense Percy watching me as I hold the baby and chat with Mary about our summer packing. Surely London's smart, literary set has spread word that the great poet Lord Byron and I are lovers. I warm under Percy's gaze, yet I refuse to soften. I am wiser now and will never allow myself to be drawn in, chewed up, and spit out as I was with Percy. I am with Albee because I cannot be with Percy. More than that, I am with Albee so Percy will know precisely what he lost.

14. A Rainy Summer

As Percy, Mary, and I retrace our route of two years ago, I am lost in fantasy. Albee, who has already been traveling for weeks, will be waiting for me at the Hotel d'Angleterre. He will be sprawled on the verandah – or whatever the Swiss chose to call it – watching my approach from under the brim of his hat. His foot will be propped on a stool and his hands folded behind his head and he will gaze at me as if seeing me for the first time. As the bold Shelley adventurers pass by, his hand will snake out to grasp my wrist. He will draw me to him and whisper his desires. "Your absence has made me wild," he will say. "You are the drug of my addiction. Stay with me, my Claire."

It is not as though Albee and I broke apart before he sailed away. No indeed, it is more the case that in his eagerness to leave England and his unhappy marriage behind him, nothing flowered between us. Here in the clear mountain air of Switzerland, I expect love to find us. I embellish my fantasy as we sail from Dover to Calais and then take a carriage across France and into Switzerland. It is a miserable journey. We endure rain and snow and an endless pit of mud.

I keep my mind set on Albee. Somewhere in the Alps, I write to announce our approach. "Our merry band makes its way to your dear company. Think of it, Albee. Sun and water and the smell of blossoms to fill your senses. Mary Godwin and Percy Shelley and me. Think what poetry will arise from such scenic beauty and like-minded company."

It is late when we reach Hotel d'Angleterre, and we are ready for slumber, yet I take time to check the register. No Albee. My knees buckle. Has he taken another route to avoid me? That is hardly his style. Albee can halt all unwanted advances with one withering word. As Percy attempts to order fresh water for our rooms, I shuffle through the stack of letters awaiting hotel guests. There in my own hopeful handwriting is the letter I mailed days earlier. Despair laps at my spirit with its heavy tongue. Then I notice a letter addressed Dr. John Polidori.

Dr. Polidori is Albee's traveling companion and said to be very handsome. I am still smiling when Percy takes my arm. "Your room is this way, Claire. Mary, allow me to carry Willmouse. We will be back to ourselves tomorrow after a good night's sleep."

Days trip on, and eventually, late one evening, Polidori and Albee's names appear in the hotel register. Oh, thank God. Immediately I send the porter to his room with a welcoming note. *We will meet soon, dear love, but we must be discreet to prevent Shelley and Mary's notice.* Oh, the complexities of a secret love.

Albee does not reply, nor does he suddenly appear before me, but the hotel is abuzz with the news that Lord Byron is in our midst. No wonder Albee is hiding. I haunt the hotel lobby, waiting and watching and making myself ill with worry. I see no one, not even Fletcher, who must be here tending to his master. I grow a bit more frantic, and then, before I can stop myself, I turn into that wretched girl who besieges her elusive lover with long letters of misery. *Oh, dear Albee, I have waited so long to see you. Please come to me at once.*

Daily Percy and Mary stroll into the sunshine with Willmouse, and they drag me along. My fresh wound of disappointment throbs as I listen to Mary and Percy enthuse over the fresh air and clear lakes and green mountains. How quickly I have forgotten their nauseating states of rapture. Percy, in particular, grates on my nerves with his endless prattle about boats and his renewed love of sailing. I think only of returning to the hotel and seeing Albee. Where, I wonder, will he keep his collection of animals?

If I were not so miserable, I, too, would be captivated by the beauty surrounding us. The lush vineyards across Lac Leman. The stunning Mont Blanc. The quaint walled city of Geneva. Today as we walk along the lake, Percy is once again enthusing. In the distant I notice a handsome man clambering out of a rowboat. Perhaps he is kin to me. We are in my Swiss father's homeland after all, and that man bears the same dark coloring as my own. What are the chances we share the same blood?

Then I notice Albee. He exits from the boat with his distinctive hop, while I exchange inquisitive looks with the handsome man, who must be Dr. Polidori. Mary and Percy suddenly cease their discussion of freshwater fish and come to stand by my side exactly as Albee regains his balance and turns to face us.

"Here we are," I say light-heartedly, as if I have nothing to do with those accusatory notes found under his door. "You remember Mary, of course, and this is the poet, Percy Bysshe Shelley. And their son, William. Named for Mary's father, William Godwin." We stand posed before him like subjects for a seascape: the gentle Mary shading fair Willmouse from the sun, the sunburned, tousled Percy suddenly struck mute, and me, overcome by so sharp a mingling of trepidation and love that I fear I will weep.

"My pleasure." Albee doffs his wide-brimmed hat, as the swarthy man leaps back into the boat and rows away. Albee's riotous laugh breaks the silence. "And that was Dr. Polidori." We stand there, awkward and anchored, until Albee adds, "I look forward to more sudden encounters along this beautiful lake."

With that, there is little left to do but move along. Polidori is heading the boat back towards shore, and even if I dare to linger here with Albee, ours will be a short-lived reunion. As much as I want to tuck my arm in his and whisper tart endearments, I, too, find myself suddenly shy. I am hopeful because he has arrived. Oh, yes. He stands before me as a living, breathing wonder, and I long to touch him.

"The very handsome man is a physician?" Mary asks as we walk toward the hotel.

"Byron travels with a physician?" Percy, the hypochondriac, is intrigued.

"Oh," Mary says. "Another delicate flower."

"Another Exotic." I smile, enjoying my secret knowledge of poets.

Eventually, in some mysterious manner known only to men, Percy and Albee strike a friendship. Their greatest bond is not poetry, but a boat, which they rent as partners and take sailing for hours at a stretch. Eventually, because Hotel d'Angleterre is ripe with speculation on how Polidori and Mary and I might fit together with the poets Byron and Shelley, Percy rents a small chalet, Masion Chappuis, in Montalegre, and Albee leases the rather grand Villa Diodati in the hills above there. Finally, here in this lovely place, and without the constraints of England to bind him, Albee is quite happy to welcome me into his residence. Stealthily we creep past Polidori's room, past loyal Fletcher's nodding presence, and into Albee's chambers. "Ah, Claire," he murmurs as he falls upon me, "you give me comfort."

"Albee is rather slight," Mary observes as we look down from Mason Chappuis's terrace to the men upon our shore. "Especially when compared to Percy, who is also slight." I study them closer. Albee and Percy lack the swarthy beauty of Polidori, yet they are made handsome by their lean frames and fine-boned faces. Albee's hair rises around his head in a curly nimbus, while Percy's honey-streaked mane blows across his eyes as a mask. Both wear linen shirts that flap around them like sails. As usual, Percy is animated, gesturing as he speaks, while Albee stands motionless, listening without a sneer to whatever it is Percy tells him.

"They have a great deal in common," I say to Mary. "These literary men from wealthy families. Besides their poetry and politics, they both have estranged wives and distant children, all of whom want their money." And me, of course. They have me in common.

"The poor man." Mary clucks. "His wife left him. He lost his fortune. He gave up his country."

"I expect Albee will always land on his feet. Rather like a cat."

Mary laughs. She is in a good humor and good health. Despite Percy's overwrought fears about Mary's health last summer, she is returned to her usual zealous self, busily making lists and planning our meals and evening entertainment. "Percy, you must read your latest stanza. Claire, you must sing for us. Albee, tell us what you are reading."

Because Mary is happy with her life, she is easier with my company. As long as Albee is around, she does not find me a threat to her contentment. Percy, on the other hand, has difficulty meeting my gaze when I spend time with Albee.

"You spend too much time with him, Claire," he says when I came strolling down the hillside from Villa Diodati. His face is scarlet, as though he has waited hours for me on this sun-struck terrace.

"No more than you. On the lake in your precious boat." I walk towards the doorway. "Where is Mary now?"

"She is napping while Willmouse naps. Babies are exhausting."

"Do not speak to me of babies." I brush past him.

"It was unfortunate timing." His hand burns into my arm. "Had it been any other moment in time, we would now have a child together. You must believe me."

"Do not speak to me about last summer ever again." He pulls me under the grape arbor and fiercely kisses me. "No, Percy," I say when I can speak. "This is not happening again."

"I have missed you desperately." His mouth is as feverish as his skin, and I am swallowed up by his heat. I am unable to protest as he lies me down in the cool dim shade where we are hidden by green vines and swelling fruit.

I am bewildered by my encounter with Percy under the grape arbor, although Percy often has that effect on people he cares about. For the next few days, I stumble about the chalet in my absent-minded state while torrents of rain blast against the walls and windows and kick up whitecaps on the lake. Willmouse turns fretful, which keeps Mary from noticing how studiously Percy and I ignore one another. I miss Albee and imagine he must miss me as the poor man is stuck at the Villa Diodati with only Polidori for conversation.

"More simpering and juvenile than a schoolgirl," he complains when we are re-united.

I laugh to think Polidori could be moodier and more brooding than Albee himself. "You consider yourself an expert on schoolgirls, my love?"

"Schoolgirls are Shelley's forte."

Yes, Albee favors older women – especially older society ladies — rather than younger. I am the exception, he tells me. I am the exception, I remind myself, because I am convenient. Nothing more. No man would turn down what is so eagerly his for the taking, and Albee makes me no promises. All the same, I am hopeful the day will come when he recognizes me as his own version of Mary Godwin, a smart, helpful lover devoted to her poet.

I now spend my nights at Villa Diodati, sneaking past morose Polidori and steadfast Fletcher, although surely they must know I am here. I am uneasy around Albee's collection of animals and his pistols and daggers, but I am happy to avoid Percy's searing blue gaze. I am content to sleep in Albee's ostentatious bed, a majestically carved, throne-like affair draped in silks and bearing the dubious motto *Trust Byron*. Usually I sleep, while Albee continues to work on *Childe Harold*. He composes well into the night before he is satisfied, and then he comes to me, stirring me awake with his warm mouth while his cool hands creep up under my nightdress. I cannot tell if he is merely tired or dead drunk or completely distracted by the stanzas running in his head, yet his lovemaking is quick and detached and mute. Without endearments. Without a touch of intimacy or familiarity. Rather like swallowing laudanum to find sleep.

When daylight seeps into the room through the shutters and silk, Albee is kinder. Not loquacious as Percy would be, yet decidedly more attentive. He takes my hand and kisses my fingers. *Oh you are delicious.* His voice is harsh from sleep. He tucks my hair behind my ear and kisses my throat. He curls himself against me like a child. *Dear Claire.* On his tongue, my name sounds like a bagpipe's hum, and I sigh in gratitude.

Upon rising at midday, Albee wanders through the house, contentedly drinking his tea and tending his menagerie, which takes more time than it would to care for a houseful of Baby Williams. He walks the mastiffs, Newfoundlands, and wolfhounds while Fletcher slices fruit for the monkeys. When Albee ambles over to Percy's chalet, I am left to transcribe his latest revisions onto fresh pages. Being here in an official capacity restores my sense of respectability, and I relish the quiet.

While Albee is with Percy and Polidori is wandering through the vineyards, Fletcher brings me tea and discreetly disappears. The dogs lie on the cold tiles at my feet, and the monkeys chatter in the parlor. The cats sleep, curled into sunny corners of the solarium. Only the crows drive me mad, forcing me to throw a cloth over their cages. I refuse to acknowledge the lizard, which is as green and as large as a baby dragon.

On days when a sudden storm chases the men off the lake, I glance up from my work to find Albee watching me from the doorway. As a cat might watch a bird.

"Welcome home." I smile.

"Greetings, mademoiselle." He leers in return, although there is deeper emotion present, too. Perhaps regret that the rain ruined his day. Or perhaps it is merely lust. He comes to me with his crooked, cat-like walk. He slides the pen from my fingers and pulls me up to him. He keeps hold of my hand to walk me past the cages of monkeys and birds and the lizard. He steers me around the carpet of dogs to his bed. There his eyes grow warm, and I recognize affection and anticipation at last. *Ah, dear lass.* He peels my clothes away. *Have mercy on me.*

Every evening, as if Albee and I are man and wife and Polidori a distant cousin, we welcome Percy and Mary and Willmouse into our parlor for drinks and discussion. Or, if the night is fair, we all scamper onto the boat, carrying our wine bottles and baby trappings with us. We sail away from a rose-scented shoreline into the tangy darkness surrounding the lake.

Albee and Percy are too shy, too superstitious maybe, to recite what they have written that day, yet they have no reluctance to speak of other writers' work. Percy loves Keats, while Albee declares him too sentimental. Percy praises Wordsworth, and Albee calls him Turdsworth. Both admire Coleridge and Leigh Hunt. Neither are pleased with Southey. At some point in the evening, Percy gasps in alarm. "Is that something moving in the water?" He points. "Right there, next to the boat." It is his nightly joke, a little exercise in frightening us with his visions of deep water dragons and elongated vipers. Relics from the ice age, he claims.

Polidori looks frantically from side to side, which is Albee's call to action. Right on cue, he stands up, pulls his shirt over his head and drops his breeches so quickly, so naturally, it becomes a ballet. He dives into the black water, his naked body as white as a bloom of lily pads. A swift, sensuous dancer flowing away from us. A work of art.

When he swims back and clambers into the boat, I wrap him in Willmouse's blankets. He shivers with satisfaction. For his ease of movement in the water. For the warmth of my hands on his skin. Maybe for having me at his side. Who can say? He is too fond of claiming he will never be satisfied.

One night when the moon is obliterated by clouds and the wind blows wildly off the water, we stay inside and read ghost stories aloud.

While we take turns, it is not long before Albee seizes control by reciting Coleridge's "Christabel" and challenging us to write our own ghost stories. "You, too, Pollydolly." He points into the shadows where Polidori is watching the rain fall. "We have the perfect atmosphere to frighten ourselves to death."

To humor our host, we take up pens and papers and write away, but I am already fearing Albee's cruel condescension. So, too, I imagine, is Polidori, although he is scribbling away with a vengeance. The dogs are restlessly prowling the halls and the birds squawk too often for me to concentrate. I notice Mary's pen quickly and quietly filling her pages, while Albee lies prostrate on the parquet floor, as if waiting for a ghostly muse to fall upon him. Across the room Percy resembles a wax figure, as pale as Coleridge's lady Geraldine. "Percy?" I call to him, but he is blank-faced, his eyes fixed on Mary. "Percy?" I jump to my feet, which startles him into a scream.

"Oh my God." He runs from the room and out onto the balcony. The rest of us follow to find him hanging his head over the rail and gasping for air. "It was a horrible and piteous face. My poor Mary."

His words are hysterical, nonsensical, but I find myself screaming in reaction to his fright. "What did you see, Percy? What unseen spirit is here with us?"

Polidori pulls out his smelling salts. Albee presses cups of port into our hands. Soon we are calmer. Percy is shaken, but apologetic. "It was a vision brought on by Coleridge and the storm and maybe the crows, but when I glanced at Mary, her breasts had turned into faces. Completely irrational, I know, but there you have it."

"I will accompany you home," I tell Mary. "I will help you get Percy through the vineyard and down the wet hillside." I, too, am shaken by Percy's hysterics, but I am also relieved to be excused from my ghost story assignment and Albee's critical disdain.

The summer storms continue, and the next rainy night finds us gathered at Mason Chappuis. "I baked a cake today," Mary says, "and want a chance to play hostess."

"You may be hostess, but Albee will always dominate the conversation," I warn. "He also refuses to be around women when they eat."

"How very strange." Mary gives me a look. "Well at least the men can eat."

Mary serves her cake, and I wait for Albee to goad us into a debate while he sits in judgement. "Is that so?" he will sneer. "That is your honest opinion?" Always I hear that slight burr echoed from his childhood, although I dare not mention it. He hates any connection to Scotland, and I prefer keeping silent to facing ridicule.

I watch the conviviality of the cake eaters and find myself comparing Albee to Percy. How can I not? They are men of similar backgrounds and talents and tastes, yet while Percy is eager to join any conversation, Albee is calculating and superior. "Books must exist for the masses," he shouts at poor Polidori. "Why literacy for only the upper crust?"

Perhaps in retaliation, Polidori brings up the novel *Glenarvon* written by Lady Caroline Lamb, rumored to be about her affair with Albee.

"She is a madwoman." Albee snorts his disgust as he helps himself to Percy's wine. "My life is haunted by madwomen. When my mistress in Greece was unfaithful, I had her sewed up in a bag and dumped in the Bosphorus. The others all kill themselves."

We understand Albee is joking when we recognize his story from The Giaour, yet I cannot bring myself to laugh along with Mary and Percy. I find his mood as chilling as the night's rain, even when he now fixates on the small details of Mary's and my childhoods. Maybe because our circumscribed, city-bred, middle-class upbringing is so different from Lady Caroline Lamb's, he studies us like rare specimens. "You are not sisters by blood?"

"Not at all." I repeat the shorter version of my mother marrying Mary's father, while Mary recounts the longer story of her dead mother and my missing father, the story of Mary Jane and Will meeting as neighbors and parents of young children.

"Claire's mother had tea parties for us." Mary rises from her chair to close the window against the wind. "For Fanny and me."

"Oh, Fanny," Percy says. "She is a sad case."

"Another Godwin sister in love with Percy," I tease.

"Christ, how many young girls did you run off with, Shelley?"

"Only three, if you count Harriet. The one he married." Mary is easier in Albee's company than the rest of us, and in return, he is kinder to her. She is relaxed, pleased to have two handsome men to praise her wit. Actually three, if I count Polidori sitting in the shadows. The poor man's infatuation with Mary is so painful he cannot bring himself to speak in her presence.

"Obviously the Serpent married Harriet before he knew you, Mary." Albee always flatters before he jabs. "Did no one in the Godwin family want you and Claire back in their fold?"

"Oh, that is another story entirely."

"Please. Do tell."

Mary reports on our ostracism from Skinner Street, and Fanny's inability to stand up to Mother. "We used to fear that Mother would kidnap me," I add. "I suspect she has lost interest by now."

"What of your father, Mary? Will Godwin strikes me as a decent gent."

"Mary Jane brainwashed him."

"Harriet swears Will brainwashed *me*," Percy offers.

Albee says nothing on that subject while Percy delivers a bitter attack on women who wrong their husbands and then keep the children from their fathers. "The very children we continue to support, I might add."

"That is the likely outcome." Albee shifts in his chair as if his leg pains him. "I shall never see my sweet Ada again."

No one dares speak until Polidori reports from the shadow. "The rain is starting," he says. "We should return to the villa."

We gather ourselves together for a walk through the rain. Polidori is soon out of sight, and I take Albee's hand, longing to soothe his loss of little Ada. He stops still. "Run back to the chalet, Claire, before you are soaked to the bone. Go. Now."

I am touched by his kindness. "I will not wash away, dear heart. I am a solid, fully-formed woman." The rain drips from his curls as he kisses me. A sad nibbling kiss that lacks desire. I press myself to him and he pulls away.

"You are far too young to suffer my ill-fated life. As I listened to Shelley tonight, it crossed my mind that I would hate for my pure, beautiful daughter to end up with the likes of me." His hands slide across my shoulders and down the length of my arms. "Go back where you belong."

I am too stunned to move. Albee may be truly sad for his lost child, yet what has that to do with me? I am hardly a babe in arms, hardly a weak and innocent child. "You have other women coming to call, Albee?" My voice rises above the wind. "I am not a fool. We see your admirers sailing by to gawk and gossip."

He pushes me away in disgust. "The last thing I desire is another girl."

His words stab me. "I remain only a *girl* to you?"

"Not at all. You are more musically gifted than most girls." Cruelty is Albee's specialty. "Stay with me if you wish or return to Shelley's house. I will pay you for your labors on my manuscript, but I cannot tend to you. I cannot be distracted by your desire for attention, nor can I pretend to care about what you think or what you say or what you last wrote in your journal."

I listen closely, as if there is a choice to be made, as if somewhere in between those words, he is saying he truly cares for me. The rain beats against us, and I am losing ground. I speak boldly as my heart cringes. "I will happily accept your wages, Albee."

I retrace my route, increasingly spongy and slick, to Percy's chalet. I enter through the nearest doorway and slosh up the stairs. Then, instead of turning toward my bedroom, I turn toward the voices of Mary and Percy. They are talking, talking, talking, as they do every night, and before I know it, I walk dripping into their chamber. I barely register their surprise, their soft exclamations, as I propel myself over their footboard like a freshly-caught fish. I drag my sodden self between their warm, comforting bodies and press my face flat into their soft, rumpled bedding, fully preparing to die right here.

15. The Bargain

I do not die. Death is not as easy as it sounds, even for the mortally wounded. No, life continues. Albee lunches with Percy as usual, and once they sail away, as usual, I walk uphill through the vineyards to my solitary labors at the Villa Diodati. It is thrilling, as always, to hold Albee's manuscript in my hands, and I tell myself that if he trusts me with his poetry, he will trust me with heart. He has been hurt by wife's desertion, by his loss of little Ada, and I must be patient. He will come around, and I will be here waiting when he does. I put those thoughts on paper and flatten them between the pages of his poetry. I weave them between the spokes of the bird cages and tie them around the dogs' collars. Albee ignores them. Our evenings are spent together as always, all of us carrying on as if nothing has changed.

It drives me mad.

Tonight, the air hangs around the boat as a heavy, moist curtain, and a very large moon scuds in and out of clouds. We are drunk on wine and the camaraderie that comes from making confessions rather than boasts. Confessions come easier tonight as Polidori is staying at Mason Chappuis with Willmouse.

"I never loved my father," Percy begins.

"I never knew my father." Albee folds his hands behind his head.

"Nor I." The motion of the lake churns my stomach.

"I never knew my mother," Mary says. "What could be worse?"

"Having a mother who ignores you," Percy answers.

"Having a mother who smothers you." Albee drains his cup.

"A mother who wishes for a better daughter."

Talk of mothers casts a gloom. "Let's swim," Percy says. "All of us. Come, Mary, this is your chance. No one but the moon to bear witness." Percy does not actually know how to swim, but he is fond of floating in moonlit water. Soon there is the flash of clothing and the glimmer of skin and then only the bobbing of disembodied heads. I paddle around for a bit near Mary until the motion of the waves makes me seasick. I round the prow of the boat to float on my back and confront the moon eye-to-eye.

The men's voices carry across the water. "So Fanny Godwin, this *sad case* sister," Albee says. "What happened to her?"

"She is home with the parents. Minding Godwin's store."

"She is also your lover, Serpent?" Albee sounds intoxicated.

"Certainly not! Fanny is a sister to me."

"In the same way that Claire is your sister?"

I hate to have Fanny belittled. So easily dismissed. I keep my eyes on the moon, fluttering my feet and hands to stay afloat. Surely Percy respects that Fanny is the sister we left behind, the one shunned from his life. Surely he senses that Albee's questions are leading him into a snare.

"Fanny is nothing like Claire," Percy says. "Not in the slightest. Taking Fanny Godwin as a lover would be an act of mercy not desire."

"Is that so, Serpent? What a shame." Even drunk, Albee is quick and clever enough to draw conclusions about Percy and me. He never pried such a confession from me. As for Mary listening there in the darkness, how could she not know that I am more than sisterly with Percy?

I flip onto my stomach and swim toward the boat. The motion of me turning combined with the moonlight and the queasiness in my stomach recalls a similar sensation. *I think I am with child*, I said to Percy a year ago in Lynmouth. Now, I must decide how to repeat those very same words and who should hear them.

I lie in my bed under the chalet's eaves, and over the crash of rain against the roof, I listen to Mary reason with Percy. "You must intervene," she urges. "You must straighten matters with Albee. I cannot bear Claire throwing herself at him one more day."

"Yes, Mary." He sighs. "Albee and I will come to an agreement."

"I am having this child." I shout from my bed.

"Yes, certainly," Mary soothes. "Do not frighten her, Percy." I close my eyes in thanksgiving that my sister has become my protector. Perhaps I will not be alone forever after all. I will have a child. I will have a family of my own.

When the skies clear, Mary and I stand on the terrace and watch Percy and Albee sail away. They are shoulder to shoulder, their hair blown back from their faces like windsocks. Albee inclines his head to hear Percy's words. Words about me, no doubt. Me and the fate of my child.

Mary turns to me with Willmouse on her hip. "How could you have allowed this to happen?" At the sound of his mother's sharp tone, Willmouse cries.

"I could ask the same of you, dear sister. You and little William here."

"Percy and I have a partnership. You are nothing to Lord Byron but an amusement. A passing fancy that did not survive the span of a season."

If I open my mouth to respond, all my secrets could spill forth in a single breath. *Percy. Last summer. My lost child. Percy under the grape arbor.* I take a breath. "Yes, Mary, I can be very amusing when I choose to be. I am quite clever at tickling fancies."

"How dare you cause Percy fresh worry?" Naturally Mary is cross over the upheaval in her idyllic summer. For the awkwardness that might arise in her *wonderfully enlightening* conversations with Albee. For the strain of having me once again under her roof and underfoot. I wait, expecting her to next blame me for the unseasonably stormy weather. Instead, she starts in on Fanny. "Not only does Percy have you to deal with, but our sister is in the doldrums again." Mary points to the table where Fanny's most recent letter is propped against the egg basket. "She bemoans the incessant rain and Father's money problems. She says our last letter was too long and thus costly for her. You must not go on as you do, Claire. You use entirely too many adjectives."

This from the woman who goes on for paragraphs about the sun in our garden or cloud formations over the lake or every inane comment Albee might utter. "Then you should refrain from sending Fanny a volume of Lord Byron's verse," I respond.

When Percy returns from his boat trip, he is dejected. "Albee refuses to believe the child is his."

"That is absurd." Mary rises up from the nursery chair with Willmose yet fastened to her breast. "Whose child does he imagine it to be? Polidori's?"

Percy fixes his blue gaze on me, willing me not to breathe a word. "He doubts she is with child."

"Even more absurd." Mary rhythmically sways from one foot to the other.

"I have a plan." Percy always has a plan. "We shall hire a nanny to stay with Willmouse and go on holiday for a few days. We shall leave Albee alone with his thoughts and the dreary Polidori. Given time, he will see reason."

"We could stand a diversion." Mary sounds distracted. "A bit of an excursion."

"It shall be an adventure! What do you say, Clarabella?"

I say nothing. I am past adventures. I am doomed to raise a child alone in poverty.

Percy reads my thoughts and comes to my side. "Perhaps you cannot depend on Albee right now, but you can depend on me, my dear girl. You will stay with us until the baby is born. I will instruct Sir Tim's solicitor to include you and your child in my will. You are to be taken care of, Claire," he says grandly. "I give you my word."

It is a generous offer, the very offer I desired from him a year ago, yet it does little to ease my heartache. I take no satisfaction as Mary recoils at Percy's promises. I experience no sense of righteousness when she quickly turns away to carry Willmouse across the terrace and into her famously sunny garden.

"All will be well." Percy's voice is strident, and I am not courageous enough to ask what was said out there in the middle of the lake. There on the boat surrounded by beauty, did Albee deny his paternity? Or did Albee's doubt merely cause Percy to wonder if he is the true father?

Percy's idea of a merry diversion is an adventure exploring the Alps. How like Percy to concoct such a bizarre plan. We spend days riding mules through the ice and snow and constant glare of white light, yet I am numb. I cannot bear listening to Percy and Mary's endless poetic discussions of desolation. Or perhaps it is isolation. Some such imagery that struck Percy upon viewing the mountain glaciers and one that Mary wants to use in the ghost story she began that fearful night at Villa Diodati. Her ghost has now become a monster man made from the body parts of other men. Oh dear God. I, too, feel like I am sewn together from other people's parts, once again carrying a child no one wants me to have.

At least our journey turns Mary from dour to light-hearted. "We must buy a gift for poor Fanny," she insists when we shop in Geneva upon our return. "Something pretty and practical. Like Fanny herself."

I am in no condition to argue that sending Fanny a gift from Switzerland is a cruel reminder of what she is missing. I prop myself against the glass-topped case as Percy and Mary choose a dainty watch with a mother-of-pearl face. It is quite pretty, and very Swiss, although I imagine it will break Fanny's heart every time she looks at it. I want to say that a gift given out of guilt is a bad omen. As it is, I am too nauseous to speak.

In the morning after our return to Montalegre, Mary feeds me dry bread and then circles the table as I take small bites between sips of tea. "I should accompany you, Percy. I will be helpful to you should Claire grow faint."

Percy sits across from me, his hands folded on the tabletop to keep himself still as he and Mary carry on their debate on how to proceed with Albee. "Claire must do this without you," he says. "She must speak for herself." Then, to me, "When you feel your strength return, we will walk up the hill together."

"That is hardly Claire speaking for herself, is it now?"

Percy ignores her and helps me to my feet. "Your color is brighter this morning. The walk will do you good."

We have done this before, he and I. A year ago, he was the one to bring me tea and toast and help me to my feet, insisting that a walk over the moors would ease my nausea. We cannot ever speak of that time again, yet the memory is there, as large and looming as Mont Blanc. The hillside between the chalet and Villa Diodoti is covered in mist, and Percy tries to distract me by making wild predictions of when the sun will burst through. "When three crows fly South. When Polidori forgets to frown. When the boatload of voyeurs from the hotel smashes against the rocks." He, too, is anxious.

While I am certain Albee is quite used to dealing with distraught, rejected lovers, I expect little to come from our meeting. Especially when the only thing I truly desire is for Albee to love me and my child. Everything else is for Percy to negotiate.

"Byron expects us," he says when Fletcher opens the door to Villa Diodati, and although I am not at all certain that is true, soon Albee appears in his dressing gown.

"My good neighbors come to call." His hair, combed straight back from his high forehead, is a mass of damp ringlets. The skin on his face and chest glow with vigor. He radiates beauty, and if he is surprised by our sudden appearance on his doorstep, he does not let on. "Polidori and I are returned from a swim." He gestures toward the courtyard where Polidari sits fully clothed and reading.

"You appear quite refreshed, my friend," Percy says.

"Exercise agrees with me." He ushers us into the courtyard, his sleeve rippling like a silken banner. "Except when I'm drinking." Barefoot and steady, he leads us past Polidori and the dogs heaped on the courtyard stone, around the many cages and onto the terrace that faces the mountains. "The air is greener here, I believe. More soft than bright." He turns to Percy. "I have some fine port. Or would you prefer tea?"

"Nothing, thank you."

I sense Percy wants to avoid distractions. He wants to speak his peace and then slide back down the hillside with a clear mind. I listen to the monkeys chatter in the background as the poets discuss their work. Without mentioning my role in it, Percy complains that our tour of the Alps has put him behind schedule. Albee, his bare, twisted foot propped on an ottoman, says his Third Canto of *Childe Harold* is complete and awaiting its journey to London. "All due to Claire, here. She never allowed one syllable to escape its line."

His attention falls on me, admiring me, desiring me in spite of himself, and at last I dare to speak. "You are most welcome, Albee. It was a labor of love."

Both he and Percy flinch, and I return to studying Albee's poor misshapen foot. Every night we were together, my fingers caressed that foot so Albee could sleep. I eased his pain with my touch. In dismissing me, Albee is losing not only a lover, but a comforter and a collaborator, and I want him to suffer his losses.

"We are here to discuss your plans for Claire's child." Percy shifts in his chair.

"Plans?" Albee rights himself from his usual slump. "My dear man, I understand quite well that you and Mary have a lasting, unconventional, marriage-in-your-souls commitment. I can also accept that Claire's child may not be yours, as I first suspected. That does not by any means conclude that it is mine."

"Claire has been with no one else." Percy is not generally a liar, although his years of evading creditors has given him a convincing manner.

"Look at me, Claire," Albee says, "and tell me true. Was I the one to father this child?"

Despite his flamboyant persona, Albee is a private man, a closed-off man not given to confidences. Never has he expressed even the mildest concern for me. Never, even at the height of our passion, has he uttered the word *love*. Now, as he leans towards me, his face is open and expectant. I see the man he might be. Mesmerized, I watch as the sun shoots a beam of light through the trees, across the terrace, and strikes his hair. Curls spring away from his head in a dark gold halo of blessing.

"I swear it is your child." I speak without faltering. "It was conceived in love, and I promise that for the rest of my life I will love this child as deeply as I love you."

His face closes as quickly as a trap, and any hint of warmth evaporates. "I do not want your love. Nor do I want yet another child I will never see."

"I beg you, Albee. Let me stay to work with you. Allow me to raise this child with you."

"Listen to me, Claire." He leans forward, his forearms braced against his bare knees. "Neither Percy nor I desire scandal. We cannot have random women and their babies clutching onto us if we wish any sort of privacy. Fletcher reports there are journalists sailing around the lake to ask about me being seen with an eighteen-year-old girl. About your underthings airing in my windows. There are boatloads of English tourists floating by with telescopes and hoping to catch a glimpse of us. I am a married man. I have a wife and child. I require some peace as I go about my day, some quiet where I can write. I cannot be with you."

"I will wait until you are free. Until you are divorced."

"My wife does not believe in divorce. Rather, she believes I should suffer from the state of our matrimony for the rest of my days." He pulls his dressing gown around him and rises stiffly from his chair. "Shelley has agreed to take responsibility for you, as you are, by virtue of his mistress, somewhat related."

"Mary is far from a mistress, Albee." Percy's tone is sharp, a badly played note.

Albee limps a few steps away and then a few steps back. I recognize his attempt to keep the blood flowing through his lame leg. His face is taut with pain, and my heart bleeds for him. "As for Claire's bastard," he says with a grimace, "I have no choice but to take responsibility for that little animal, yet only on the condition you will turn it over to my sister Augusta. She is a fine woman and an excellent mother to her own adoring brood."

"Your sister Augusta?" I am dumbstruck. Does Albee not remember confessing his lust for Augusta during our own moments of intimacy? Augusta, who is rumored to have borne Albee's child, a daughter named Medora, and thus sent his wife fleeing with his beloved Ada? "That is an absurd proposal." I rise to face him eye-to-eye. "Completely unacceptable. I will keep our child with me."

"You are incapable of keeping yourself, dear woman, let alone a child. Kindly spare your progeny as dismal a fate as you have brought upon yourself."

I am no stranger to Albee's caustic remarks, yet Percy grows agitated and tips back his laudanum. "I beg you to be civil, Byron. Kindly do not distress her."

Albee responds by pouring himself a glass of port.

My fury is too dark and pulsing to remain in their company. I wander through the house cursing both men. Percy's rejection last summer thrust me into my seduction of Albee, who has proven himself to be a despicable human being. How could I yet love such a man? In the dining room I feed Santa Maria, the smallest of the monkeys. Not because I am fond of her, but because I admire her for scurrying across the draperies and swinging from the chandelier. I admire her fierce determination to pluck the grapes from my hand and leap away again before being captured. Santa Maria is a perfect kindred spirit for Albee.

When I return to the men, I find them mellowed. "I can be reasonable if I must," Albee says to me. "I am willing to provide for this child, and I will entrust it to your care on two conditions. You must relinquish it to me when it is old enough to leave you, and you will proclaim you are its aunt, not its mother. Nor I the father. You may visit the child as often as you wish when it is in my care, yet you shall have nothing to do with me during those visits. We are not fated to become the glorious family portrait of your imaginings. Is such comprehension within your feeble grasp?"

I allow Percy to protest for me. Except for Albee's promise of provision, nothing about their arrangement pleases me. Yet I reason that by the time my child is old enough to leave me, every condition Albee demands could well change. Every single one. In this moment, I desire nothing more than to keep my child, and I will agree to anything that keeps my baby away from Albee's sister Augusta.

"I accept." I speak loudly to be heard over the men. "I accept your conditions." I turn in time to see Santa Maria swing past the window. I have time, I tell myself. I have plenty of time to persuade Albee of my love and devotion.

16. Bath, England, Autumn 1816

Ancient Bath is a splendid place for an unwed mother like Mary Godwin and me, her unwed pregnant sister. I adore the city's liveliness, its cobbled streets filled with shoppers and tradesmen and visitors to the Roman baths. It is a drastic change from Lynmouth, where every soul was a hiker passing through the gorge or a villager quick to gossip about any stranger. In Bath, no one pays us any mind. Perhaps that is why Mary hates it.

"My dear Elf," she begs Percy, "please find me a house in the countryside. Without Claire."

Naturally, Mary is in agony now that I am once again under her roof, yet I am not convinced she detests Bath as much as she claims. Our residence at 5 Abbey Churchyard, next to the Pump Room, is in the thick of society. Here she takes drawing lessons and attends lectures and the theatre, and when Percy returns from London, they gad about town, leaving me to languish with Willmouse and Elise, the nanny they brought home with them from Switzerland.

I believe Mary complains about Bath because she resents Percy's absences. First, he traveled to London to deliver Albee's manuscript to his publisher. Then he went there to battle his latest debts and keep himself out of prison. While we were in Switzerland, it seems Percy lost his Bishopsgate house and all its furnishings to creditors. None of which has anything to do with me.

"I am not to blame for us living in Bath," I tell Mary. "If you must have a scapegoat, blame Albee for your discontent."

She does not want to discuss Albee. Nor do I. The great Lord Byron has loaded up his mammoth Napoleonic coach with books and animals to journey to Italy, and I am spinning fantasies. Come next summer, I tell myself, I will meet Albee in Venice with our child in my arms. At once glance, Albee will immediately and completely fall in love with both of us, and we will live together as a family in the beautiful city of canals. Venice is said to be lovelier than Amsterdam, the city which first enchanted me. Ah, such an exquisite life my child and I will have in Italia.

For now, Bath suits me fine. I, too, can walk about as freely as Mary until my condition becomes too advanced for proper society. "We shall not have it whispered that Percy is the father of your child," Mary warns me.

Percy and Albee are in collusion to spare their good names. Come the New Year, I am to be shut away in my own quarters in some lesser part of Bath until I emerge – rather like a butterfly – as the nanny of a newborn child. Considering Percy's earlier schemes for adopting children off the street, such a plan is not as far-fetched as it sounds.

If I might see you again, I write to Albee, *I could remind you of how it was for us to be together. Our heat. Our rhythm. The perfect symmetry of our souls.*

Not a word in reply.

I imagine Albee misses Percy more than he does me. Although I write faithfully, Albee is too gleefully tearing his way across the Continent to respond. If it were not for his correspondence with Percy, we would know nothing at all of the great Lord Byron.

We would also know nothing of the Godwins if it were not for Fanny, who wants to be here with us as much as I want to be with Albee. "I crave fresh air and a change of scene, dear sister," she writes to Mary. "I would happily tend to little William and grant you time to spend with Percy." Mary Jane, she adds, is causing her headaches.

"Precisely what I need." Mary drones when she reads Fanny's letter. "Another sister to look after."

"You know Percy. He likely encourages Fanny to call on us."

"Percy is overly generous. He will have no time for his writing with yet another sister hanging on him. Especially one as tedious as Fanny."

"Percy is never here in Bath long enough to write."

"All that is about to change, Claire. Now that your condition is becoming noticeable, we cannot have *anyone* around. Especially not Fanny. She will go tattling right back to Skinner Street, and then scandal will brew."

"Fanny could live with us."

"Now you sound like Percy."

Percy is away. Mary is resentful. Fanny is sad. Albee is disgusted with me. I spend longs days wandering Bath alone. Some days I want my mother, who cannot know that I, her only daughter, am expecting a child.

By the time Percy returns to Bath, the changes in my appearance take him by surprise. "Clarabella. You have grown." His blue gaze runs the length of me, admiring me, but also pronouncing judgment. My condition has jeopardized his poetic camaraderie with Albee, the friendship I prompted in the first place. C'est dommage. For better and worse, I have changed Percy's life, and I feel no pity toward him. Only a rare concoction of love and gratitude and disappointment.

With Percy in residence, life becomes animated. He throws himself into his writing, his extravagant peek-a-boo games and finger-plays with Willmouse, his strolls with Mary, his exploration of his new community. He talks nonstop, and while he keeps me at arm's length, he watches over me constantly. "You are well, dear Claire? You are keeping up with your studies?" And every evening, he asks me to sing. "Tonight could you favor us with a love song that does not involve tragedy?"

"Does such a song exist, Percy?"

His laugh is high and piercing. A blasting whistle of joy.

On the eighth morning of October, Mary receives a letter from Fanny. *Good tidings, dear sister! I am at this very moment at the Greyhound Inn near Bath and looking forward to seeing every one of you. I doubt I will recognize Baby William, yet it is a challenge I anticipate. Awaiting my soonest opportunity to call on you. Love, Your Sister Fanny*

Mary quakes, the thin paper pulsing in her hand. "Oh, Percy. You must go to her. Tell her Claire and Willmouse have a touch of fever and could be contagious. Tell her we regret her long journey. Buy her some dinner, and then put her on the next coach to London."

I want to grab Percy's sleeve and shout. *Bid Fanny to come and save me from Mary.* Percy buries his face in his hands until Mary speaks sharply. "Quickly, Percy. What if she grows impatient and hires a driver?"

His hands swipe the length of his face as his chin rises toward the ceiling. "Why must I be the one to lie to Fanny? Why can you not meet your sister for dinner? She misses you greatly, and I had the opportunity to see her at Will Godwin's barely a fortnight ago."

"She would be very suspicious of you taking care of fever patients, and she will enjoy having you to herself. You can feed her tales of Lord Byron. Do not speak of Claire, and all will be well."

Grumbling, Percy leaves, and Mary goes about her normal routine: her drawing lesson, her afternoon walk, and her listless reading of Clarendon's histories. Yet, her thoughts are elsewhere and anxious. Fanny is the sister Percy chose first, the sister who loved Percy with all the innocence of a woman much younger than her age. Of us three sisters, only Fanny remains the pure, good-hearted girl that Percy greatly admires.

"Why does he tarry?" Mary frets as she rocks Willmouse.

"Percy appreciates an attentive audience."

When he returns at teatime, he is red-faced and more disheveled than ever. "It was vile to leave her there, Mary. She misses you and Claire and longs to see Willmouse. She said to thank you once again for the watch."

Ah yes, the watch. The trinket from Switzerland Mary sent as a pacifier. "Did she ask to call on us again?" Mary wets the tea and slices the bread and waits for Percy to collect himself.

"Fanny said she *wishes* she could be with us. That her life is hopeless, and our life is a dream and she regrets not going to school when she had the chance."

"What did you say, Percy?" I ask.

"I told her our life is not the dream she imagines. I told her Harriet is keeping my children from me and I, too, am heart-sore."

"Might you have sounded less disenchanted with our life?" Mary snaps.

"I *am* disenchanted with Harriet, just as you are disenchanted with Fanny's loyalty to Will and Mary Jane. In the future, you attend to your own sister. I hated turning her away. I hate myself for that unkindness, and I refuse to do it again."

"We did this for you, Claire." Now Mary fumes at me. "We turned poor Fanny away for the sake of your reputation."

We eat our tea in silence. I am furious with Mary, yet I say nothing because one more word could bring Percy to tears. He consumes his bread and cheese and stewed plums without comment, while I bow my head over my teacup to secretly observe the roundness of my belly and wonder at how much my fatherless child has grown.

Fanny's next letter, addressed solely to Percy, arrives on the evening of October ninth. Percy stands in the open doorway, holding the letter in his hands just as the angelus bells begin to ring. Not only are they deafening, but then, smack, the wind blows the door shut and startles us all. Willmouse begins to cry, and Mary croons to him. Percy runs his fingers through his hair, always a signal of trouble. "I must leave at once," he shouts. Then he grabs his coat from the peg by the door and runs toward the stables.

Mary and I are left to read the letter for ourselves. It begins as a bread and butter note thanking Percy for dinner and apologizing for any inconvenience that Fanny caused him. She missed seeing Mary and me and Little William, she writes, and then she apologizes for being *the forgotten sister, the sister who expected too much.* Fanny has perfect penmanship, yet her words grow small and shaky by the bottom of the page. "I shall leave now. No longer to be a worry to you. Percy, please bury me with my mother at St. Pancras."

"We have killed her." My heart pounds, and I shiver. "We have killed our dear sister Fanny."

Mary says nothing. She sits in the chair by the door and smooths the letter across her lap. Again and again, her fingers flatten the page as if she is ironing out a crease. When Willmouse cries, I go to him. I lift him into my arms and tuck him to my chest. I kiss the top of his soft blond head and walk him around the flat as I recall what daring it took for Mary and me to run away from Skinner Street. Fanny, our tragic, eager-to-please sister, was never brave. She would rather die than admit failure and return home to Will and Mary Jane Godwin. Oh, our poor sister. "If Percy can reach her in time, he will save her," I tell Mary. "Fanny will listen to Percy."

"Do you think Percy once loved Fanny as he loves me?" Mary's face is distorted. Her lower lip is bloody, all but bitten-through. To have my wise, composed sister confess her doubt is a revelation to me.

"Of course not," I say at once. Yet, again I wonder at what might have happened if Fanny had gone with Percy when he first asked.

Our next two days are torture. Percy tracks Fanny from Bath to Bristol and then returns to sleep a few hours before taking post horses to Swansea. The hours tick on painfully as we wait for his return. Too lethargic to move, we watch Willmouse, so pure, so innocent, bat at his blocks. The agony of waiting boils inside my brain like water over the flame, and words bubble from my mouth.

"I wish my child to be a boy as boys can do whatever they please. They do not require male relatives to protect them. They are not frowned upon for lacking an education or a spouse. Nor are they required to take care of their women or children." My voice grows in volume. "Though my son will, of course. My son will be a fine man. A good father."

"Yes, yes." It is Mary's turn to soothe me. "Of course he will."

My son, I say to myself, will be as good a man as Percy himself.

Night falls. The sun rises. Willmouse cries. Mary stirs. The kettle whistles. I stay abed and listen to Mary making tea and warming milk. I sense her worrying about Percy and blaming Fanny for dragging him away from us. She comes into my room to worry aloud. "What is keeping Percy so long, do you think? Should we send for Hogg? Or Father?"

"Would Father come?" The thought is chilling. "Perhaps Percy is on the road this very moment," I say to comfort us. "On his way home to us. Let us take Willmouse for a morning stroll. Let us fill our heads with fresh air. Is that not what Fanny would wish for us?" From the other room, little William laughs, and I am struck with sadness. Willmouse may never know his Aunt Fanny, the only aunt to share his maternal bloodline.

It is after midnight when Percy returns in a state of agitation. He is pale and shaking as if he has been to war and witnessed all its atrocities.

"I went to Swansea," he begins, "to the Mackworth Arms. I bribed the desk clerk let me into Fanny's room. I was too late." A sob catches in his throat. "I am deeply sorry, Mary, not to have better news."

Mary, also sobbing, embraces him. His cheeks are hollow, his eyes deep-set and staring. His chin is stubble, and he smells like rotting onions. She eases off his coat and rubs her fingers over his chilled face. Their tenderness is too painful to observe, and I bury my face in my hands. Our dear, plain sister, the naïve girl with a passion for songbirds and fossils, was cold to his touch, Percy tells us. A laudanum bottle and suicide note lay by her side. There is nothing more to say.

I stand before Percy and force his eyes to meet mine. "I did what had to be done, Claire." He sips from his own vial, and I shudder. "I did what had to be done," he says again.

Much later, after Mary is asleep and Percy has washed away his road dust, he comes to perch on my bed, precisely as Mary had that morning. "Ah, Clarabella. I regret I could not save your sister." The laudanum causes him to sound like an actor reciting lines. "I am haunted by wondering what tenderness I might have offered. What would you have done in my place?"

I have little sympathy for his melodrama. "If I had gone to meet Fanny at the Greyhound Inn, I would have told her to stop pitying herself. I would have told her that if she was brave enough to leave Skinner Street, she could go anywhere – with or without you and Mary and me. I would have told her I was sorry we had no more than a pretty little watch to offer her when she needed us, and from now on, we would do better by her."

Percy grows tearful again. "The watch was with her."

The thought chokes me. "Where is she now?"

His eyes flicker towards me like a blue flame. "Now?"

"What arrangements did you make for my sister?" I whisper as loudly as I dare.

"I did what Will Godwin instructed me to do." Percy lies down beside me, his words floating up toward the ceiling. "Not a pleasant task."

"Father is traveling to Swansea to bring Fanny home? We will go to London for her funeral?" Immediately I fear being left behind. "I will wear Mary's heavy cape. No one will detect my condition."

"There is no funeral. No burial service. Nothing." Percy's voice grows so flat, so completely without emotion, I worry that he, too, has consumed too many draughts.

"Percy." I shake his arm. "Where is Fanny? What did you do with her?"

"Nothing. I did absolutely nothing." He cups his hands over his eyes. "Will sent word for me to take her identification, take the note she left, and remove myself as quickly as I could. I followed his orders."

I am on my knees, twisting towards the limp, spineless man that Fanny loved. I pull his hands away from his eyes, eyes that remain closed. "You left her there alone? Even after she specifically asked you to take care of her? To bury her with her mother? Oh my God, Percy, how could you?" I begin to beat at him with my fists. His chest. His shoulders. His face. "Damn you, Percy. Damn you to hell."

He grabs my wrists and sits up. His eyes are wide open and his words as measured and precise as a metronome. "Will said that news of Fanny's death would lead directly to us. We could be called as witnesses at the post mortem, and the press would never leave us in peace. Your child would become yet another scandal attached to us."

The cruelty of the world makes me weak. Percy loosens my hands, and I sit back on my heels. "Fanny is paying for all our sins. Fanny is our scapegoat."

"Fanny is dead, Claire. You are speaking nonsense."

"We were the ones to run away and live in sin. We flaunted our love for one another, and now Fanny will be dumped into the ground hundreds of miles from her mother's grave. She will have no proper grave, no headstone. Her body faces desecration by common thieves. Her soul shall spend eternity among those who were unknown and unloved, and yet Fanny was the best one of us. The very best."

I weep silently as Percy's head bounces, a slight up-and-down motion that goes on too long and too steadily. Like he is keeping beat to a sprightly melody. "Yes," he says. "I thought those precise thoughts on my long ride home. I told myself that Fanny would be pleased to be a martyr. Pleased to be remembered as the sister who saved us from high-minded gentry and the moralists of the world."

Percy is parroting Mary. She has eased his guilt by assuring him Fanny was content with her role, the good girl who did whatever anyone asked so she would be loved. It sickens me to the point of biliousness. I lie back on my pillow and close my eyes to stop the room from its dark spinning.

"Claire?" His voice is barely a whisper. "Speak to me. Tell me your thoughts."

My thoughts. My thoughts are clouded and unforgiving and hopeless. "Oh, Percy, to speak of Fanny as a martyr is like giving her that watch. Both are totally meaningless."

"That watch and her brown berry necklace could yet be traced to us. Her stays and stockings bore her initials."

"Those are her mother's stays, her poor dead mother's initials. What became of the note?"

"I left the note and tore off her signature."

"What did she write?"

"I cannot recall."

I do not believe him, yet I do not press him. Who wants to recite someone's last words? Who wants to hear them spoken out loud?

My son, I tell myself again, shall be a good man. A better man than Percy Shelley.

As the dreariness of autumn falls around us, we slowly let down our guard. We breathe easier in those rain-greyed days as Percy calls on Will and Mary Jane and reports back to us that they are holding up fine. Mother tells anyone who asks – including my dear brother Charles -- that Fanny is visiting her dead mother's sisters in Ireland, while Will tells those very same sisters that Fanny is touring France with friends from Wales and might possibly be traveling on to Italy for the winter. Having herself a lark.

Death forces us not only to lie, but to invent a world filled with impossible promise for our lost sister. When Percy pens *this world was all too wide to thee*, I know he is writing of Fanny and their last meeting. Or perhaps he is quoting her suicide note. *Some secret woes had been my own.*

"She loved you, Percy," I remind him out of spite. That the great Percy Shelley cannot find a way to grant Fanny's final wish without attracting attention to the rest of us is unacceptable to me.

"Fanny comes to me in my dreams," I tell Mary. "She complains she cannot sleep."

Mary does not raise her eyes from her needlework, does not raise her voice beyond a hiss. "Rubbish. Do not start up with your hysterics again, Claire. It will harm your child, and I cannot abide listening to such drivel."

This from the sister with the excitable husband and her own monster man creation. Fanny comes to Mary, too, I surmise. And Percy. Surely, I believe, Fanny comes to Percy first. My baby moves like the clock on Mary's mantel. Slow steady ticks with sudden jerks of his hands. Please God, a boy. Not a girl at the mercy of men who ignore her needs and desires, her final wishes.

Eventually Will and Mary Jane announce to friends that Fanny died of inflammatory fever while in Wales. To others, Mother confides that Fanny killed herself because Percy did not love her. If we depend on Percy's love to live, we are all doomed. Percy has not been himself since Fanny died, and I take some comfort in his suffering. Unlike the man who bounds into the house and hoists Willmouse high above his head, this poor creature is too distracted to notice his son crawling across the hearth.

Mary is napping so I am the one to rise and snatch Willmouse from his steady progression towards the grate. I distract him with a handkerchief doll and sooth his hurt feelings while Percy stares into the fire, one leg crossed over the other, his foot bouncing without rhythm.

"Percy?"

He startles, pivoting toward the sound of my voice. Then he blinks, returning from wherever he was. "I cannot find Harriet."

"Harriet?"

"She left my children with the Westbrooks and then disappeared. None of us can find her, and I am worried."

"You despise Harriet. Why search for her now?" Money, I think. Any search for Harriet must relate to his ongoing lack of finances.

"Oh, Claire." He bows his head into his open hands. "I fear she is carrying my child."

My own child kicks in response to this announcement, and Willmouse squirms in my grasp as the fire blazes up.

"How could you do this to us, Percy?"

He attempts to explain, his voice dipping into that flat monotone I detest as he meanders on about Harriet and her deceit with other men. I stop listening. I know Percy's charms all too well. His sweet words of a life together. *We shall be a true family once again.* We have all suffered from Percy's promises, albeit Harriet, that young beautiful girl he first chose for his wife, has suffered most of all. It sickens me to think he has seduced her yet again with professions of love he can never honor. The man spreads his seed like a milkweed, camouflaged in pure white airy clouds.

"My friend Hookham, the bookseller, is looking for her," he says. "We cannot speak of this to Mary."

Yet another secret to keep from my sister. I rise from my chair and hand Percy his son. I, too, am in need of a nap.

Once again Mary and I are alone together, left waiting for Percy to return with news of another dead woman. In this case, his wife. How quickly we have grown from those young girls waiting in a fever for the poet Shelley to stride into Will Godwin's bookshop and let his blue gaze sear us. Now we are fully-formed women kept waiting for tragic news.

From London, Percy sends one dire message after another. The Westbrooks confirm that Harriet became despondent in October and went missing from her place on Elizabeth Street in November. On the tenth of December, her body was fished from the Serpentine, and she was buried as Harriet Smith rather than Harriet Shelley to prevent scandal from falling upon her children.

To make matters worse, Harriet's sister Eliza will not relinquish those children to Percy, and he is furiously indignant. "Oh, poor Percy." Mary clutches her copy of Othello to her breast. "After all he has done for that wretched woman and those dear children, you would think Eliza would be more tenderhearted towards him."

I refrain from saying that Percy was the one to make Harriet wretched. "Percy loves children." I choke on my words as I think of Fanny and Harriet and my own lost child. The child that never was. Thomas, I have named him in my heart.

"Hogg says Harriet was with child with when she died." Mary's announcement comes as a defense of Percy. "Her pregnancy was reported in all the papers. Percy believes the Westbrooks disowned her and she became a prostitute."

I imagine Percy's voice screeching upward in pitch as he rants about Harriet and her fall from grace once she could no longer have him. Once upon a time, I believed Percy's claims against Harriet. Sadly, I now know him too well. By declaring Harriet an unfaithful wife, Percy allowed himself to seduce first Mary and then myself. I want to remember the Harriet that Fanny so admired. The high-spirited young wife in her splendid purple dress who teased her serious new husband. Fanny and Harriet and her unborn child are together now, I hope, laughing with my Thomas and Mary's Clara in some celestial city.

I observe my sister, her face flushed with outrage, and I want to weep. "Oh, Mary. We are no different than Harriet waiting for Percy to come home with a glad heart and love her once again."

"Do not be foolish, Claire." Mary slaps Othello onto Percy's writing desk. "Given your circumstances, I will forgive your unkind remark."

"I know Percy loves his children, but I cannot bear to think they will shun Harriet's memory. Consider how you and Fanny honored your mother's memory. Consider how you would wish for Willmouse to honor you."

"Certainly." Mary avoids making eye contact by fussing with the combs in her hair. "Percy and I will raise Ianthe and Charles now. As we always vowed. Marriage means nothing to us, although if that sacrament grants Percy his children, I won't object."

How very noble. For all their scorn of the conventional, marriage is precisely what might grant Percy custody of his children. Marriage will re-establish Mary's relationship with her father. Marriage will remove the stain brought upon the good names of Shelley and Godwin. I am not duped by Mary's pious tone, yet if I accuse her of abandoning her own mother's cause, she would accuse me of jealousy.

And she would be justified in such an accusation as I, too, long to marry the father of my child.

It is barely two weeks since we learned of Harriet's death, and Percy and Mary are exchanging wedding vows at St. Mildred's. Will and Mary Jane are there to celebrate the revered union of their remarkable daughter to a gifted poet. They are so filled with joyful propriety they will host a small reception. They will boast that Percy is the eldest son of Sir Timothy Shelley, Baronet, and thus Mary is the future Lady Shelley.

In my heavily pregnant state, I am left here in Bath while Mary is left to explain my absence. Health concerns, she plans to say. Which is closer to the truth than not. Willmouse sleeps and Elise is out and I have only the tick of the clock and the fire's crackle for company. I struggle not to consider those circumstances that led Fanny and Harriet to their deaths. Rather, I choose to believe that Percy loved Harriet right to the end, and he, instead of a random stranger, fathered the child who drowned in her womb. That on the day Harriet's baby was conceived, Percy returned to her not for financial dealings, but because their eternal love bound them together for all time.

I want to believe eternal love is possible for me and Albee and our child, and yet Albee has not responded to me in months. Worse, he instructs Percy that I am not to write to him ever again. So I refrain. Soon my fatherless child will be born and then what will become of us? I stare out on the Abbey Courtyard, so frosty it gleams under the lamplight, and vow to not lose hope like Fanny and Harriet.

17. The Wonder

My newborn daughter immediately wraps herself around my heart. My life is hers. My days are hers. Every moment of my existence is hers, and I am weak with love. How completely childish of me to assume a mother's love would resemble my affection for Willmouse or one of Albee's monkeys. I have a beautiful daughter, and if any of us harbored doubt of her father's identity, we now have no doubt at all. She bears the delicate shape of Albee's face, his dimpled chin and grey eyes, his fair skin and curls. Her spirit, I believe, is mine.

"We should name her Albe." Mary is elated, her faith in Percy restored by the sight of my daughter.

"Alba," I insist. "The feminine form." I caress her cheek as she suckles, awed that we have both survived the ordeal of childbirth. How arrogant I was to think I would not suffer like Mary. That because I am descended from the sturdy Mary Jane Godwin, rather than a bloodline of dead mothers and frail children, I would feel neither pain nor gushing emotion. I was wrong on both counts. "Sweet Alba deserves a father," I say to Mary. "How sad to pass my legacy of a missing father on to her."

"At least she will know who her father is." Mary hands me a folded parchment. "Percy sent word to Albee, remarking on her beauty and bright spirit and her keen resemblance. This is his reply."

I unfold the note and hold it above my sleeping daughter's head to read Albee's words. He goes on for paragraphs about Italy and *Childe Harold* and their friend Hobhouse, and then in a postscript he adds *another little B to grace dim England's distant shore. I choose to name her Allegra.*

"Allegra." I say to try the sound, to test the roll of syllables across my tongue. "Allegra." I smile at Mary. "A name with promise."

Allegra, meaning *lively*, is the perfect name for my daughter. Unlike Mary's delicate flower babies, Allegra is hearty, a child of light and wonder, and despite her female state, I am hopeful for her tenacity. Consider her parentage. No one is likely to think of either Albee or me as frail.

I spend this winter here in Bath knowing I am safe. There is no chance of banishment now that I am the mother of Lord Byron's love child. Who knows what I may say or do if I were sent away again? In that regard, I hold all the cards, and I am content to remain in Percy's house and help Mary with the chores. I make the tea while she writes away on the ghost story that has grown into a novel. *Frankenstein*, she calls her monster man creator.

When Mary and Percy go into London, I am content to stay with Allegra and help Elise with Willmouse. Unlike poor Harriet and Fanny, I will not be worn down and tossed away because a man refuses to love me. And Allegra is my proof that once I was loved. "Allegra." I speak slowly, smiling as Willmouse watches the movement of my lips. Rather like a squirrel he is, wide-eyed and alert. He reminds me of Fanny.

Our Fanny did not quite fit in anywhere, yet I always imagined she would marry someone like Will Godwin, an ordinary man who desired her tender care without being asked for much in return. Now I realize Fanny was as earnest and childlike as Willmouse, and would never have found such a man. Did the loss of her mother at a young age cast her doom? Or was it Percy?

"Are you ready for your tea, dear Willmouse? Some bread and jam and milk?" He nods solemnly, but he is happy for my notice of him, happy to know he will not starve while his parents are off hobnobbing with London's smart literary set. I kiss Allegra's cheek, and, tucking her head under my chin like a nest-warmed egg, I rise to my feet and hold out my free hand. "Come, my darling boy. Let us find Elise and have our tea."

Naturally Percy has a plan to explain a new baby in his family. Once his grand new home in Marlow is refurbished with its sculptures and paintings and a massive library of new books, I am to deposit Allegra in London with the Hunts, one of the smart literary set who apparently have more children than they can count, and go to live in Marlow village with Mary and Willmouse. Next, Percy will appear with his reclaimed children, Ianthe and Charles. Then, the Leigh Hunts and their brood will arrive with Allegra to spend the summer. When they return to London, Allegra will stay behind with me. "We will say she is the child of Hunt's cousin, and we have adopted her," Percy instructs us. "Voila! Fait accompli." He speaks as if he barters with children's lives on a daily basis. Then again, perhaps he does.

I am quite enchanted by Albion House, a stately Georgian at the end of Marlow's West Street, and Mary rules her new home like a queen bee in her hive. "Finally I am a proper bride." She grasps my hand to lead me from one grand room to the next. "Large as a ballroom," she says of the library. "Notice my beautiful statues."

"Lovely." The statues, life-sized versions of Venus and Apollo, stand as sentries on either side of the library doors. *A bit of a show*, I can imagine Mother saying, yet truly she would covet them.

I am awestruck by how much Mary is spending on furnishings and am tempted to remind her of all they lost last summer when their belongings were sold to pay Percy's debts. Instead, I study my sister for signs of exhaustion. A new babe is due in late summer, but here in April she remains energetic and good-humored. "At last, a family home of our own, with rooms aplenty for our London guests and a splendid nursery for all their children and ours."

After a tour of the five bedrooms, she leads me to the third floor, where the nursery, high-ceilinged and airy, causes me to sigh. I envision myself here, happily tucked under the eaves with the lovely Allegra in my arms. "The summer shall be a good one, Mary. A good one for us all."

"I am happy you can share it with us, Claire." She smiles. "You and Allegra are most welcome for the summer." Thus Mary makes it clear that Albion House is not to be my permanent home. Like one of the smart literary set from London, I am to be merely a guest, and that is fine by me. Albee is expected to join us in the heart of summer. Surely he will find Allegra enchanting and in turn recognize me as her mother and his fate. Surely by the end of summer we will be together and as happy a family as the Shelleys themselves.

Mary and I cheerfully go about unpacking the household crocks and bowls and linens, items from the various homes where Mary and Percy lived during the past year. Every day new items arrive from London merchants, and we unpack goblets and china and pewter. The only thing we do not touch are Percy's books. Nothing makes him more ecstatic than crates of new books. "He will spend hours simply sniffing the spines." We laugh like girls.

In between chores, we walk through the gardens, into the Berkshire woods or down the country lanes until we come to the Thames. We breathe in the rich green dampness before re-tracing our steps, pausing only to admire the budding trees, the pussywillows and primroses, or listen to the call of a robin. Anyone seeing us might assume we are young maidens without a care, good friends or sisters, dreaming of future husbands. If only they knew.

When we return to Albion House, Elise is directing the men unloading a very large crate from a delivery wagon. "What can that be?" Mary scurries ahead. "Best to place it in the parlor until we determine where it belongs."

"'Tis a piano," one man reads from the label. "Addressed to Miss Claire Clairmont."

With one twist of her neck, Mary's cool grey eyes are on me, and I understand at once that our sisterly sojourn at Albion House is under threat. "How very like Percy to think so kindly of you, Claire. What a dear man my husband is."

As for me, I am dumbstruck with joy. What man, in the entire history of time, ever presented his sister-in-law with a piano? The very gift he knew I would find most precious, whether it suited Mary's decorative scheme or not. Percy bought a piano so I would sing for him. I bite the inside of my cheek to staunch my rush of emotion. Percy imagines us here together in this lovely place, sharing poems and songs, taking walks and being carefree. Precisely as we did when we lived on Arabella Row. Before Baby Clara died. Before I was sent away to Lynmouth. Before Albee. Before Allegra. Before we became so old.

Percy misses me and wants me returned to his life.

There is no talk of songs or pianos when Percy at last arrives at Albion House. He stands before us, empty-handed and shaking with fury. "Ianthe and Charles are to go to a guardian. *My* children. Living with a stranger. A preposterous notion."

"Oh, darling." Mary eases him out of his long brown coat. "Why a stranger?"

"I cannot bear to speak of the Westbrooks and their falsehoods. Their vile path of revenge took those children away, and now we all will suffer their loss." Mary gently brushes road dust from his neck and shoulders. He takes a deep breath, lifting his head and straightening his shoulders. "Let us talk of more pleasant things. Let us retreat into our new home, our books, our music, our small comforts. Let us forget the outside world." He embraces Mary and then me. "Welcome, dear Claire. Welcome home." Then he slips his arm around Mary's waist and draws her toward the grand staircase. "Come, love. Now, where is my son, my darling Willmouse?"

Percy has little time to retreat before London's smart literary set rains down upon us like a refreshing summer shower. First to arrive are the Hunts with Marianne's sister Bess Kent, their many children, and my own darling Allegra, whose little face brightens at the sight of me. "Your little one shall be happy to have some quiet moments with her mammy after our noisy brood," Bess says with a laugh.

Marianne, a painter and sculptress, is voluptuous, rather like a gypsy with her scarlet shawl and wide smile. "Ah, at last," she says as she kisses my cheek. "The mother of the charming Allegra."

Leigh Hunt is darkly handsome, his coloring much like my own, and he, too, greets me with enthusiasm. "Claire, my partner in duets! The piano has arrived, I hope?"

When Percy's good friend Peacock, who lives in Marlow, comes to call, I notice his face also brightens at the sight of me. A true indicator that he is between women at the moment and growing lonely. Such a droll man. I find his sad eyes and serious manner are quite deceptive. "Dear Claire," he whispers in greeting. "A ray of sunshine in our gloomy hamlet."

Lastly there are Thomas Hogg, a welcome comfort for Mary, and Will Godwin himself, who gives us all pause. Surely, Will must observe the grandeur of Albion House and question why Percy, his esteemed sponsor, is behind in his patron payments. "Your mother regrets not coming along to see you," Will says to me.

"It is a pity," I say. Mother refuses to be under Mary's roof, and while I miss her to some degree, I cannot risk her discovery of Allegra. In my mother's mind, I am a traitor, and she has no idea that I am a fallen woman who bore Lord Byron's daughter. For that reason, I also keep my distance from Will. Let him dandle Willmouse on his knee and counsel Mary and chat with poets while I tend to the nursery.

I am on my way to pick peppermint for the children's tea when Will looms up from beside a garden shed. "Hello, Daughter." He blocks the sun. "Your mother sends her love, dear. She misses her Clara Jane intensely."

"Give her my best, Father." I step along, not willing to face his questions. Should he ask about Allegra, we are to say she is the child of Leigh Hunt's cousin, a child that the ever-charitable Mary and Percy will adopt. All the same, I am anxious.

"I understand the custody matter did not go well for Percy," he says as I tiptoe among the herbs.

"Such a shame for a man who loves children as deeply as Percy does."

"The Westbrooks claim that Shelley had nothing to do with those children from the time his son was born until Harriet was found dead. No court would entrust children to a father who cannot be bothered to see them."

Was that true? I clearly remember the time Percy called on Harriet to see the newborn Charles. It was the dreadful winter Mary and I moved from place to place while Percy hid from his creditors. The winter Hogg came to call on the pregnant Mary. The winter Percy took me for his own. He has not seen his children in all that time? How can that be? "Does Mary know?" I ask Father.

"I do not want Mary to know. She is Percy's wife now, and they have a promising life together. No, your mother and I worry for you. You should free yourself from Shelley, Claire."

For a dazed moment, I am certain the Godwins know about Allegra and believe her to be Percy's child. Head spinning, I melt forward, first crouching and then kneeling, my hands gripping the earth. "Percy and Mary have been very gracious to me." I pluck a sprig of parsley and wait for the return of my senses.

"You are most welcome in our home. Your mother wants you to understand you would be forgiven."

I would be welcomed on Skinner Street with Lord Byron's illegitimate child in my arms? I would be forgiven?

"Thank you kindly, Father." I shade my eyes to look up at him. "Come autumn, I expect to take a position as governess." It is a complete falsehood. Come autumn, I expect to be with Albee and our Allegra.

The Albion House nursery is my sanctuary. There with Allegra, Willmouse, and all the little Hunts, I glory in their small joys and tragedies. Their spilled milk, silly songs, clapping chubby hands, or eyes brimming with tears. Marianne's sister Bess and I take the children to visit sheep in the adjoining field. Allegra laughs uproariously at the lambs' frolicking, and Thornton, the eldest Hunt, chases them about to renew her mirth. "Ah, the joy of innocent minds," Bess says.

Bess possesses Marianne's beauty, and she is pleasant company for a walk in the Berkshire woods while the children nap. I curl against a tree trunk to read while Bess observes nature in the same studious manner as our poor dead Fanny. "Isn't this a wonder?" She holds up a grotesque toadstool. "Oh, I could live in a forest."

"I am certain you could." I smile at her pleasure. Oh, so like our Fanny's.

One afternoon when small clouds skim across the sun with the speed of Percy's paper boats, Bess is less cheerful than usual. "We suffer the same fate, Claire," she says as we sit under an elm. "We are both women who love our sister's husband."

It takes me a breath or two to respond. "You are in love with Leigh Hunt?" The idea seems preposterous. Leigh with all his many children and the affable Marianne?

"We are lovers." She tucks her magnifying glass under her arm to re-tie her bonnet. "Never to be a wife now. Never to be more than what I am. I should have left years ago. Easier than it sounds, is that not so, Claire?"

As with Father in the garden, I am caught off guard. What does Bess know of me? If she knows all that Percy passed on to Hunt, then she knows Allegra's father is Albee not Percy. I repeat what I said to Will Godwin. "Come autumn, I plan to leave."

"That is wise." Bess nods. "I tried to leave before Spring and was not successful. I wish you better luck, dear."

Now the clouds block out the sun. Here in the woods, the air grows chill and damp as I recall Mary's words from February. *Poor Marianne. Her dear sister tried to drown herself in a pond. I hope news of Harriet's misfortune did not bring about her desperate act.* I draw my shawl closer. In this moment, with Allegra tucked into her cradle under the solid eaves of Albion House, I cannot imagine what circumstances would ever lead me to throw myself into water, whether as shallow as a farm pond or as deep as the Serpentine.

I have not yet properly thanked Percy for the gift of my piano. Now that Albion House is full, Percy is no longer accessible. He rises early to walk with Leigh before each man takes up his writing. Although Mary set up a study for Percy, he prefers to wander off into Bisham Wood or to contemplate the Thames from under a grove of beech trees. Marlow locals are used to seeing him, leaves stuck in his hair, books and paper in hand, and reciting lines from his day's work. He eats berries from the woods, not returning until teatime. If Percy is late to return, Mary sends little Thornton Hunt to search for him. Usually, he is found lying in his rowboat and reading. "Solitude," he tells Mary. "I crave solitude in the midst of all this socializing."

Even so, Percy enjoys taking the children for daily rides in his boat and tromps in the woods. Together, they fly kites and sail paper boats and chase fireflies. Every day their skin turns darker and their hair lighter. Everyone is the picture of health, except for Mary, who despite her jolly tone, grows paler and more strained as the summer passes by.

"Are you well, sister?" I stack freshly laundered serviettes on the breakfront.

"Perfectly fine." Mary smiles to prove her point. "Marianne and I have become fast friends, and she is excellent help for our household." Mary sighs as she shakes out a serviette. "Is this not the best summer we have ever had, Claire?"

"Certainly." Neither of us wants to recall our last summer in Geneva, which was also *the best summer* until Albee lost all interest in me.

Yes, this summer has been good for my sister. No matter her weariness during the day, Mary recovers her wit and charm during the evening gatherings in her grand drawing room. She is quick to join the endless discussions of politics and poetry. Most especially poetry. The smugness of Southey, the purity of Keats, the sensuality of Byron. I accompany Hunt on my new piano as we sing the beautiful lines Percy wrote for Mozart's music. "My thoughts arise and fade in solitude," we sing. I wonder what Mary thinks of Percy's musical cry to be left alone. Percy's peace and quiet may be gone, but the rest of us are aflutter with gay sociability. At last, I am a flicker in their glorious, sparkling company, and I sense Thomas Peacock is watching me.

He stands there by the doorway, a shade taller than Apollo's statue and wearing his usual heart-sore expression. Though I find him to be a reasonably attractive man, I cannot comprehend his attention to me. He is Percy's longtime friend and privy to the complete sordid history of my life. He is also the friend who urged Percy to leave me in Lynmouth and return to Mary when she became pregnant with Willmouse. If not for Peacock, Percy and I would yet be together, living in that rose-covered cottage overlooking the sea with our own child Thomas. Of course, then there would be no Allegra.

"Miss Claire, you are a lovely creature tonight," he murmurs in a sideways manner, not daring to look directly into my eyes. Perhaps he fears he will burst into flame.

"You, dear Peacock, are a charmer."

"A horn-player with a cobra?"

"Precisely."

Thomas Love Peacock is a fine man, an intelligent man, a man of means, and I am flattered that he finds me alluring. He admires my singing, he asks my opinion on literature, he fusses over Allegra. He is the friend to clean up after Percy's messes, a man who would take good care of me. And yet, he lacks the passion of Percy and Albee.

"I love you, Claire," he whispers as we stand in a cool patch of moonlight. "I am mad for you." He pulls me into the center of the rose garden and kisses me. A kiss that is as sweet and natural as the perfumed air around us, a kiss that promises what could be: a simple, honest life.

"Is your love born of pity, Thomas? Pity for Percy's poor sister-in-law?"

"Not at all." He straightens his thin frame in denial. "Become my wife, Claire. Allow me to give you all you deserve. A home of your own. A life you do not have to share with Mary and Percy." Again, he kisses me. Gently, respectfully.

"I have Allegra." I allow his chin to rest against my forehead and his breath warms my face. "Allegra is my life."

"I shall raise her as my own daughter. She shall have the best of everything."

What to say to such assurances? I cannot confess that Allegra is promised to her father's care, and that more than anything, I want to re-attach myself to Albee when he comes to collect our daughter. Once I wished for nothing more than the love of a tender man. Now I know that tenderness is no substitute for passion, and my sigh is swollen with regret.

"Claire?"

The kindest act is to say nothing at all, so I do not. Soon he will take my hand and lead me carefully across the dark gardens and into the well-lit merriment of the smart literary set where he belongs.

Suddenly, just as it did a year ago in Geneva, the weather changes. Storms lash our lovely Albion House and leave it dank and cold. The Hunts and Bess return to London, and while they leave my darling Allegra behind, Percy's plan does not go as smoothly as we hoped. Known locally as the poet in the long brown coat who lies about in his boat or on the leafy ground with his books and papers spread around him, Percy has become a suspicious character in Marlow.

A furious Mary waves an anonymous letter. "They – whoever *they* may be -- seem to think Allegra is Percy's child and that he is guilty of bigamy. Despite his generosity, forever handing out blankets and shillings to the poor and tutoring that schoolgirl Polly Rose, he is accused of corruption."

Allegra cries at the tone of Mary's voice. She twists herself this way and that in some nameless misery, and I put her head on my shoulder and rub her little back. Percy remains silent, his hand pressed to his forehead. The wind wails in the chimney, and Mary shouts to be heard.

"We must notify Albee to come for Allegra at once. How else we can live here in our beautiful new home, Percy?"

"You are right, Mary," he says without conviction. "I shall notify Byron at once."

Albee coming for Allegra is what I most desire, what I most fear, yet I sense that Percy is wracked with regret. He does not want us to leave. He is sorry to have taken on the grandness of Albion House in the first place.

We worry for naught. Albee, when he finally replies to Percy, claims he has no interest in retrieving Allegra, and if we want his daughter to live with him, then we must take her to Italy ourselves. His words chill my hopeful heart. No matter his lack of love for me, how can he love our child if he cannot be bothered to come for her? "I suppose he would prefer she take wing and fly to him? As his daughter, she, too, must possess the gift of flight."

Mary shushes me. "Please, Claire. You are no less a child than Allegra."

Percy embraces me. "Never fear," he murmurs to me. "I will take of you and your child. It is my promise to you."

Late at night when Allegra's cries wake me, I glance out the window to see Percy pacing along the garden paths. I hold Allegra's warm body against me and watch his brown coat flapping around his legs with every pivot of his heel. He is not terrified by unseen creatures now. He is terrified by loss.

"I fear the courts Mary," he says in the morning. "Now that Ianthe and Charles will be sent to live with an abhorrent clergyman, I fear the Lord Chancellor will also take possession of Willmouse and Allegra. I think we should flee to Italy before our next child is born."

"Impossible, Percy. Our baby may come at any time. I cannot risk traveling now."

"Of course not," I say, as Percy retreats to his study.

We spend our days shut inside as the rain falls and the cold and damp rise into every room. We hang on until Mary's draperies turn limp and spongy, the rich colors of the brocade upholstery turn dark, and all the pristine books in Percy's splendid library are spotted with mildew. In September Mary gives birth to another delicate flower child she promptly names Clara. Oh, what redemption can ever come from that? She sinks into her usual state of melancholy that follows every birth, and when Percy returns to London to deal with creditors, he insists I go along. "I require you to lighten my mood, Claire, with your enchanting songs."

Nothing good can come from this either, but bad sister that I am, I am happy to leave with him.

18. Italia, Summer 1818

Mary is ecstatic over the splendid villa she discovered on the shore of Lake Como. "It has two great halls with lake views from one and mountain views from the other. It is the perfect place for Albee when he comes to visit Allegra. Percy, you must write to him straightaway."

Percy, busily enchanting Willmouse with his own descriptions of Lake Como, nods agreement. "I will. At once."

"Do not forget to tell him how much it resembles Villa Diodati. Stress that he would have his own grand quarters. Unless, of course, he chooses to share them." Mary cocks her dainty head to smile at me. As if Allegra and I are the bait to lure the great Lord Byron into her glowing summer plans.

Mary writes to everyone she knows about the beauty of Italy. She wittily describes our treacherous journey over the snowbound mountains from France to Switzerland and our descent – through yet more snow – into Italy. She is ebullient as she bustles around offering me advice. "Even if you live separately from Albee this summer, you will live close enough to share Allegra. A perfect opportunity, do you not agree?"

"The very thought of seeing Albee makes me retch." I stack Percy's books on the dining table of our simple flat. "I love him one day and hate him the next. Some days I never want him to know the beautiful daughter we have."

Mary's cheerful expression evaporates. "He is Allegra's father, and he is the one to care for her. And for you, if he so chooses."

"He does not love her as Percy does." A volume of sonnets slips from my hand and crashes to the floor.

"Compared to Lord Byron, Percy is a poor man. He cannot support you and Allegra for the rest of his life."

"For the rest of Sir Tim's life, perhaps?"

Upon the death of Percy's father, we will all benefit from his estate, a fact she and Percy often joke about. Yet now she appears shocked. "Do not be so disrespectful, Claire."

Once more my sister wishes me gone from her life. The pall of last autumn haunts us with memories of mildew and coughing children and the Hunts coming and going. Not only did Mary suffer melancholy after Clara's birth, she had to manage the household while Percy and I cavorted in London. Then poor Percy, sick-at-heart over Ianthe and Charles, was jailed for his debts and became sick in body. I blame Albee for not sending support. I blame Albee for every awful thing that happened to us last year.

Ignoring Mary, I retrieve the book of sonnets from the floor and place it on the bookshelf. This year is looking better. Not only are we here in beautiful Italy, but Mary's monster man novel, *Frankenstein*, has been published to great success. We are hale and hearty, and Albee will soon arrive to meet his daughter. Perhaps he will fall in love with her mother and our fairy tale will begin at last.

While Allegra naps, I take Albee's old letters from my glove case. I have no new letters to read and likely never will, yet a sense of her witty father rises from these pages like a genie from a lamp. He is condescending and gossipy; he is romantic and earthy; he is self-deprecating and skilled at keeping his emotions tucked away. A deeper being, I might say, than the average insatiable man.

My Claire de Luna, he wrote when we were staying together in the Villa Diodati, *the sight of you sleeping beside me rouses me faster than Salome dancing with John the Baptist's head roused old King Herod. So wake up, darling, let us rise and shine as one.*

I have every letter, every note, every little scrap of poetry instructions he wrote for me, and someday, likely on my deathbed, I shall present them to Allegra. "See, darling daughter, your famous father did once hold me in high regard." Or in high desire, at the least.

The letter from Albee, the one we have been awaiting to make our summer plans, finally comes to us in Milan. When Percy unseals it, his hands are shaking, and when he looks up from the page, he summarizes, protecting us from whatever is truly on that page. "Albee will not, under any circumstances, be spending the summer with us, nor will he come anywhere near us to collect Allegra." Mary and I gasp as though pelted by an icy rain blowing through our sunny quarters. Percy speaks like he is delivering a eulogy for a lost friend. "He will send Mr. Merryweather, his trusted messenger, to return Allegra to him in Venice. *After that time,*" Percy reads directly, "*Claire is to have no further contact with either father or child.*"

No further contact. I push past Percy and scoop up Allegra. She is bathed in sunshine, her skin and hair warm to the touch. I bury my face in hers, making promises only she can hear. "Oh, Claire." Percy wraps both of us in his embrace. "Albee is suffering a foul mood and lording it over us. His good sense will return to him shortly."

"I agree." Mary stands behind Percy, her face pinched in worry. "Albee will come to his senses soon enough, and until then, we will ignore such threats." She takes Allegra's sweet hand. "Sending a child off with a stranger – where is the man's mind?"

"Most likely in the gutter," I say, "with the rest of his fine self."

At this moment I hate Albee with a passion so akin to love that I fear I will burst into flames from the heat of it. I must cool down. I must give myself time to think. I wait until nighttime when Mary and the babies are in bed, and then I go to Percy. "You must convince Albee that Allegra belongs with us."

Percy looks up from his late-night writing. He wears his pained expression, which means he detests my interruption or that I have won his compassion. "I will gladly write to Albee on your behalf, Claire, although you must understand that he does not consider us fit parents to raise Allegra."

"Why would you say such a thing?"

"Apparently Albee believes any child of his should be raised in a more conventional household than ours."

"*More conventional?* The man who has one mistress after another — the man said to have a child with his own sister — has the nerve to condemn *us?*"

"Albee boasts he only loves one woman at a time, that he prefers to woo a woman rather than have her toss herself at him, and he emphatically does not want any child of his to be in the public eye."

I blink at the cruelty of his words. While I do not believe either the one-woman-at-a-time claim or his preference for wooing, Percy does, so I do not debate it. "No one knows Allegra is his child," I say instead. "Albee's lack of responsibility has cast the spotlight on you, and you, thank God, are man enough to stand up to public scrutiny. Who would guess Albee is such a coward?"

"That is unfair, Claire." He speaks sharply. "I will do my best, but no promises can be made when dealing with Albee."

"I cannot bear to lose Allegra. To never see her again. She is all that I possess." My voice cracks. "I cannot do this, Percy."

He rises away from his poems and holds me, paying no mind to my tears dampening his chest. He caresses my hair and rocks me back and forth like I am the child who is leaving her mother. I hear Mary pad into the kitchen, her bare feet slapping the floor, yet Percy does not relinquish his hold on me.

My lively Allegra not only walks, she runs through the garden like a rabbit, her great bounding leaps often dumping her onto her bottom. Today she is a dancer, grasping fistfuls of grass and letting it trickle from her dimpled hands as she twirls, giddy from the motion. "A Whirling Dervish," Percy insists as he catches her mid-spin.

"Pa-pa," she responds with a laugh.

Mary frowns over the top of Clara's bonnet, although Percy is delighted.

"Say Ma-ma," I coax.

"Pa-pa." She laughs at her own joke. "Pa-pa-pa-pa-pa."

When the sun grows too warm, Mary and I carry our sticky, grass-stained children into the house, bathe them, and put them down for naps. I caress Allegra's damp curls, so like her father's, and pray she does not have his heart as well.

Perhaps Percy is correct in thinking Albee's harsh words are spun from the heartbreak of losing custody of his daughter Ada. When another diversion comes along to amuse him, he may be more like his old self. Arrogant and caustic, but somewhat reasonable. Perhaps I overreacted. If I remain calm, if I act in a sensible manner, perhaps I can enchant the great poet once again. I can reclaim my roles as his muse and the mother of his child.

At first, I pay no attention to the familiar sound of Percy chatting below the nursery window. His conversations with the locals are a mix of Italian and English highlighted by elaborate gestures, like those of a mime. Yet when I hear a man's reply, also in English, my heart leaps. *Albee.* Albee regrets his cruel words and is here to make amends. He is here to discover his beautiful daughter.

I reach for her, angelic in her sleep, and then withdraw. No, let him wait for her to wake. Let him wait for the pleasure of his daughter's company. For once, let the great Lord Byron wait. Quickly, before Mary wakes from her own nap and takes charge, I tidy myself. I smooth my frock and re-pin my loose curls. I walk down the stairs at a pace befitting a queen.

There in the front doorway, Percy stands chatting about the weather or the condition of the roads or some other such triviality. Then I see that our English visitor is not Albee. "Ah, yes," Percy says when he sees me, but there is something not quite right in his voice. It is restrained and low-pitched, a shadow of its normal self. "This is Mr. Merryweather, sent to safely deliver Allegra to Lord Byron's home in Venice."

Percy's cautious tone drapes me with a mantle of composure. I coolly regard this ordinary, run-of-the-mill-Englishman assigned to take my child. There is nothing in his appearance to comment upon. Nothing that reflects Albee's wealth or power or wickedness. "I regret your journey, Mr. Merryweather. Allegra is too ill to travel at this time. Please excuse me while I return to her bedside."

I am trembling from head to foot by the time I reach the top of the stairs, and the sight of Mary, wide awake and hurrying towards me, stiffens my spine. "Precisely what did Percy and Albee agree to that day on the lake in Geneva, Mary? What price did you place on my daughter's head?"

"Calm yourself, Sister. Percy and I have nothing to do with Albee's demands."

The sounds of leave-taking float up from below. Mr. Merryweather says his farewells, and Percy promises to contact Albee when Allegra's condition improves. "I have no one left to trust," I say as Percy bounds up the stairs. The three of us stand there, wary as wild beasts.

"You knew Allegra was to be raised by her father, Claire." Mary is stern. "You knew this moment would come. Releasing her to Albee is for her greater good."

"For your greater good, perhaps."

From behind the nursery door, the babies stir and coo. Percy raises his head, his eyes damp and red. "We must keep her, Mary. Allegra is a precious little girl. A perfect playmate for our children."

"I refuse to share you any longer, Percy."

"Allegra is my life." My words are thick and sodden. "She is the only thing that is truly mine."

Mary and I battle all through the day, each of us fighting for what bits of family we have left. By morning though, Mary wins. Her only compromise is to send Elise along with Mr. Merryweather. "She will stay in Albee's villa as Allegra's permanent nanny. She will be your eyes and ears at Percy's expense. Surely you know this is all for the best, Claire. Albee will care for your daughter far beyond our limited means."

It is the best I can expect under the circumstances. Instead of sending my daughter into the unknown, where I will hear only tidbits from Albee's correspondence with Percy, I will have Elise report to me directly. Elise, who gave up her own daughter for the good of her family in Switzerland, is perhaps the only one to comprehend the state of my heart.

Not that I will cease from holding Albee's own shrunken heart to the fire. While I wait for the sun to rise and Elise to pack up Allegra's things, while I listen for Mr. Merryweather and his fine carriage to pull up to the door, I shape my wretchedness into words for Albee to read. *My twentieth birthday came and went yesterday, and there was no cause for celebration. I am losing my only love, my only joy in life, and my tears have turned to blood. For me to send dear Allegra into your care, shows my highest regard for you, Albee. Do not disappoint me. Think of me as a mother who loves her child above all else, a mother who suffers for the good of her daughter. Treat her well.*

Because Allegra is a sunny child, she waves gaily as she departs in Elise's arms. "Bye, bye." She laughs. "Bye-bye, pa-pa."

She will never call me ma-ma. The thought burns my mind until I have to take a dram of Percy's laudanum and lie down for a few days. Once again, I do not die. I continue to breathe, and even in its damaged state, my own heart beats a forlorn staccato. Eventually I must rise from my bed and pretend to be alive.

From Venice, Elise writes in glowing detail about Albee's villa on the Grand Canal and his exotic mistress Teresa, daughter of Italian aristocrats. Allegra is in fine fettle, she reports, and eagerly charming everyone she meets. Albee's scribble of a few agreeable words at the bottom of the page lifts my hopes a fraction. Perhaps, I tell myself, Albee will relent and allow me to see Allegra again soon. Nothing, after all, is forever. In between letters from Elise, I calm myself by repeating *nothing is forever.* Especially when I assist nanny Milly with Willmouse and baby Clara and it takes every fiber of my being not to hate them.

Soon we all travel from Milan to Pisa to Leghorn and then finally on to the house Percy has rented for the summer. Casa Bertini at Bagni di Lucca sits among the mountains at the top of a steep, winding street, which is more Percy's idea of a perfect setting than mine. I prefer the sight of water, although the River Serchio is said to lie somewhere below us.

Mary soon discovers the many English folks -- more fashionable than literary -- who summer here, and she insists on Percy squiring us to the balls in the town's old casino. Not that we dance. We are more at home at the local riding stable, and when I immediately fall and injure my knee, Percy and Mary ride off every day by themselves. No matter, I content myself with lazing about and reading as we now have, in addition to nanny Milly, a cleaning woman named Estella, and the handyman Paolo, who does a bit of everything.

Our summer glides on its narrow, mind-numbing way as does any stretch of time that follows loss. Mary is always enchanted by new places and warm weather, although Percy grows homesick when Peacock writes of his walks through the Marlow woods. "I miss England," he confesses to me.

"Nothing is forever, dear Percy," I chirp. I sense him pulling away from Mary and her newly-found fame as novelist. I sense her watching me with Percy and wondering why I am still here, a thorn in her side. She does not win my sympathy. I know her role in dispatching Allegra. What a pity she chose the wrong one to send away.

In August, Elise writes that she and Allegra have moved to the home of the British counsel. "Countess Teresa says I am too young to care for your daughter, Miss Claire. You must come at once."

"What am I to make of this, Mary?" I wave the letter in her face. "Where is Albee? And who are these strangers?"

"Let me see." Mary takes the letter and hands me a saucer of custard to feed to Clara.

"I shall leave at once, Mary." I dip the spoon towards Clara's mouth, and she smiles warily. "I shall walk down the hill and hire a coach. How can Albee make promises to us and abide by them for less than a season? How dare he deposit Allegra in the home of a stranger?"

"I would guess this turn of events has more to do with Elise and Countess Teresa than with Albee and Allegra. I doubt the Hoppners are strangers to Albee." Mary eases the spoon from my fierce grip. "You cannot rush to Venice like an angry fishwife, Claire. Allow Percy to contact Albee."

"Not this time. This time I shall go directly to Allegra and bring her back with me."

Mary is silent. She is the less impulsive sister, the one to act after she thinks things through and through. Thankfully, Percy acts with more alacrity. He, too, worries for Allegra. He must detest losing her to Albee as much as I, and in no time at all, he and I are on our way to Venice. When I am not beseeching God to allow me the return of my daughter, I am peppering Percy with questions. "What has Albee said to you of Elise and the Countess? Who are these people keeping Allegra, these Hoppners?"

"Very little. I cannot be certain. We shall soon see." While Albee is the silent one and Percy the conversationalist, both men are experts at secrecy. Percy's evasiveness causes me to wonder what he is keeping from me. His luster has worn thin. Part of me loves him for making this journey; another part hates him for allowing her to be taken from us in the first place.

"You believe Allegra is well and in good hands?"

"I do. Albee has her best interest at heart, and you must not attack his good name when we arrive at the Hoppners' home. Promise me you will refrain, Claire."

"Oh, I shall behave. I shall be as sweet as honey to retrieve Allegra."

"Perhaps Elise is merely overwhelmed by her new circumstances. You can imagine a young girl working for someone like Albee with his many homes and his boat and his exotic animals. She was dazzled. Perhaps the Countess Teresa's jealousy will force Albee to return Allegra."

"Truly?" I grow light-headed with promise.

To reach Padua, we cross the Apennines in a blaze of heat and then take a gondola to Venice through a torrent of rain and windstorms, and yet my heart is filled with hope. Oh, if our journey grants me my daughter, I will never complain about one more drop of rain. *Oh, please God.* I make promises with every stroke of the oar. *Let her be well.*

The Hoppners' home is on a canal, and there to greet us is Elise and, spinning beside her like a large golden top, is my daughter. "Allegra, my love!"

Somehow she has grown taller. She steps toward me, flushed and listing from her spin. "Mama," she says as plain as day.

I open my arms and sweep her skyward, spinning myself. "How are you, darling? How is your mama's little girl?" I have no idea what she says after that, although it is a happy-sounding babble, and I know by the solid weight of her in my arms, the wholeness and perfection of her, that she is fine. That we will both be fine now.

The Hoppners, a rawboned couple wearing fine clothes, are gracious in their greetings, yet they eye Percy and me in a manner I find stiff and chilly. They have little to say. No praise for my daughter or Elise's fine care of her. No words of admiration for either Percy or Albee. Even as I compliment them on their home, their many pieces of carved ivory, their generosity in tending for my daughter, I sense they are thinking *heathen. Wanton, depraved heathens. The lot of them.*

All the same, Percy accepts their suggestion that he call on Albee while I spend the day with Allegra. "I will ask him for visitation privileges," he tells me, and when I protest, he adds, "it will be a starting point, Claire. If I can convince Albee to allow us a week's visit with Allegra, then perhaps he will agree to more permanent arrangement in the future."

"I do not trust the Hoppners." I whisper. "Their home is a museum, hardly a suitable place for a small girl. Let us leave Venice with Allegra right now. We can deal with Albee when he notices her gone. If he bothers himself to notice."

"He is Allegra's legal guardian, and we would be charged with kidnapping. Now stop your talk of abduction and allow me to first discover his state of mind."

I let him go. Off to Albee's grand palazzo to present his meek little petition for my daughter. Signing Allegra over to Albee was more in Percy's best interest than anyone's. It saves him from Mary's wrath, and it saves him the cost of raising another child. Then I chide myself for my lack of appreciation. Where would I be without Percy?

My darling Allegra and I thread our way through Venice's narrow, winding streets. "I can scarcely believe we are here," I tell her. "Together!" Rain-cleansed and glistening in the soft sun, Venice is beautiful. "Once upon a time, I thought we would live here with your Papa."

"Papa and Mama." Allegra smiles in agreement, but then perhaps she is imagining Percy as her father instead of Albee.

When Percy comes to collect me at the Hoppners, he is bit more frantic than usual. His fingers fly through his hair. "Albee was most considerate, but he believes Mary and the children are with us. If he discovers that you and I are here alone together, it could go very badly for us. For Allegra. He is offering for us to stay in his summer home in Este, and Mary must come to us at once."

"Albee cannot be bothered by Allegra's presence in his own home, why should he care who is here in Venice and who is not?"

"I believe Countess Teresa is very devout. Very proper and conservative."

"And yet she is with Albee?" I am scornful. I am tired. I am fretful over Percy's plans for Mary. "Surely there is no rush for Mary to travel now in this heat."

"I have already sent for her," he says. "She is to pack up the house, gather up the children, and journey to us as soon as she can."

"Oh, Percy." I do not want to dwell on his mad, treacherous scheme for Mary to travel across Italy with her delicate children in the heat of the summer, yet Percy is good at being Percy, and we both know Mary will agree to whatever he asks.

"Sleep well, Claire. You must rest for tomorrow when we shall retrieve Allegra and Elise and leave for Este to begin anew. We shall be a family once again."

I have heard Percy's rallying cry too often to be convinced. As I shut myself into my airless room at the back of the inn, I resent knowing Percy's laudanum will ease him into slumber, while I remain wide-eyed and anxious for us all.

By the time Mary, the children, nursemaid Milly, and the handyman Paolo join Percy, Allegra, and me at Albee's grand summer villa, we are all deathly ill. Percy has food poisoning, and I am too dizzy to stand upright, while the new arrivals look like they wandered for days across a land eaten by a plague of locusts. Percy blanches at the sight of them. He reaches for Clara, who is red and limp from the heat or a fever or both, and Elise gathers up Willmouse. Mary staggers through the door on her own power. "Why must we all suffer so?" She pants.

Fortunately, the servants remain on their feet. Elise feeds us and cleans up after us while repeatedly reminding us that Albee is indeed a generous, thoughtful man who values our friendship more than we imagine. When Percy recovers, he returns at once to Venice to call on the *generous, thoughtful* Albee, while the rest of us, save for baby Clara, revive sufficiently to enjoy the beauty of our new setting. The Euganean hills, the fruit gardens, the vines and trees and lush greenness are restorative. Ahh, we breathe deeply. Perhaps all will be well.

We also have Albee's exotic menagerie to amuse us. Oh, not the mastiffs. Countess Teresa must have allowed them to remain with her. Yet we have the birds, more birds than ever, a blue aquarium filled with colorful fish, and in a cage as large as a hut, we have the green iguana. Allegra loves the monkeys. In addition to the self-absorbed Santa Maria, there is the more affable Saint George. He and Allegra chatter to each other in lengthy, give-and-take conversations.

"Monkey talk," Allegra says with glee.

"Indeed." I kiss her. "You too, love, are a little monkey." I kiss her again.

Poor Mary is completely preoccupied with Clara, so Elise and I establish our own routine. Every morning, before it grows too warm, we take Willmouse and Allegra along the vine-covered walkways. In the heat of the day, we spend our time on the shaded terrace. Allegra naps while Willmouse draws sailing ships or tries his hand at folding paper into boats. He is so like his father.

During our afternoons together, Elise and I chat about the weeks she and Allegra spent in Venice. "Is Albee good to Allegra? Does he treat her well? Does he show her proper attention?" I ask that same question a hundred different ways, and her answer never varies.

"He loves Allegra," she insists. "Lord Byron is a good man."

Sometimes Mary joins us, her wan face as distant as the moon. Our conversations are mainly a variation of the day before. "Albee is a passionate man," Elise insists.

"Passion comes slow and leaves fast," I say. "Like the man himself."

"Albee possesses a brilliant mind." Mary remains his staunch defender.

As grateful as I am for these long, leisurely days with Allegra, I tire of the praise for Albee. My impatience flares. "He seduced you, did he not, Elise? He read you his latest poem and his passion spilled all over you."

"Claire! That is enough." Later Mary lectures me out of Elise's hearing. "Kindly remember, you were the one to seduce Albee. Trailing after him with your songs and your stories about Percy until you wore the poor man down. You have only yourself to blame for your lost virtue."

I am to blame for my lost virtue? Does Mary not realize that by the time I *wore down* the great Lord Byron, I had long ago lost my virtue to Percy Bysshe Shelley? I say nothing.

Here in Albee's summer paradise, we are prisoners, and poor Clara grows worse with every passing day. At last Percy sends another detailed directive to Mary. She, Milly, and baby Clara are to journey to Padua, where Percy will meet them for transport to Albee's excellent Dr. Francesco Aglietti in Venice. Paolo and I are to accompany them as far as Padua. It is a simple enough plan, given Percy's usual roundabout approach to practical matters.

We start before dawn to avoid the highest heat. Heat that bakes down from the sun and boils up from the ground until it meets in the middle and sends hearts and heads into a tremulous state. The road shimmers before our eyes and perspiration turns our skin slick and shiny. By the time we meet Percy's carriage in Padua, Mary and baby Clara resemble ghosts, mere diaphanous shapes. Paolo blesses them with the sign of the cross as I wave them off.

Returned to Este, we have little more to do than wait. Elise and I calm Willmouse's worries about his mother and baby sister. We praise his bird drawings, so like his Aunt Fanny's, far more than is good for him. We laugh too loud and too long at Allegra's conversations with Saint George, as if our merriment will keep bad news at bay.

When Elise wipes her eyes, I realize she is frightened not only for Clara, but for her own uncertain life. I study her pretty face, which is fuller than I recall from last spring, and her decidedly fuller form, and find myself remembering my summer at Villa Diodati. The summer when I thought I would spend the rest of my life with Albee and my baby.

"I am not one to pass judgment, Elise," I begin. "You have my promise that your secrets are safe with me. Yet allow me to share what I have learned in my own short life."

Elise's stiffens, drawing away from my words.

"I appreciate that Lord Byron can provide any possible thing Allegra will ever want, but if I were to do it again, I would never tell Albee he was her father. I would claim somebody else. Anyone with whom I might have had the slightest contact. The laborers in the vineyards. The fruit vendor, the peddler, the cobbler. I would claim an Immaculate Conception if it meant I could keep Allegra with me."

Elise shrugs indifferently. "It was necessary to leave my first child with my family, Miss Claire. Lord Byron will allow me to keep this child. That is the difference between you and me."

"Is that so? What of his new love, Teresa?"

"The Countess." Elise scoffs. "She does not even care for Albee's pets."

"Imagine that." From the corner of my eye, I catch a green flash of the iguana in its cage. "What of the two hundred Venetian women he claims to have slept with before he found Teresa? Are they not also lining up for his affection?"

"Love in Venice is a different matter."

I let it go. Exhausted from waiting for news from Percy, I retire early. My narrow child-like room is next to the nursery where Willmouse and Allegra dream their innocent dreams. Here amid garish pastels and the ticking of a fancily painted china clock, I fall into dreams of forests and streams. Percy, Allegra, and I are hiking up a hillside. She twirls ahead of us, and I call her back. "No, darling, stay with us."

Percy laughs, unconcerned. "She is a good girl," he says. "We have ourselves a good one, Claire."

It is a dream I crave, and I force myself not to wake, but to dive deeper into the landscape, to dip my toes into the rushing stream, to smile into Percy's loving blue gaze and hold Allegra between us until we merge into a bubble of complete joy.

My dream bubble bursts with the arrival of a messenger, and I am immediately returned from the forest to Albee's splendid house in Este. I rush to down the stairs where Elise holds out a letter addressed to me in Percy's hand.

C -- Our dear daughter is gone, and we are broken. We were delayed at the border, and then while Mary waited at the inn for Dr. Aglietti, Clara died in her arms. Kindly comfort sweet Willmouse in our absence. – PBS

I bundle the sleeping Allegra from her bed. "Come here, darling," I whisper. "Come sleep with mama." She is squirmy at first and then her spine relaxes against my chest. We breathe together as if we are one. I sigh. Mary will blame us for Clara's death. She will say my great hunger to be with Allegra led to this tragedy. She will do everything in her power to get rid of us, and I cannot blame her one bit.

I curve myself around Allegra until she complains. "Hot, mama."

Frantically I press my palm to her damp forehead. There is no fever, only the warmth from my body. I check on Willmouse. He sleeps with the same solemn expression as his father, and he, too, is cool to my worrying touch. I wander out from the quiet house, where every sound echoes, across the terrace and into the moonlit garden. Here in late September the air is cool and moist. Autumn is coming. I sit at the edge of the fountain, pulling my knees to my chest and contemplating what tragedy might befall us next.

19. The Grey Season

We tiptoe around Mary as she sits at Percy's writing desk to copy stanzas for Albee's *Don Juan*. Mary has a careful hand, and she is a diligent worker, but we all know her assignment is pity work out of guilt. Each of us feels responsible for Clara's death. Albee was the one to recommend Dr. Aglietti, and Percy to order the hot trek across Italy. I am to blame for going to Allegra in the first place. We are all guilty.

"Mary believes she is cursed," Percy says when we take our daily walk with the children.

"How so?" I watch Allegra take Willmouse's hand and tug him along like a stubborn goat.

"She believes the loss of her babies is her punishment for Harriet's misfortune. That she played a part in Harriet's suicide. Even though I reassure her it is only her imagination."

"That is hardly reassuring." I pry Willmouse loose from my daughter's sturdy grip, and he sits down next to his favorite man-shaped rock. "No woman wants to hear she is imaging things. Mary *did* have complete disregard for Harriet, but she was too young to know better. We knew only one side. Your side."

Percy, too, is grieving for Clara, so I do not confess that Mary and I believed every bad thing he told us about Harriet. I also do not confess that we three sisters wanted Percy for ourselves and rejoiced when Harriet lost her hold on him. He stops under an arbor and the sun plays across his face. His eyes are in shadow. "You will come with me again in the morning, Claire? You will walk the hills with me and listen to my new poems?"

"I will. Certainly." I nod my assent, even though I find his new poems too beautifully painful. Every striking image casts his despair at falling out of love with Mary. No wonder my sister now claims to understand Harriet's tremulous mind during the years Percy left her.

"Mama, mama, mama." Allegra grasps my own hand in a quick, harsh tug. "Willmouse dead."

My head snaps up from her anxious face to see Percy running toward the rock. Jutting from the side of the hill like a pearly grey ghost, the pillar shades Willmouse, lying there with his face to the sky and his arms stretched out like wings.

Willmouse is not dead but suffering from fever. Mary and Percy rush away with their last remaining child, leaving me blissfully alone with Allegra. Every day is a gift that I do not take lightly. "Albee will reconsider," Percy writes from Venice. "Given time, he will allow us to keep Allegra."

I know Percy is wrong. After losing Ada, Lord Byron will never let go of another child, and I know that, like anything truly magical, these days with my daughter are destined to end. I tell myself if she leaves here as a happy child who loves nothing better than to run and sing and dance, Allegra will remember only that I love her. Not that I sent her away because I am an unmarried woman with no means of support.

Unexpectedly, Percy arrives from Venice. Breathless from fear, I run out to meet his carriage. "Is it Willmouse? Mary? What is wrong now?"

"They are quite well, Claire." He smiles at my panic. "I am here to escort you and Allegra to the Hoppners, remember?"

"You are too early. We have days before we must leave."

"Yes," he says with a flash of his old vibrancy, "we have days ahead of us."

"And you assume you are welcome?" I tease.

"I know that I am. Isn't that true, Allegra?" He picks her up. "Do you welcome your Uncle Percy?"

"Papa." She laughs, raising her hands to pull leaves from a low-hanging chestnut, and Percy gloats.

"There you have it, Claire. Let's take a walk before the sun sets. My legs are stiff from the journey."

I wonder why I am the girl who will never turn him away.

"Let this be cure for our misery," Percy says on those evenings when Allegra is safely asleep in her bed and Willmouse is on the mend in Venice and Mary is too haunted by Harriet to think clearly. "Let us take pleasure in the time that we have."

He kisses me and leads me up the curling stairway. There in the grand bed where Albee and Teresa will sleep, we sink into tenderness. Unlike the driving, forceful lover of his youth, Percy is gentle and measured in his kisses, his touch. His voice is soft rather than strident. "Death hovers behind every door, Claire. Let us live while we can." For me, about to relinquish my daughter, our intimacy is a tonic. "Remember, my love, nothing – good or bad – lasts forever."

#

Mary and I stand aside when Percy starts packing for our trip to Naples. "A new adventure," he crows as he shoves our trunks out the door. I know better than to interrupt, and Mary is guarded, no doubt contemplating Albee's remarks that Percy's journey to Naples with three women and a young lad was *foolhardy.*

Does Shelley not comprehend what a dangerous part of the country he is entering? Albee adds to his note about Allegra's tranquil re-adjustment at the Hoppners. *You should thank God that your daughter is safely in my care, Claire, rather than with you and your reckless leader.*

Albee's warning frightens me, yet I am beyond caring, and Mary is barely speaking since Percy spent those days with me and Allegra in Este. "The lost weekend," she repeats with scorn.

Tolerant of her anguish, I keep my distance. I caused Mary to lose Clara that day on the streets of Venice, and, in turn, my justice was served when we returned Allegra to the Hoppners. Always, I believe, we are suffering for the suffering we cause others. Percy and I deserve Mary's wrath.

Now bound for Naples, I am on my best behavior. As we ride headlong into what Albee claims is certain November death, we encounter filth and discomfort. We endure Percy's endless accounts of the passing scenery, the beauty of the pine forests and the danger of the Pontine Marshes. Not to mention his bold tales of thieves and murderers and soldiers along the Appian Way. He points out ancient temples and Roman numerals carved into stone. "There is Monti Ausoni." His voice rises with excitement. "And the Tyrrhenian Sea."

Mary and I, numb with our separate losses, are not impressed. "What is left to take from us?" I ask Mary. "In our forlorn state, no self-respecting murderer would bother with us."

Eventually, at some point along the way, Mary revives. She, too, chimes in about the marvels of the landscape. "Oh, the sea is a lovely deep blue, and look there." She points. "Is that not Monte Circeo, the mountain of the enchantress Circe?"

Their spoken duet doubles my misery, but relief comes when at last we arrive at Percy's rented lodgings on the luxurious Riviera di Chiaia. "Mary needs a distraction," he says of our spectacular water views with Vesuvius rising in the distance.

I, too, desire distraction as Albee's words about Percy's reckless nature continue to haunt me. If I separate myself from Percy, would Albee allow me to raise Allegra? If I could support myself as a governess or a music teacher, would he send Allegra's support payments to me rather than the Hoppners? Is it possible for me to change my daughter's fate?

Here in Naples, we soon settle into our usual comforts. We explore the city. We read endlessly. We study Italian. We pretend our lives hold promise, even as winter looms ahead. Winter always brings melancholy, followed by Spring and her rains of misfortune. Perhaps, we tell ourselves, winter in a warmer clime will be kinder to us.

Anxious to see everything there is to see, Percy plans an excursion to Vesuvius. "A splendid bit of exercise for our bodies and our souls," he exclaims as we set out. I distrust his optimism, yet I am certain this excursion will be nothing compared to climbing the Alps, and I do not want to be left behind with the household servants.

Elise and Willmouse see us off. He is slight and solemn, and she is gay and growing larger. I wonder why neither Mary nor Percy notice her expanding girth. "Arrivederci," we call as we walk to the dock. "Buona giornata."

Clouds gather over the Bay of Naples, yet the sea is brilliant on our crossing to Ercolano. Flecks of sunlight bounce around us and every foam-tipped wave shifts in color and shape, yet our journey is smooth. "A pleasant crossing brings good fortune." Percy jumps ashore first and offers his hand.

I am dismayed to discover Mount Vesuvius, so promising from a distance, is nothing more than a grey ash pile. Immediately I want to turn back. With every step, heat seeps up our legs from the cracked, crusted earth like we are being burned at the stake. When I dig in too deeply with my walking stick, it catches fire! Percy, our natural leader, bounds upward, while Mary and I follow steadily behind. Tarry too long, and we might also burst into flame.

Over my shoulder I notice the clouds have dispersed. Fresh blue sky is reflected in the sea below us. If I cannot be with Allegra, I must keep moving. I must stay fit and ready for her return. Whenever that may be. Then, quite suddenly, as if blown in from across the bay, there is a skip to my thoughts, a pulse beating in my brain like a stone skimming over water. Keep climbing, I tell myself. Stay fit. Yet discordant images splash before my eyes: Allegra. Willmouse with Elise. Elise with Albee. Albee with Allegra.

Above us, Percy halts to examine some specimen at his feet. He falls to his knees as he and Mary observe whatever charred object he has discovered. Yet I stand stock still, blinking away the obscene image of Elise lying in Albee's bed. Elise, wide-eyed and adoring, as Albee stretches over her, the naked length of him obscuring her in my jangled vision.

"Claire!" Mary calls to me. "Percy is ill. Come, help me."

I cannot move. I, too, fall to my knees, watching as Percy retches over the blackened crust and Mary wipes his brow with her handkerchief. I kneel here as Elise's words from our summer afternoons on the terrace trickle into my bouncing brain. "Albee likes young girls," she said with an offhand shrug. "Allegra will grow from a child to a young girl someday."

I rise to my feet with a vengeance and haul Percy upward with the strength of a Roman goddess. "We must return to Venice," I shout at him. "We must go for Allegra now. Before she grows a day older, we must bring her home."

Somehow, despite my hysteria and Percy's illness and Mary's fright, we make our way down from the volcano and across the Bay of Naples to our own quarters and our own beds. "Nothing good can come from this day." Mary frets as she tends to us. "Something is amiss."

"All that fire and ash." I breathe slowly through my tender lungs. "A foreshadowing of Hell."

"Shhh." Mary presses a damp cloth to my forehead. "Percy does not believe in Hell."

I remain abed for days to regain my strength. The recovery of my mind is taking much longer. My sense of reasoning has lapsed, forcing me to calm myself by repeating *as long as Albee is with the Countess, Allegra shall be safe*. Which is totally ridiculous. Albee has never shown the slightest interest in young girls. "Young girls are Shelley's obsession," he always said with derision.

Along with Allegra, I have lost my spirit. Christmas comes and goes without my participation, as does the birth of Elise's baby. "She is a beauty." I scrutinize Elena Adelaide for Albee's features, for intimation of Allegra herself, yet see nothing obvious. The infant's coloring is darker, more like my own, and her hair is straight and thick. The shape of her face might resemble Albee's. And perhaps her dainty fingers and feet. Not that it matters. Perhaps in an ideal world, where women have a say about their futures, Elise and I could raise our daughters together as sisters. We could start a tribe: The Daughters of Byron.

I present none of this to Elise. I do not ask *and where is the great man now?* Mary has already said plenty about Elise's naiveté. If Mary has no room in her heart for Allegra, she has even less for the illegitimate daughter of a nursemaid. The second illegitimate daughter, she continually points out. "Wasn't leaving her first daughter with her parents enough of a lesson for Elise?"

Thus begins our new year of 1819. A new girl child arriving in our household as if by magic does little to fill in the void left by the missing girl children Clara and Allegra and Clara. If anything, Elena Adelaide causes us to mourn more deeply.

Not that Percy comprehends the depth of our emotions. To Percy, Elena is a wonder, a miracle cure for Mary's grief. "We shall adopt her," he decides with a renewed passion for his mythical love commune. "We shall make her our own."

"How dare you consider such a notion?" Mary's fury is tightly curled, an icy flame that causes us to shiver even in the sunshine of Naples.

The flu has hollowed flesh from Percy's face. His voice is harsh. "It is the proper thing to do, Mary. Elise delivered this baby in our household. She conceived this child while in our service. I am responsible for her."

"Not, I hope, as Albee is responsible for Allegra. Albee fathered Allegra." Mary grows frantic. "Please swear to me that Elena Adelaide is not your child."

"There is no father for Elise's child." Percy's cough is ragged. "Whoever he is, he is now gone."

"We cannot replace our Clara with a stranger."

"This our dream, Mary. To care for unwanted children."

"It is your dream, not mine. I do not want her. Do not ask me again."

Before January draws to an end, Elise marries Paolo the handyman, and they depart Naples without Elena. Neither Elise nor I speak of Albee before her leave-taking. Perhaps she is ashamed, or perhaps she does not want to jeopardize her marriage or her hope that Percy and Mary will raise Elena. As for me, I am selfish in my silence. I want every gram of Albee's fatherly love to go to Allegra. Although I yet wonder how Percy and Mary cannot subtract the months and come to their own conclusion.

Perhaps they have.

By the end of February Percy ceases his campaign to keep Elena Adelaide. He registers her birth, naming Mary and himself as her true parents, and then leaves her in Naples as a foundling. It is too shocking for me think about.

The following day, as if nothing tragic has occurred, we depart for Rome, where we lodge at the Palazzo Verospi on the Corso and fall into our customary life of riches: drawing and singing lessons, and walks to view all the wonders Rome has to offer. Percy begins work on *Prometheus Unbound*, writing mainly among the ruins. Mary takes Willmouse to play in the Borghese Gardens. Not yet recovered, I float along.

In time, Mary forgives Percy, and by March, she is expecting another child. A pattern which anyone with half a brain could have predicted: no sooner does Mary lose a child than another is on the way.

Such an unkind thought. Like sentiment sprung from Albee's heart rather than my own.

A letter from Mrs. Hoppner finally finds us. *Allegra pines for her mother*, she writes. *Only an incompetent mother would leave her daughter as Miss Clairmont did. Only a selfish mother could have produced such a selfish child.*

"What rubbish!" Mary throws the letter towards the hearth.

"She is not to be trusted. I shall write to Albee at once." Percy turns to comfort me and finds me stiff and unyielding.

Mrs. Hoppner has given voice to my own conviction that I am a bad mother, and I want to prove her wrong. "We must return to Venice. We must assure ourselves that Allegra is well."

"This insult springs from Mrs. Hoppner's own failure, not yours." He takes my hand between his ink-stained fingers. "Remain strong in heart, Claire. Think of Allegra as we left her. Lively and laughing. Ignore Mrs. Hoppner's fondness for casting blame."

It is too late. I fall ill again, and this time, Willmouse does too. By June, the first sweet month of summer, William, the solid, steady bloom among those frail flower children, suddenly worsens.

Mary and Percy are never wise in crisis. "We shall leave Rome for a healthier climate," Percy says. "We shall move to the mountains."

"We cannot move now, Percy. Let us send for Dr. Bell, the Scottish doctor I found here."

Mary and Percy dither, Albee dryly says of them. Percy and Mary dither, malaria takes its grip on our little Willmouse, and Death leads him away.

"It is retribution for my wickedness toward Harriet," Mary cries. "It is precisely what I deserve."

I know at once we will not survive such a crushing loss. So many losses. "I must leave," I tell Percy.

"You cannot leave your sister now. Mary needs you more than ever." As always Percy persists. As always, I stay.

Somehow we survive the summer. I care for Mary's household and listen to Percy's poems, and that occupation saves me. Percy's poetry saves him. The anticipated birth of a new baby saves Mary.

We move to Florence, so Mary can be attended by Dr. Bell for the birth of Percy Florence Shelley. We take one look at that vigorous newborn – not one thing frail or flower-like about him -- and immediately perceive he will live to adulthood. "He will outlive us all," Percy announces. It is a holy moment of joy, and yet Mary is already sinking, fast and deep, into her post-natal sadness.

My devotion to Allegra keeps me sane during these lonely days of caring for baby Percy. Mary is lost in her gloom, and Percy is lost in his writing. Milly is no longer trusted, and Elise is long gone, so I am the one to take charge. I cheerfully bathe him and change his nappies and rock him to sleep as I once did with my own daughter. "You will live a long life," I tell him every day, "and my Allegra will return to me again. When she is old enough to declare *I wish to be with my mother*, Albee will send her to me with a glad heart."

I convince myself only good will come to us even as Mrs. Hoppner continues to send spiteful letters. *Lord Byron will never allow you to see Allegra*, she threatens. *You and the Shelleys are immoral, godless creatures who deserve eternal damnation.* Fortunately, I know Albee better than Mrs. Hoppner does. No matter how respectable and moral he is under Countess Teresa's influence, Albee would only laugh at Mrs. Hoppner's extreme sense of self-righteousness. Albee is always the cynic.

Here in this new year of 1820, I believe we have found ourselves a guardian angel, but perhaps that sounds a bit too Catholic. Percy the heathen is more apt to call her a goddess. As Lady Mountcashell of Ireland, she bore seven children to Lord Mountcashell before leaving them all to come to Italy with her lover. Here in Pisa, she is known as Mrs. Mason, and as a friend of both Mary's mother and my own, she treats us as though we are her natural born children. Oh what a blessing. I miss my daughter. I miss my mother. I miss my sister's goodwill. After our long, sad year, I rejoice to have found this woman, who takes us under her wing and soothes our broken souls.

At the Masons' house on Via Mala Gonella, we read Thomas Paine and discuss Irish independence. Individually, she gives Percy counsel on his health and Mary counsel on her household duties. She tells me to detach myself from Percy and Mary and find my way in the world.

"You are an intelligent young woman, Claire," she says again and again. "Fly away. Establish your independence."

While she eases Mary's practical concerns regarding servants and shopkeepers and doctors, I follow Percy's example and retreat to our terrace to write. There in a quiet corner shaded by bougainvillea, I become Albee's faithful correspondent. Or is *correspondence* the wrong word when the sender receives no reply? Although the great Lord Byron once admired me as a woman of spirit and determination, I am very cautious not to cross that narrow line between being forthright and somehow offending him. Forcing my tone to be pleasant and maternal, I request that he allow Allegra to spend the summer with me under Mrs. Mason's supervision.

I receive not one word in return.

I wait six weeks, and write again, keeping a copy for the sake of my own sanity. I keep my tone light and honest, even when I defend myself against Percy's non-beliefs. *The nights grow warmer here in April, the days are green and sweet-scented, and I miss my daughter. Please grant a mother's dearest desire for the company of her only child. Let me also assure you, Albee, that I do not share Percy's views against religion. Yet, I do remain grateful to him for his many kindnesses to me over the past five years. C.*

Still no response. Mary blames me for the fractured friendship between Albee and Percy, and she has no sympathy for me, a mother missing her daughter. "At least your Allegra is alive," she reminds me, as if that is sufficient. We sisters battle all summer long until our nerves snap and fray like kite strings.

Mrs. Mason straightens us, although not in a manner either Percy or I would choose. The dear woman finds me employment as governess in the Florence home of Dr. Antonio Bojti, physician to Grand-Duke Ferdinand III. "It is a splendid opportunity for you, Claire," she says of her feat.

"I do not want to leave Pisa." I pout like a child. "I must stay to help Mary and the new baby. What if Albee brings Allegra with him to Pisa?"

She places her hand on my shoulder, like a saint bestowing her blessing. "It is for the best, my girl. You must allow Mary and Percy to live their lives. You must establish yourself so Lord Byron will grant you time with your little daughter."

Once again, I am destined to be alone in a strange place.

"Please, Claire, do not go," Percy whispers as he lifts me into the carriage bound for Florence. "Remain with here with me, I beg you. Mary will calm herself, I promise."

"Mary and I bewitch each other with misery. We will be better sisters when I return at Christmastime." I wave farewell to Mary, who holds baby Percy at her breast. "Until December," I call to her.

Percy's eyes are as blue as broken sky. "You will miss me, my sweet Clarabella."

"Yes," I promise him. "Yes, I will miss you."

He is fearful of Mary's moodiness, I think. He knows that when I am absent from his household, Mary is happier, but he is not.

Part Four: Percy

20. The Cloud

Living in Florence with Dr. Bojti's family is a bit like living in a cloud. Everything is soft and airy in this city, and the Bojti children are sweet, eager learners. To be a good governess and keep my wits about me in their innocent, blissful world, I imagine Allegra is with me. Here she sits at the breakfast table wearing her blue frock with the white collar, and her eyes shine brightly above her cup of milk. When we walk in the gardens, she runs beside me through the palmettos, her arms stretched wide to rattle the fronds. During our English lessons, I shape my mouth to enunciate *th* in *thank you*, and Allegra mirrors me, her tongue caught between her perfect rosebud lips. I place the fingers of the Bojti children on the piano keys as Allegra places her own smaller fingers an octave away. When I smile at her, as I often do, I am careful not to praise her, not to show favoritism. Occasionally, I slip. "Very good, Allegra," I say of her drawing.

"Olivia." The youngest Bojti corrects me. "My name is Olivia."

"Of course," I say as I pat her hand, a hand much plumper than Allegra's.

People are kind to me here, and I wonder how deep their kindness might run if they knew about my dearest Allegra. Or Albee. Or my life with Percy Shelley. I would be cast out on the street in the blink of an eye. Which speaks little of Christian charity.

In the evenings when the Bojti children dine with their parents, Allegra, too, deserts me. Here in this lovely place, my world again turns white and airy and completely unsubstantial. It is a perfect match for my mind, which is also void of colors and sound. I meander among the

Florentine hills. I sit at the feet of Ceres and curse Albee's shriveled heart. For all my pleasing surroundings, I may as well be back in Devon, sitting on the stone bench above the bay and watching the fog wrap around me. I am as alone in Florence as I was in Lynmouth.

Mary and Percy remain my faithful correspondents. Mary's letters are irksomely chatty and cheerful while Percy's are flirtatious. *My cousin Medwin is gathering friends to travel to the Middle East,"* he writes. *"I say we should join him. I can think of no better adventure than to be with you in a new, exotic land, Clarabella. Then before he closes, he adds, not that you should mention this plan to Mary. She has grown cold and distant to me of late, and I miss you more than you can imagine.*

Oh, I can imagine quite well. Percy always misses me when I am gone and finagles to bring me back. As for Mary, whose life alone with Percy is not going as well as she hoped, I have little sympathy. I blame my sister for the loss of my daughter. If not for Mary, Allegra would be with me still.

When I return to Pisa in December, my cloud of aloneness fills the carriage even as Florence falls behind me. As does my hate for Albee. The thought of spending another Christmas without Allegra makes me ill, and I close my eyes to shut out any cheerful scenery, any wholesome family tableau along the roadside. When we arrive at Casa Galletti, an unimposing house next to a marble palace on the Lung'Arno, I gather my courage like a shield.

"Dear Claire!" Percy and Mary greet me with smiles. "We have missed you." Percy bows as if I am visiting royalty, his knuckles brushing the dusty road. Mary, her cheeks as pink as her frock, embraces me with warmth. "Welcome, dear sister."

"You look quite fit," I say, "and happy." I breathe in the scent of pine. Oh, I have missed Pisa. "Where is Baby Percy?"

Baby Percy is the chubbiest of Mary's babies, which surely must be a good sign. He is a fine, solid bundle to hold on my lap while Mary fusses with the tea and Percy tells tales. The bustling energy and teatime chatter is all very familiar. Mary and Percy are experts in smooth facades.

"You know with the help of Mrs. Mason we have made the most charming Italian friends," he says.

"Actors. Professors. An exiled prince from Greece." She sets a plate of dainty tea cakes before me. "Wonderful characters for my novel, don't you think?"

"Mary is making great progress, despite our busy social schedule." Percy, who ordinarily *despises* sociability, speaks rapidly, as if confessing a sin. "Her latest character Clorinda is based on a young girl we have come to know. Under tragic circumstances, I might add." His voice rises.

I ease Baby Percy's hand away from the tea cakes. "Tragic how?"

"Would you believe this young beautiful girl is shut away in Saint Anna convent, visible there on the hill, until she will be forced into an arranged marriage?" He fusses with his shirt sleeves, rolling them up and down, to avoid meeting my eyes. "Emilia is a lovely young girl with raven black hair and skin as white as marble. She is as pure as a goddess."

Percy is so obviously in love it takes my breath away. *Emilia.* He all but sings her name. My heart cracks with envy. "Do you know this girl, Mary? This Emilia?"

"Oh yes, Emilia." Mary nods, her face dewy from the teapot's steam. "Such injustice exists here in Italy, Claire."

"A great injustice." Percy's face is also flushed, although likely not due to the teapot. "A girl of her beauty should choose the man she loves."

"Why a forced marriage?" I ask. "She is a ward of the nuns?"

"Not at all. She is the daughter of Pisa's governor. Can you imagine such an outrage ever occurring in England?"

"I know a daughter of Governor Viviani," I say. "A pretty girl with my coloring named Teresa." I hold my teacup away from the baby's reach as Mary pours. "Will she face the same fate as Emilia?"

"Emilia and Teresa are one and the same girl." Percy takes his son from my arms. "Emilia is our pet name for her."

"I visit her at her school every day," Mary says. "Perhaps you will be kind enough to write to her, Claire? The unfortunate girl needs our encouragement." Does Mary suspect nothing of Percy's new infatuation, I wonder, or is she merely playing along for her own peace of mind?

"I will persuade Mrs. Mason to rescue her." Percy rocks the baby in one arm and gestures with the other, still not daring to look at me. Such a coward.

"Mrs. Mason?" I have the sensation of re-reading an old familiar novel where the passionate hero rescues a beautiful school girl named Harriet and they elope to a foreign land. "How would Mrs. Mason rescue Teresa from her very expensive private school?"

"Dress as a man and claim to be a suitor."

His bravado is ridiculous considering how poor Harriet's story ended. "Our Percy, always the hero." I refrain from scoffing. "I doubt kidnapping is in Mrs. Mason's character."

"I agree." Mary passes a tin of dates.

"Mrs. Mason believes in freedom of women." At last Percy's eyes flicker towards me. "You know that as well as I."

"I do indeed." Since there is no point in arguing that "Emilia" comes from a family of wealth and power and has no need of rescue, I change the subject. "The weather has been quite odd in Florence. Have I mentioned the frequency of fog in my letters?"

Returned to my cloud in Florence, I find Allegra comes to me now only in flashes. I catch a skipping movement from the corner of my eye. An echo of her laughter hangs in the air as I lift my fingers from the keyboard. When I wake in the night I touch the warm hollow beside me where she has lain. None of these sensations sustain me for long.

Percy sends me verses from his latest poem, the story of a man imagining life with a new woman while mourning the love he lost. Mary, always the moon in Percy's poetry, is now winter personified, a woman of ice and cold, while Emilia is a glimmering moonbeam. It is difficult to read, even for me, yet I forge on. *This line is for you, Clarabella: my beautiful comet, so fierce and bright that I burn when we touch.*

The man will never change. That thought returns to me again and again as I thread my way through my foggy winter. Percy, Mary, and I know entirely too much about each other. Our histories are too painfully snarled to ever completely disentangle. As for Albee, I cannot think of him without hate, and I cease sending letters he will never read.

When Mary sends long, chirpy accounts of life in their new home in San Giuliana, I know she has not read Percy's latest poems. Rather, my sister is very excited by the news that Edward and Jane Williams are spending the winter in nearby Pugnano. *We have only to sail down the canal from the Arno to the Serchio, and we are there. What a joy to see old friends and hear news of London. Percy has renewed his interest in sailing. Only last week a storm caught them on the river, and I remain most thankful for Edward, who guided the boat to shore. Albee and Teresa may rent a house farther down the river, and you shall be able to visit Allegra here at our home. Does that not ease your heart?*

I fear giving my heart ease. When I reply to Mary, I remark that Jane Williams has been known as a gossip, and Edward is a bit of a dullard.

Envy, I imagine Mary saying as she holds my letter in her hands.

In March, she writes in a more restrained tone before adding this: *Even though Albee and Teresa left Venice for Ravenna to avoid political unrest, the situation has grown worse. For the sake of Allegra's safety and education, he has entered her into the Copuchin Convent of Bagnacavallo. Alas, this is not the news we desired, and Percy and I will encourage him to reconsider. Be of courage, Claire, and know that Albee has your daughter's best interest at heart. Your loving sister, Mary.*

Oh, dear God. Albee has vanquished Allegra from his various exquisite homes overlooking water and fields and mountains to live in a plain colorless cubicle with loveless tyrannical nuns. Miles from the sea, from the hills, from a good sturdy forest, what joy will my high-spirited daughter find in a convent?

Here in Florence, this place of lightness, my cloud burns away in a flash. I am blinded by the bright colors of Spring and deafened by clamor of laughing children. I cover my ears and cower beside the piano until little Olivia Bojti, her eyes wide and dark, pats my knee in comfort. "Sei malessere, signora?"

Unable to speak, I take her small hand, so unlike my Allegra's, and hold it like an offering until I can once again pretend that I am still alive. I go about my day afire with a fresh anger, and then sit at my desk to dash off a letter:

Albee—

Long before our daughter was born you vowed she would never be raised by strangers, and, as you are esteemed as a man of your word, I believed you. Not only have you broken your vow, you have *condemned your own flesh and blood to a joyless life among barren spinsters. No matter what you may say to your cynical mates, you <u>know</u> Allegra is your child and she deserves the love of her parents. If not the love of her father, then the love of her mother. Allegra is my sun, my moon, and I shall do anything you ask to have her returned to my care. <u>Anything</u>, Albee.*

You are, as you yourself once proudly claimed, a sadist, a man whose ecstasy comes from the suffering of others. I fear this cruel, despicable act is to punish me for once loving you, and if I could reach you now, I would kill you with my bare hands. I would silence your famous words of love and passion once and for all.

The act of writing and posting my letter allows me to breathe, even though I know Albee will never read my words nor respond to my pleas. I lie sleepless as my heart bounces like a child's wayward ball. Then I climb from under my coverlet and light the lamp.

Dear Mary and Percy,

How can you claim outrage over the lovely Emilia locked in her convent and yet not extend that same sense of outrage to my own dear Allegra? How dare you consider Albee a responsible father? Do not speak of him again. Do not speak to me at all until you have a plan to return my daughter to me.

Albee, likely in a moment of boredom while Countess Teresa was in the marketplace and the dogs and monkeys were sleeping, lowered his high standards to read my letter and became immediately enraged. He wrote spiteful letters to Percy, and, fearful of losing the love and affection of the great Lord Byron, Percy apologized profusely. Claire is unreasonable and distraught, Percy told Albee. She hardly knows what she says. That part, at least, is true.

When Mary and Percy insist I, too, must apologize, I am terse. *I regret my hasty words, Albee, I never imagined you could become so easily wounded by words.* That also is true. Why would he care what I say? Perhaps he is vainer than I imagined. Or the truth filled him with guilt. I no longer harbor the illusion that he will regret his ill treatment of me and be filled with new desire. I am too old for such romantic notions.

My nightly dreams are filled with harrowing dramas of Allegra. Always, I am fleeing with her in my arms, running through the night for all I am worth. Always Albee pursues us on a tall dark horse. Some nights I drop her, and he swoops down to catch her mid-fall. Some nights the nuns tear her from my arms, and I must run past Albee's rearing horse to evade their clutches. Unlike most nightmares, Allegra and I escape. Always, we are reunited. Every morning just before dawn, my breathing calms and I sense her lying beside me. Together we breathe in unison. We sigh. Ah, at last, we are together again.

All spring, while I teach the Bojti children in this beautiful city and dream my dreams of Allegra, I ignore the missives that arrive from Mary and Percy. Oh, I read Mary's sunshiny chatter and Percy's promises to thaw Albee's icy heart. I simply refuse to reply.

Mrs. Mason and I carry on a more positive correspondence. *When summer comes and your time with Dr. Bojti ends*, she wrote, *do not be tempted to return to the Shelleys, dear Claire. At Percy's bidding, I have secured reasonable accommodations for you in Leghorn via a family friend. It will be good for you to spend your summer as an independent woman, as a mother preparing for your child's eventual return.*

I find Mrs. Mason's proposition appealing, and it is also my only possibility. Although Percy can talk Mary into anything, I cannot bear to be under their roof for another summer of sisterly strife. I prefer to live alone in quiet reflection, and if I give Mary peace, perhaps the return of Allegra will be my reward.

I am surprised when Percy, obviously with Mary's and Mrs. Mason's blessings, comes to Florence to escort me to Leghorn. He stands before me like a vision, this handsome, rumpled, excitable poet of note. "I have sorely missed you, my darling Clarabella, and I am sorry for your misery, but I vow to set things right. I promise Albee will send Allegra to you."

I cannot respond to Percy's vow to right wrongs. Especially not when his eyes are wildly blue in the sunlight. He hops into his carriage like a schoolboy and extends his hand. The driver eases me inside. "Luigi is also a builder." Percy offers as introduction. "We hope he will build us a new boat before summer's end."

"Who is this *we*, Percy? You and Mary are building yourselves a boat?"

"Edward Williams and I. We are becoming expert sailors and could use a swifter, sturdier vessel." He kisses the back of my hand and holds it to his heart. "Please do not leave me again, Claire."

"Leave-taking is beyond my control. As you well know. Besides you have Edward now. And Jane. How is she?"

"Jane is good-humored, a good listener, a good companion to Mary." His blueness dims a bit. "She is not you."

Nor could she ever be, I say to myself. I slip my hand from his grasp. Let him earn the privilege of touching me. Let him charm and wheedle and squirm. My forgiveness shall not come easily.

By the time we reach Leghorn, I have heard Percy's many tales of marital woe with the cold, distant Mary. He is lonely, he tells me. He is bored with Jane and Edward Williams and Mary's collection of local gentry. He misses his smart literary set. He misses me.

"What of Emilia?" I ask now.

"Oh yes, the poor girl is now betrothed. We see her not."

I sense there is more to be said about *the poor girl*, although I let it pass. His eyes are in shadow, and there is no wild, blue throbbing. His hands lie still atop his book of Keats, glorified for dying so horribly and so young. "Only you and I can speak so honestly. We can be witty in one moment and silly the next. I miss that. I miss your childlike, carefree manner."

His words punch air from my lungs, which he mistakes as a laugh. Such is the state of our estrangement. Despite being a brilliant man, Percy does not comprehend that I have lost the joy that he so admires and misses. I have lost a piece of myself. I have grown old and sullen. "Oh, Percy. Our lives shall never be what they were."

He comes back to his normal state of excitement then. "But they shall, Claire! Our children will grow up together, I promise. There will be hikes and boat trips and picnics in the garden. Mary and I will have a loving household filled with even more children. You and she will live together as sisters once again."

We were never sisters. I do not say it. I allow his imagination to run free, and when we arrive at my summer lodging, a plain, tidy apartment on a tree-lined street, I do not extend an invitation for him to linger. Again, I vow to be a good woman who will be rewarded with the return of her daughter.

"I shall see you often, Claire." He kisses me farewell. "I promise to return with good news of Allegra. I shall pursue Albee like a hound from Hell."

As poets who are careful and precise with their words, Percy and Albee are superb letter writers, and yet in their exchange of letters during those warm summer days, I learn from Mary that careful wording does not change the meaning and the tone of their messages. Percy is warm and wary; Albee is aloof and defiant, reiterating his claim that we are all worthless as parents and a convent would do a better job of raising any of our children, and his in particular.

Percy is not easily dissuaded. When he suddenly appears on my doorstep clutching a bouquet of wildflowers, I laugh out loud from the simple delight of seeing a familiar face. "Oh, Percy. Come in. Quick, before the neighbors see you standing there like a nervous bride."

He swoops down on me like a bird of prey and gathers me in his embrace. Flowers spill across the plain wooden floor of my flat as he spins me around, not lessening his hold, not missing a beat of our jolly dance. "I am here at last, dear Claire, and I never want to let you go."

"I am growing faint." I laugh anew at his antics. "Stop twirling us about so I can breathe. Stand still and tell me why you are here in sad, beautiful Leghorn."

He slows our spin, but he does not loosen his hold. We stand face to face, swaying slightly to music only Percy can hear. "I am here, dear lady, with good tidings. I am here to commemorate the day of my birth."

It is the fourth day of August. The day Mary always celebrates with her exquisite gifts: hand-stitched kites and love poems in her beautiful penmanship, a picnic in the park and a basket full of paper boats, a quiet day on the water for the two of them alone. Yet, here he stands before me. His hands grip my waist, and he acts as mischievous as a schoolboy.

"Where does Mary think you are?"

"With Albee in Ravenna." He is pleased with his deception, his clever plotting to spend his twenty-ninth birthday with me. "It is a partial truth, Claire. I have been to call on Albee." He raises his hand. "Now, hear me out. Come sit and allow me to share what I know."

We sit on the parlor settee, our knees knocking together as we face one another. "When it comes to reports on Albee, I can only bear small portions."

"This portion is quite small, Claire, yet it is promising. He vows he will not keep Allegra in the convent forever, only until the political strife in Ravenna is settled. I suggested boarding school in England, and he dismissed that idea. He finds travel too troublesome for a small child like Allegra, although he claims he and Teresa have discussed a return to England."

"Which fate is worse, the convent filled with nuns or the miles lying between me and England? Although I could return to England and better my chances of seeing her there, don't you think?"

"Albee's poetry is doing very well in England, yet he claims a return to London would draw too much attention to his personal life. He says he might spend the winter season in Pisa, and permit Allegra to stay with Mrs. Mason. I will encourage him every way I know how, Claire, and I hope he will agree."

"Hope is a slippery creature." I take his hand. "I thank you for your efforts on behalf of our sweet Allegra."

"Oh, there is more, dear woman. On this day of my birth, I celebrate by bringing you news of your daughter."

"Allegra was with Albee?"

"I called on the convent to see her with my own eyes."

"Oh, Percy. You saw her?" My eyes ache for such a vision.

"I did. She is a most beautiful little girl, Claire. Aside from Byron's curls and dimpled chin, she looks precisely like you."

"She is well? She is happy?"

"She is indeed. She wore a white dress and a black silk pinafore and showed me around the convent by pointing out her bed and her dining table. She shared the sweets I brought with her little friends and then danced around the courtyard chasing butterflies. She is taller and thinner, and perhaps quieter, but she remains the same charming child she was with us."

"Oh, Percy." I can barely speak for the relief and the longing pressing against my throat. "What of the nuns?" Again, I imagine the nuns of my nightmares, their twisted virgin fingers grasping at my child.

"They dote on her, especially her favorite, Sister Marianna. Aside from the Catholic-ness of it, the prayers and saints and such, it is a beautiful place with lush gardens."

I laugh at Percy's fear of Catholicism. "She is happy?" I ask again, because I cannot bring myself to ask what I most want to know. *Did she speak of me?*

"I promise you she is quite at home there. Allegra is an enchantress. That is the word Albee chose to describe her, and I would agree. She has your soul, Claire. She has your heart. You must believe you will soon be together again. She calls you *her dear little mama.*"

Even a woman with a stronger resolve than mine would have difficulty turning away from the charms of Percy Shelley. And a man who celebrates his own birthday by bringing her word of her heart's desire? He is unable to resist.

I am suddenly euphoric and hopeful, and I behave as frivolously as I did in my younger days. "Let's pretend we are lord and lady of the manor," I say as we stroll past the villa said to belong an Italian knight. "We are out to see how the common folk live, Sir Percy."

"Ah, what a fine afternoon to mix with mere mortals, Lady Shelley."

"Lady Shelly? You claim I resemble your mother?"

"Only in beauty, Lady Claire. Thankfully, beauty is the only trait you share with my mother."

We carry on as any couple might. We admire Leghorn's many canals as Percy lectures me on the effects of the Napoleonic Wars and the city's Greek influences. We walk along the sea front as he announces that some of London's smart literary will also winter in Pisa. He and Hunt and Albee are planning a new journal, he tells me, one that will grant them freedom to say what they want from the safe distance of an Italian shore. As we stand staring out at the water, his mood shifts with the wind. Our charade ends.

"I am lost without you, Claire." Percy's tone rises. "Emilia is threatening to blackmail me, and Mary is more my partner than my wife. I regret the turn of our lives."

I watch the gulls rise and soar. The sun glints off the water, and I shade my face. "If only you had chosen me on Skinner Street. If only you were Allegra's father. If only I had waited for you instead of enmeshing myself with the great Lord Byron." Percy's hair blows around his handsome face, and his eyes reflect the sea and sky. "We would have made a good life together."

It is little wonder that, as in those previous times when we are alone together, Percy and I fall into our usual patterns. Like lying together under the stars. Like falling into bed together. Like waking up and making love as if it is our own discovery. When Percy leaves, he begs me to come along. "Mary will not react as badly as she has in the past," he promises. Oh foolish man.

Not unlike the lovely Emilia, I resort to my own form of blackmail. "If you arrange for Allegra's return, then perhaps we will all live together again, Sir Shelley." It is a plan Albee will never approve, and yet in Percy's presence, I bloom with optimism.

"You must never again live with Percy," Mrs. Mason says when she learns of his visit. "You are too intelligent to be caught up in such a dark web, Claire. Consider instead how you will live out the rest of your life as a respectable mother, not a desperate woman grasping on to a married man."

"Yes, ma'am." I smile at her concern. "I shall restrain myself."

Like any wildly romantic dream, the intensity of Percy's company fades after his return to Mary. It is the end of August, and summer is dying. My quiet quarters echo in the stillness, and yet I am at peace. I continue to pray that Albee will bring Allegra to Pisa this winter. I assure myself that great possibilities lay ahead. At twenty-three years, my life is hardly over.

21. Sins of the Mother

*D**ear Claire,*

The Hunts are on their long, slow journey to Pisa, and Percy and I must travel along the coast in search of winter lodgings fit for a poet and his countess. Are you free to join us? We would welcome your excellent company.

Love, Mary

As it has been only a week since Percy's departure from my apartment, I recognize his hand all over this scheme. Once I would be distraught at the prospect of finding a house for Albee and his mistress. Now I am merely eager for some company and a change of scene. Mostly I welcome the prospect of once again traveling with Percy and Mary.

"We balance one another," Mary says when we start out from Pisa on the eighth of September. "You and Percy lighten the mood when I am too fixed on one detail. Percy and I calm your excitable nature, and together, you and I ignore Percy's fondness for romanticizing the worst of places. As if Albee and Teresa – especially Teresa – would find a view of treetops through a crumbling rooftop *exquisite*."

Mary and I often make Percy the brunt of our jokes, and he takes no lasting offense. "Ah, the laughter of women is music to my soul." He is happy to observe us sisters on cordial terms. Evaluating, no doubt, how well we might co-exist in the same household once again.

We easily fall into our familiar patterns. I listen to Mary and Percy read aloud to one another in their adjoining room as I lie alone staring out at the night sky. I am unusually well-behaved. I do not invent scrabbling vermin or the unwanted attentions of the bellman to burst in on them as I did on our earlier journeys. I remain in my bed and listen to their murmurings and realize that what Percy shares with Mary in no way rivals what he shares with me. Together, they are intellectual commentators, while he and I are fanciful players.

After several pleasant days of searching out coastal villas with seascapes and sunlit vistas, we return to Pisa, where Percy and Mary settle on the villa Palazzo LanFranchi. Across the Lung'Arno from their own spacious apartment, the Palazzo LanFranchi is enormous, easily able to accommodate Albee's menagerie and his household staff. We hone our bartering skills to accumulate beds and chairs and tables and a sideboard or two. "Hardly luxurious," Mary says, "but it will suffice." She shakes her head at the notion of pleasing a Lord and a Countess. "I hope she can overlook a crack or two in the marble tops."

"It will all soon be covered in dog hair." I laugh at the thought. "Until Albee finds grander accommodations." Truly, if Allegra stays with Mrs. Mason in Casa Silva, I care not at all where Albee and the Countess Teresa lay their fine heads. "We have come a long way from Skinner Street, sister. Thank you for including me on this lark."

Mary smiles serenely. "Yes, we are good together when we choose. Not that Percy should know that."

I am sorry to leave the hum that surrounds Mary's household. Despite my small comforts, my books and writing, my existence in Leghorn is lonelier than ever. My apartment echoes like the owl-filled barn at Este. Soon, that will change, I remind myself. Nothing is forever.

I raise my aching arm to again read Mary's latest letter. *My dearest sister*, she begins. *The Countess will be arriving soon, and Albee will follow, but I am very sorry to tell you that Allegra will not be joining them as we once thought. Albee does not want to disrupt her education, and he believes Pisa will be too much a distraction for her young mind. We hope you will visit us again soon, Claire. Be strong of heart until then. Love, Mary*

The hard wooden floor presses into my back, reminding me of the times I lay under my bed on Skinner Street to escape from my sisters. Here, instead of looking up at a mattress, I watch as the wind loudly shuffles Cypress branches against the window. I fear I might go mad from want and hate. Want and hate are emotions that can never be sated. Or so Percy says. Our poor Fanny never knew hate, yet she knew want, and Harriet knew both. I have failed as a mother and a sister and brought this anguish upon myself for misbehaving with Percy, for giving up Allegra, for causing Clara's death, for ignoring poor dear Fanny, for every wrong I have done.

I push myself up until I am kneeling, reeling. Slowly I rise to my feet and walk to the window. On the street below, leaves from the neighbor's aspen lie like tossed coins. I open the window and lean into the salt-tinged wind. If I could fly, I would go now. Into the sky and out over the water like a great sea bird. Oh, I am in the depths of despair, *il più profondo.*

This is how it was with Harriet and Fanny. The fluttering in their chests grew louder and louder until it forced one poor woman into the river and the other dear woman to extinguish the sound with laudanum. I understand completely. But I am not as weak-hearted as Fanny. I am not as neglected as poor Harriet. I withdraw from the window. I withdraw into myself. I will not send Albee another furious letter. I will not raise an alarm with Mary and Percy. I will reform my bad behavior and, please God, be spared the fate of the other women who loved Percy.

Here in October of 1821, my life stands before me like an empty vat. I am totally without purpose. I walk along Leghorn's leaf-strewn streets, waiting for a sign of hope, but when it arrives in the shape of Percy Shelley, I hesitate.

"Mary has sent me," he says before I can object to him standing on my doorstep. This time he has no air of mischief, no flowers in his hands. "Mary insists you deserve a little holiday in Bagni di San Giuliano."

"My reward for readying the Palazzo Lanfranchi for the man I hate?"

"Precisely. And San Giuliano is delightful this time of the year." He takes off his long brown coat as soon he is through my door. "Mary has arranged for you to stay with Jane and Edward, but you may come and go from our house as you see fit." He rubs his neck and glances out my window. "It is a pleasant four-mile walk. Time aplenty for quiet meditation and wildflower picking."

"Why not Pisa? I can stay with Mrs. Mason if you and Mary prefer."

He stops pacing. "The Countess is in Pisa now, Claire."

"And you fear I might find her and somehow assault her?"

"It is always better to keep the flame from the tinder."

I laugh at his caution. "I *might* be tempted to rant at the dear woman for Albee's actions, but mostly I would pity her for falling in love with him. Loving the great Lord Byron is an unholy calling, and she, poor thing, is said to be a devout woman."

Percy lands on my settee, stretching out his legs and watching me with his wide blue beam. "We have three days before we must leave here, Claire. Three whole days to be together."

"And you assume I want to be with you?"

"I do." He pulls me down beside him and kisses my forehead. "I am sorry I could not do better for you, Claire. I know I am no substitute for Allegra, but I can be tender. I can ease your heart." His eyes are full as fountains.

Percy shares my sorrow, and I cannot resist his comfort. I do not ask how he secreted this time away from Mary, what tales he spun to win her understanding. Is it possible my sister no longer cares that her husband is with me?

My time in the hills outside Pisa passes in a sweet blur, because nothing truly awful happens. I fall into old patterns learned from previously living with the Shelleys and their various hangers-on. I help Mary with meals and play with baby Percy. I teach Italian to Edward Williams, who is rather a slow student. I listen to Jane Williams's tales of motherhood and her *great good friendship with dear Mary* until I think I shall retch. I read Percy's poetry and study German. I walk the four miles between Pugnano and San Giuliani, which is, as Percy promised, most pleasant. Often he accompanies me. "I wish you to remain here for the winter, Claire," he says at every turn. "Allow me time to soften Albee's pride and bring Allegra to you."

It is precisely what I want to hear, and despite my best intentions to become a better sister and mother, Percy and I misbehave again and again. It begins, as it often does, with teasing and silliness. "You believe fairies would prefer living in an olive grove to living in a vineyard, now why is that, Claire?"

"Too many creatures in the vines. Birds pecking away at the grapes and the fairies' dear little faces will not do at all, Percy."

"But they can hide under the cool green leaves. They can grow drunk on one sun-ripened grape. They would be forever jolly." Percy turns to my sister, who is hanging nappies out to dry. "What say you, Mary? What is your take on the wee fairy folk?"

Mary shakes out a wet cloth. "Claire is expected at the Williams' villa within the hour. None of us have time for talk of fairies."

Our frivolity – such a blessed escape from our troubles — makes Mary dour, which makes Percy desire me more acutely. "Claire is spending tonight here, Mary. In fact, she may be here every night."

"Then I shall be the one to stay with Jane and Edward." She flings her wet laundry onto the grass. "Claire can take over the household chores once she clears her head of fairies."

"Allow me to drive you and our son there at once." Percy's tone is even-keeled. "I do not want to keep you from the company of your friends."

I wait for one of them to back down and apologize, and when that does not happen, Mary quietly gathers up the baby and Percy quietly loads her into the cart. I turn my attention to the laundry, expecting at any moment their abashed, dewy-eyed, hand-in-hand return. Instead, Percy stands here before me with his arms open wide.

Always there is my deepest hope that he will stay away from Mary and tie himself to me, but then our summer in Woodbine Cottage floats into my mind like a warning buoy. This time with Percy will be short-lived, I tell myself, and I will enjoy it while I can. I sing for him, and he recites verse to me. I cook his vegetables, and he picks me flowers and grapes and mushrooms. We are the young romantics, cavorting around like nymphs and sleeping under the stars. "Do not leave me, Claire. Do not leave me again." I am so unlike Mary, and that is why he loves me. In these brief, passionate bursts of time, Percy loves me best.

Eventually, Mrs. Mason shows up at our door. Tall and red-haired, she is hard to ignore. "I understand what it is to be in love," she says with a sigh. "I, too, love a man who is not my husband." Mary's best tea cup and saucer fit like a pincushion into the palm of her large hand. "You, Percy, cannot leave your wife and child when they have no means of support. You and Claire cannot live here as lovers when all the upper crust of English and Tuscan society will be arriving in Pisa for the winter season."

"You and George have survived scandal."

"True." Her eyes are as green as new grapes. "Many unmarried couples live here as man and wife, and at one time you and Mary and Claire might have lived together as a family. Not now, I'm afraid. Too many people know about Claire and Lord Byron. Think of what scandal would do to your friendship with Bryon and to Claire's reunion with Allegra."

We sit here in the dying light of late October and let reality settle around us.

"I will take you home with me today, Claire." Mrs. Mason pats my shoulder. "We will have a delightful visit before you return to Florence. We must do everything to keep negotiations open with Lord Byron. For the sake of Allegra, we must play by men's rules, not lovers' impulses."

Once again it is better for me to be banished than for Percy to incur the great Lord Byron's wrath. I spend my last few days in Pisa sulking at Casa Silva, where Mrs. Mason is generous and kind, yet practical. "Focus on what you most desire, Claire. Is it Percy or is it Allegra?"

It is always Allegra. Always. And Mrs. Mason is a woman to envy. A woman to emulate. Eventually I forgive her meddling and allow her to return me to Dr. Bojti. I persuade Mary to send my belongings, because I cannot bear to look at Percy and hear his pathetic whining about how he must choose Albee's affection over my own. Then I climb aboard the carriage, and Mrs. Mason waves me away. "Be strong, dear Claire," she calls after me. "Be smart in love."

At the edge of Pisa, I sense a change in the air. Winter is coming, and the temperatures are dropping. I pull out the lovely blue shawl Percy gave me and wrap it around my shoulders and across my throat. I close my eyes and imagine him watching my departure. His head would be bent. His mouth pursed. His hands hanging still.

I open my eyes to see the approach of a carriage, a dark green monstrosity that extends in all directions. Huge and hulking as an earthbound ship, it is filled with trunks and servants and dogs and a massive bed. I blink. Very large dogs and peacocks and parrots and monkeys. In a flash, like a dream, I see a pallid, plumper version of the man I once loved. His head turns. Our eyes meet. I do not stare after him. Let it remain a dream, I tell myself, rather than a bad omen.

The specter of Albee in his outlandish coach haunts me all the way to Florence. Albee is in Pisa, and I am sent away. Oh, the irony. For ten minutes of happiness with the great Lord Byron, I am to suffer in exile. Alone. Again. Without the company of my dear Allegra.

Letters from Mary and Percy increase my suffering. Percy and his mates, the Corsair Crew, they call themselves, are behaving like schoolboys with their pistols and billiards and boats while Mary attends fancy dress balls and dances until dawn.

Dear Claire—

Percy is feeling better since Edward William's friend Teddy has arrived to design his boat. Teddy is quite handsome in a pirate-like fashion; tall and dark and full of stories. I believe you would find him amusing. Percy is hard at work on his poetry and encourages Jane with her music. He gave her a beautiful inlaid guitar for inspiration.
Love, Mary

I am quite good at reading between the lines: Percy has fallen in love with Jane Williams. Such a pathetic choice. All while poor, stoic Mary is missing the brilliant company of literary minds. The smart literary men are too involved with sporting to offer her intellectual stimulation, while the women are hopelessly enthralled with selecting ball gowns. Her new friends Countess Teresa and Jane Williams are no match for Mary's quick mind. My sister, too, is suffering.

To distract myself from what I am missing in Pisa, I go to the Saturday market and stroll through the vendors' pitiful displays. It is too cold, too out-of-season for anything of worth, although I could buy a hen, if I choose. Or a brown-spotted goat. A donkey. Which recalls memories of traveling with Percy and Mary in our glorious youth. My eyes well.

"Miss Claire!"

I spin toward the voice. "Elise?" Could this thick-bodied matron before me be the same pretty girl who dutifully tended my Allegra, the same girl who loved Albee and married Paolo the handyman before leaving her own daughter in Percy and Mary's care?

She speaks with a world-weary tone. "Oh, Claire, it is my pleasure to see you. You live in Florence now?"

"For the moment." I am guarded, recalling Mary's account of Paola's attempt to blackmail Percy, yet my impulse is to embrace her. "I am sorry for the loss of your daughter. Little Elena was a beautiful child, Elise."

"Yes." She picks up an artichoke, cupping it in both hands. "Very sad."

"My Allegra is with the nuns near Ravenna now. Apparently Teresa and Albee lost their patience with her."

"The Countess is to blame, not Lord Byron." Oh mercy, she yet defends Albee. "The Countess and Mrs. Hoppner, the lady who lies."

"How so? What lies did you hear from Mrs. Hoppner? Aside from her claim that I am a bad mother? I heard that aplenty."

"She tells Lord Byron you are Elena's mother. She tells him you and Percy are the parents of my own dear daughter." Elise returns the artichoke to its bin. "As if that babe was never mine."

I am sad for Elise, and angry for myself. "It is unforgiveable that we have lost our daughters, but now poor Percy must take the blame for Albee's child?" I am about to say more about Albee's fecklessness when Elise shifts her attention to another market stall. It is a slight movement, nothing more, but in that moment, a new awareness sweeps over me. I have it wrong. All this time I have been wrong about Albee. "Elise, who was Elena's father?"

Already she is moving away, her head bent and her steps determined. "I cannot say, Miss Claire. Kindly do not ask."

Albee did not father Elise's child. Then who did? The sounds of the vendors and the monkey grinder and the goats and donkeys assault me. Not Paola, obviously. Not Percy. That man would never give away his own flesh and blood. Then I remember my exiled summer in Devon, the summer Percy determined I should end my pregnancy. Suddenly the marketplace noises swell in my ears and all my senses grow numb. No, surely Elise never slept with Percy.

The artichoke vendor tosses a heel of bread near my feet, and pigeons swirl around me, squawking and flapping, and pecking. Dizzily, I back away. It is too late to fret over little Elena's father. Worse yet, it is too late for me to save Allegra. Thanks to the vile gossip of Mrs. Hoppner, Albee believes Percy and I are the parents who gave Elena away without a backwards glance. No wonder he is keeping Allegra from me. Who can blame him?

The depth of my loss hits me like an executioner's blade. *Albee will never relinquish Allegra to me.* I grow desperate. Since I cannot have her, I will leave Italy forever. Bella Italia has granted me no favors, and I am done with her.

I send farewell letters to everyone in Pisa, including Albee. *By all that is holy, pray let me see my child one last time before I leave,* I beg him. He ignores me, while Mary and Percy and Mrs. Mason send letters instructing me to remain calm and reconsider. What sort of life, they ask, do I imagine I could make on my own?

I do not respond. My life as a governess in Florence can be replicated anywhere. I have nothing to lose now, and should Albee ever reconsider, I will return to Allegra from wherever I am. This evening when I make my nightly sojourn to Boboli Gardens, I ask Ceres where I might go when I bid Italy farewell. Holding her harvest basket and waving her bouquet of wheat, she shows no interest in my dilemma. She is too smug for my own small world, but she seems to say *oh, cease dithering and be gone with you.* Which is really all I require for validation. I will pack tonight and leave in the morning before the Bojti family is awake.

I am too absorbed in my thoughts to pay much mind to the beggar sitting under the chestnut tree on the corner. With nothing left to lose, I have no fear, yet I sense him studying my approach from under his coal black nest of hair. All at once, he looms up like a wild beast, his huge hands outstretched and menacing. I scream until he shouts over me. "Claire! Claire, Mary sent me."

I take a closer look. Teddy the Pirate is a tall, broad-shouldered fellow with long black hair, beard, and moustache. His nose is hooked and his eyes are as deep and black as a coal mine, but he is, as Mary vowed, dashing and handsome. "You are Edward Trelawny?"

"I'm here to return you to Pisa, Miss Claire. Your sister is worried."

"I cannot possibly leave at a moment's notice."

"Then I shall wait."

If he were anyone else, I might leave him to wait for the rest of his life. Yet Mary is right, The Pirate does interest me. Teddy is nothing like Percy or Albee, and that arouses my curiosity. And I am prepared to leave.

All the way to Pisa, Teddy tells me his sailing stories, fighting stories, smuggling stories. Names of exotic places roll from his tongue. Bombay. Constantinople. Madagascar. He has been shot and stabbed. He has loved many women. He has worked as a spy and a swordsman.

I am unconvinced of his veracity, but his liveliness is infectious. "I take pride in workmanship," he tells me. "I am the man chosen to perform specific skills. Like building a bridge or shooting an elephant or fetching a friend's sister from hours away." He gives me a wink. "I am building Percy a fine dinghy to transport him to and from shore whenever he is anchored in the bay." His black moustache frames sensuous lips. "I am also a writer. Accounts of my travels, mostly."

A writer. The combination of Teddy's storytelling and his adventures doing the work of real men in exotic places must send Albee and Percy into a fever of excitement. I smile as Teddy comically describes the English society now orbiting the Shelleys in Pisa. The Corsair Crew with their fishing and sailing and pistol shooting. The women hanging at the edge of the smart literary set. "Pretenders." Teddy dismisses them all with wriggle of his moustache. "Except for Mary," he adds. "Your sister is genuine, and when she said she wished to speak to you, I said I was the man to deliver you from Florence. Never thought to hesitate."

I press him for more. "You enjoy the company of poets, Mister Trelawny?"

He snorts. "Lord Byron is the only one who considers himself a poet. Shelley is more a crusader, a man who believes in the power of words. Those other gents simply take advantage. They lord about eating and drinking and speaking in high-minded tones, while your sister is reduced to cooking and cleaning up after them."

I imagine that is precisely how Mary exists among the Corsairs, and I appreciate this honest account by Teddy, the freewheeling pirate. Many stories later, we arrive to find the Shelleys' riotous household has grown quiet. Jane and Edward Williams are nowhere to be seen. Albee has likely slithered across the river to his palace of iniquity. I alone am left to face Mary's furrowed forehead, Mrs. Mason's serene manner, and Percy's stern blue stare.

"Why," he demands, "would you abandon what precious little you have here in Italy to begin your life over again?"

"Where would you go, dear Claire?" Mrs. Mason takes my hand. "You could never take Allegra to England without Albee's past haunting you."

"You could consider America," Percy offers.

"America? The home of Fanny's true father?" Mary leans towards me. "What, precisely, would you do there? Are you mad, sister?"

And so it goes. I allow them to have their say. I promise to remain in Florence. And then, I make a silent vow. *A year,* I promise myself. *I will give Italy another year. If I am not living with Allegra by the time I am twenty and five, I shall flee this country unannounced.*

22. Dream State

I am the errant sister carried off by a pirate and then returned to Florence with a warning to be sensible. Instead, I contemplate Teddy's parting words: *The promise of reward is the only thing to nurture the human spirit.* Allegra is my only promise of reward, and thus I write to Percy, likely distracting him from Jane Williams and her beautiful inlaid guitar, to suggest that we rescue my daughter from the convent.

It seems a *sensible* plan as Percy was the man to plot schoolgirl Emilia's rescue, and, in Harriet's case, to carry it through. *You know the way to the convent, dear Percy, and once Allegra is in my grasp, I will secret her away. Neither Albee nor the nuns will find her. My darling daughter deserves a life outside the walls of her prison, and I will remain forever grateful to you, my dear.*

Despite his demanding schedule of writing and boat-designing and seducing Jane Williams, Percy responds at once to my plea. *Not only is your notion of rescuing Allegra foolhardy, it would eliminate any hope of ever seeing her again. Albee would charge us with kidnapping before the day was done, and Allegra would be sequestered for the rest of her life. Please be patient, Claire. Allow me this winter to convince Albee of our ability to care for his child.*

I am dismayed by Percy's response, and I am wounded by his harsh tone. When would he find time in the midst of his frivolity to persuade Albee of anything? Mary's missives about their glorious days in Pisa do nothing to raise my spirits. *Teddy ordered Percy's new boat, Mary reports, and is completing the dinghy.* Perhaps Teddy the Pirate is a wiser choice when it comes to bold talk and grand actions. Alas, Teddy is devoted to Percy and Mary, and he would report me as a traitor.

Sleep is my only solace. There, Allegra flourishes in my dreams. She runs ahead of me through Boboli Gardens. She laughs at the winter rain and speaks Italian like a native. *I piccoli uccelli marroni. Dove sono, Mama?* She sings as she flies into my arms. *Mama.* I stroke her pale blonde hair, although she is too impatient to remain in my grasp. She chases after a lapwing. Her motions, so quick and decisive, are precisely those of her father's.

I dread mornings when I must wake and traverse my day, and thus, I make my own plans to rescue my daughter. First I will travel to Ravenna. I will hire a coach with a driver as large and forceful as Teddy the Pirate, and he will transport me to the Copuchin Convent of Bagnacavallo where Allegra is shut away.

Over and over, I soothe myself with this scenario. I will see Allegra from afar, her blonde head bouncing as it did when she chased butterflies with Percy. I will call to her, and she will come to me. She will scale the wall or swim the moat or cross whatever horrid barrier the nuns have in place. She is strong and daring, not one to hold back. When she runs into my arms, we will ride away to some civilized land where the seasons are balanced and dark days only promise the glory of sunshine to come. Some place where little girls are not sent away from their loving mothers on the whim of their wicked fathers. This is my plan.

A sharpness now appears in Mary's letters. She offers little hints of displeasure with the great Lord Byron, who orchestrates the social gatherings where she and Percy once presided. Conversations over leisurely dinners apparently feature Albee's sarcastic wit, which wears on the Shelleys' compassionate souls. As well it would. I refrain from comment. Instead I take perverse satisfaction that others are suffering under Albee's grandiosity.

Dear Claire,

We have had an unfortunate occurrence. On our return from the men's shooting outing yesterday, we were confronted by a soldier. A scuffle ensued and Percy received a slight injury. Then Albee's servant stabbed a soldier who likely will die from his wounds. It was truly a shocking event, and I remain stunned that men who are smart and resourceful become useless en masse. Percy shall recover, have no fear, and we expect no charges will be pressed against Albee's servant. Nonetheless, Albee and Teresa have departed Pisa.

I worry this Spring shall be as unfortunate as Spring often is for us. Perhaps when you visit us in April, good fortune shall shine on us again.

Love, M

Poor Mary. I have yet to receive Percy's version of this event, yet I know plenty about his discontent with Mary. *She remains cold and cheerless*, he laments, *so unlike you and I, who enjoy nothing better than to throw back our heads and laugh simply for the sake of laughing.*

Such laughter, I think, will never come again. I walk among the Florentine scenery and envision the incident with the soldier in Pisa. I see Albee, his chin raised as he taunts the unfortunate fellow, his eyes snapping as he challenges him to duel over Percy's perceived injury. And of course it would be a servant to carry out the attack. Stabbing is too intimate an act for Albee.

If I were a truly awful sister, I would respond at once by saying *I told you so, Mary. I warned you of Jane Williams' devious nature and Albee's blindingly cruel streak.* I say nothing of the sort. Not because I am a good sister. Not in the slightest. I say nothing because Spring finds me as morose as Mary. I have lost my spirit. I have lost hope of rescuing Allegra and blame myself for not defying Albee all those years ago at the Villa Diodati. The sole thing in my life I had to lose was Allegra. Why did I care if Albee took offense at my demands?

When I feel able to respond to Mary, I ignore Albee and Percy's altercation with the soldier. *Oh, dear sister,* I write. *I sense that Allegra is unwell, and I am beset with terror.*

By the time I board the carriage to Pisa in mid-April, I am filled with a quiet grief. Somewhere in my wounded motherly heart, I know Allegra is dead. By not fighting for Allegra's living, breathing presence, she is lost to me forever, and I shall never forgive myself.

In Pisa, I spend a week with Mrs. Mason, who always nurtures my soul. "You have done your best for Allegra, dear Claire," she says as she served me a true English tea, complete with potted meat, delicate cakes, and clotted cream. "Even if you possessed a title and a fortune equal to Albee's, you are a woman. Women have little say on how to raise their children, and a woman with a child out of wedlock is looked upon as a child herself."

"I am now twenty and four, and I am ancient. Only Percy offers me mirth."

She frowns. "Please do not think of Percy as your savior."

"Percy has his own woes. There will be no laughter from the Shelleys on this visit."

Although Mrs. Mason disapproves of my relationship with Percy, she does not censor me. She allows me to speak freely and does not flinch when I complain. "I detest being shuttled about like a creature too hideous to be seen in the light of day. Truly, I feel as welcome as Mary's pieced-together Creature. Albee and his Countess are reported to be in Leghorn, yet Percy and Mary are taking new quarters outside Pisa to increase our distance from them. Do they fear Albee will expire at the mere sight of me?" I ask. "Or that the Countess may have an apoplexy?"

In the end, I find the result of all this shuttling to be a complete disappointment. Percy and Mary's cottage on the Sea of Lerici is named Casa Magni, yet there is nothing *magni* about it. Set between the Caprione mountains and a bleak coast, it is miles and miles from anywhere of note, and barely large enough for the Shelleys, let alone the Williams family and myself. We are squashed into the upper floor with a terrace balcony that bravely overlooks the endless sea. The dining room is at the center with bedrooms along either side. Mary and little Percy are on the left, facing the sea, while Percy's room, also on the left, is off the terrace. The Williams brood are on the right and facing the hills, which leaves me the last room, on the right and also off the terrace. My arrival displaces the housekeeper, who unhappily moves to a lower, damper level with the nursemaids. We are a household of discontent.

"You do not worry about being away from civilization?" I ask Mary.

Gaunt and nervous, she wears the bemused expression I associate with her early pregnancies. Her frock hangs loosely from her shoulders. Her golden hair has lost its sheen. Yes, I decide, Mary is expecting another child.

"It is a quiet place for Percy to write," she says, "and we have privacy."

"Even with Jane and Edward?" Truly, how much privacy could there be? I gather little Percy into my arms. "It is a blessing he is such a hearty child."

"He is that." Percy lays his hand across his son's shoulders. "Fit and happy."

I observe his fatherly tenderness with envy. If only, I think. If only Percy had fathered Allegra. "Are you writing, Percy?"

He blinks, his blueness dimming as a cloud scuds over the horizon. "I intend to return to my writing at once. Now that we are settled in, and you are here at last." It is Percy's way of reminding me I am his muse, yet there is something awkward, something odd, in his manner. Perhaps an acknowledgement that Jane is more his muse than I. Never before has Percy been so distant with me.

As subterfuge, he immediately launches into a description of Lerici and the joys of living among fishermen and young Italian families. "We could pass for natives ourselves, is that not so, Mary?"

"Highly unlikely." She turns back to sorting linens, while Percy, left to face me alone, turns away.

It is Albee, I think. Some unsettling news about Albee that Percy cannot reveal to me.

When Jane and Edward return from their walk, they greet me effusively, as if we are long lost kin rather than mere acquaintances. "I hope your journey was pleasant, Claire." Jane is comely in her robust way, all teeth and bones and freckled skin, yet she is less forthcoming than I recall of our earlier times together. Blessedly, there is no prattling about her children's beauty or her guitar playing accomplishments.

"Has Percy regaled you with tales of his new boat?" Edward asks. Unlike Jane, he is talkative, an easygoing chronicler of nautical feats.

Percy continues to be oddly restrained as I watch for sparks to ignite between him and Jane. I watch for evidence of her famous charms as we dine on the terrace. Our simple fare consists of bread and cheese and a bit of bacon.

"Bacon is a rare commodity in this village," Mary says as she passes the platter. "Take an extra slice of bread in its place."

"We shall adjust to our new locale soon enough," Percy assures her. "We shall exist on whatever the natives eat." This from the man who obsesses over his diet and has no interest in bacon at all.

Wishing I was back in civilized Pisa with Mrs. Mason, I claim my day's journey as an excuse to retire at the same time as the children. I listen to them settle into sleep, their murmurs and sighs as soothing as the surf. I watch the sky darken and the lamplight flicker on in the neighboring cottages. Rather like the fireflies of my childhood. Like the night in St. Pancras Cemetery when Percy seduced Mary and left me to fend for myself.

Conversation from the balcony terrace drifts through my window in small waves of words and phrases. Their voices drone, lulling me into troubled dreams of rising water, blazing fires, and discovering my skin covered in large black spots. Like a leper.

I awaken when the voices change pitch. Jane's voice lifts sharply, while Mary's turns tinny. Percy's is high and fast, and Edward's is a steady bass. Something is amiss. Something has gone terribly wrong, and no one wants to tell me about it.

Slowly and stiffly, rather like Percy when he sleepwalks, I rise from the bed and walk toward the voices, toward the flicker of lamplight. The flame distorts their faces and sets them wavering. Their mouths appear to move at the same rhythm, as if they are reciting a chorus. When Jane notices me in the doorway, they fall silent. Even excitable Percy and easy-talking Edward are struck mute. From somewhere out of the night, in an echo of my dreams, awareness strikes me in one hard stroke.

"This is about Allegra," I accuse them. "She is gone, is she not? She is dead, and none of you have the courage to comfort me."

Now they rush to me. Mary makes me tea and buttered bread, and Jane rubs my shoulders until they ache. Edward grows weepy and holds my hand. Percy takes me out on the boat where stars fill the sky and lay scattered in the ocean, and we float through an orbit of quiet.

Their kindness does not matter. I am beyond sympathy and not about to be bought off by pity. I am here to make demands. "Tell Albee I want to see her," I say to Percy. "To touch her. I want a lock of her hair and her miniature. I want to attend her funeral as a family member. Tell him I refuse to be hidden away with the servants in an outer chamber."

At first light, Percy sails away to meet with Albee in whatever fine villa he is presently hiding, and upon his return, he bids me to come aboard. Here, away from the others, there is only the sound of water and gulls. "Do not speak his name," I warn before Percy can open his mouth.

"Oh, dear Claire." His eyes are blinding as he wraps me in an embrace. "There shall be no funeral. Allegra is to be buried in the family cemetery in England. At Harrow Church." He reaches into his pocket and pulls out a small envelope. "This is for you."

Allegra's hair is as yellow as forsythia. A curl tied by a string, like a parcel for a bird. So fair and fine, it could blow away in an instant. I tuck it back into the envelope and take out the miniature. She is smiling and saucy, a look that says *I shall do that if I so wish.* She is whole and healthy and happy. How can I bear to see her any other way?

"I shall treasure this, Percy. Until I die, I shall keep these small remembrances close to my heart and bless you for bringing them to me. As for her father, I shall write to him at once."

To Lord Byron – You deceived me in sending Allegra away to that hideous place. You broke my heart, and you broke our daughter's heart. Thanks to your own arrogant, wicked heart, you killed the only goodness either of us ever had. Now I long for Death. Death cannot come soon enough for us now, Albee. – C

23. The Storm

I sit on Casa Magni's balcony overlooking the sea and pretend to read as I listen to Mary and Jane quibble in the scullery. Since Allegra's death, I despise any blue-sky, sun-shining day, and Jane and Mary's disputes help to distract me. Quietly I listen as Jane persists in her desire to bake Percy a berry tart, while Mary claims there is no pan suitable for such a creation. "Then I shall order my own pan," Jane says. Mary's voice fades away as she retorts something about Percy's diet not tolerating fruit covered in pastry.

I am amused, mostly because their disagreement has nothing to do with me. Also because I notice Percy fusses less about his diet since Jane is around to feed him formerly forbidden foods. He is now known to indulge in meat on occasion, and he resembles the Percy of his youth. More full-bodied and cheerful, he again absorbs himself in his poetry and his solitary walks and his newly arrived boat, which Albee stealthily christened *Don Juan*.

"How can you wander off now, Percy?" Mary offers a daily recrimination. "Claire is beside herself with grief, and we have another baby coming. How dare you treat us so?"

Poor Mary. She hates Casa Magni as much as I do, and we grow weary from encountering Jane and Edward at every turn. After one unusually spiteful outburst in which Mary accuses Percy of treating her like a servant, he responds by ushering Mary onto his boat and sailing out into the bay with her for the rest of the afternoon. There, Jane and I watched them, anchored and bobbing ever so gently until they returned to shore subdued. No longer quarreling partners nor contented husband and wife, yet somewhere in-between.

The ruckus over the fruit tart subsides, and I put my Wordsworth aside to stare out at the sea. Soon I see Percy winding his way home through the pines. He has spent the day writing in the forest, and he appears quite happy. His head bounces in tune to his steps, and I imagine he is singing to himself. One of his songs about Jane, maybe, or he is reciting new verse, editing a word here and there as he walks. The poor man, who can blame him for escaping three quarrelsome women?

Although I have calmed considerably. With Allegra's death came intense hate for Albee, and yet also strange relief. The worst calamity that could befall me is past, and while I am bereft, I am no longer anxious and fearful about Allegra every moment of the day. And, oh blessed release, I am no longer under Albee's control. I am free to say and do as I please. Albee cannot hurt me anew, and Mrs. Mason thinks me mad to remain in this house I hate, to again envelop myself in the confines of Mary and Percy's world.

"They are family," I tell Mrs. Mason. "My sole remaining family." Neither of us mention my brother Charles, who is off exploring the world, or my mother, who would happily re-claim me under certain exacting conditions. "Mary is with child and unwell." I remind Mrs. Mason. "She needs my help with little Percy now." Neither of us mention Jane Williams or why she cannot offer assistance in my place.

As Percy approaches the cottage, he sees me and waves. He doffs his misshapen hat and bows to make me smile. He disappears from my view, and I hear him greet Edward, who rests in the garden after a day of tinkering with the new boat. Then he moves on to little Percy, who walks with his nanny Caterina. When Percy comes upon Jane in the pantry, he murmurs quietly, but her voice is clear. "Mary is napping."

So I become the next one to receive his greetings. His energy, vibrating like wings of a honeybee, precedes him onto the balcony. His face is sun-speckled despite his floppy hat, and his mood radiates pleasure, such a contrast to his demons. "I see Allegra running in the surf," he confessed to me one morning. "It is a comforting vision, but then I have nightmares where Edward is drowning, and Jane is broken and bleeding. I see dead children coming out of the sea."

"We have borne too many dead children, Percy. My nightmares died with Allegra, but I often hear babies crying. We suffer from grief."

"Oh, Claire," he says to me now. "What a mighty spell the forest casts upon me. Not a sound to be heard over the slapping of waves." He spins around a bit with his arms flung wide, and an olive leaf shakes loose and falls from his tangled hair. "You must join me. Perhaps later when the nightingales begin to sing?"

As if such an opportunity exists under Mary's reign. "What of your boat, Percy? Certainly you and the Williams will be sailing tonight precisely as the nightingales sing?" I speak in jest, knowing how anxious Percy is to return to the water. His brand new boat is now being re-fitted with top masts and elaborate sterns to better compete with the size of Albee's boat. Hopefully it will also hoist a new sail that reads *Ariel* instead of *Don Juan*. Oh, the pride of men.

"Soon," Percy promises. "Soon we shall set sail once again."

A clamor rises within the house. Jane dropping her precious tart perhaps. Or little Percy playing with pans. Then an outcry. "Percy! Claire! Come quickly!"

At the doorway to Mary's bedroom, we find a knot of women: Jane waving floury hands, a servant girl screaming, and Mary's ghost, white as a cloud and moaning.

"For the love of God." Percy takes hold of her shoulders. "Mary, what is it?"

She is wide-eyed and trembling. "The pain woke me. The baby is coming. I feel faint." She swoons, and as Percy gathers her up to carry her back to bed, I notice her skirt is stained red. Then I comprehend that the red is blood. A great deal of blood.

As Percy lays her on the bed, a fresh gush of blood soaks through her skirt. "Call for the doctor. Fetch cloths. Order ice." Percy, the one most given to hysterics, speaks like the steady commander of a fine sleek vessel.

We follow his orders. Jane and I fetch water, while Percy calms Mary. The servants are sent in search of ice and a doctor. We dampen cloths. We mop, fan, and murmur prayers. Percy and I have been through Mary's previous miscarriages, although never have I seen so much blood. Never has Mary appeared so lifeless. Her face is without color, as gray-white as the sky before a storm. We are miles from nowhere.

The servants return with ice, but still no doctor appears. Jane hacks at the ice with an ice pick, and I wrap it in a cloth to place on Mary's brow. She jerks away with a moan, and Percy grows impatient with us. "We need ice to stop the bleeding. We cannot depend on a doctor arriving here any time soon."

Jane and I exchange helpless glances. Our history with childbirth involves midwives or physicians, knowledgeable people who act with speed and precision. Not hesitant women raised with little practical experience. Not cowering servant girls who squabble amongst themselves.

Percy raises his searing blue gaze from Mary's face to scream at me. "Claire, bring the ice."

In the scullery, the ice is melting at a rapid rate and filling the washbowl that holds it. With one downward thrust of the meat cleaver, I break off a cup-sized chunk, wrap it in a tea towel, and run with it. Percy, his sleeves tidily rolled above his elbows, moves with the grace of a lover in lifting Mary's skirt and positioning the ice between her legs. The remaining ice, he declares, is to fill the washtub where Mary shall recline until a doctor arrives.

We follow his orders. We splash the ice and melted water into the tub, and Percy lowers the lifeless Mary into it. She jolts upright with shock of the coldness, and again, Percy speaks in commanding tones. "Lie back, Mary. Jane, fetch her shawl. Help me rub her hands, Claire." He keeps vigil at her side as the sun sets and the lamps are lit and the children put to bed. Hours later, when the doctor at last arrives, he declares Mary will survive. Percy has saved Mary with his own bare hands.

At dawn, unable to sleep for my dreams of those who are dead and those who have outwitted Death, I wander onto the balcony. Percy is there, slumped into a chair and staring at the water. Percy the poet, the savior. I slump down beside him. "How does she fare?" I whisper, aware of Mary sleeping nearby.

"She is weak. Very weak." A yawn muffles his words. "She will recover."

I smooth his hair, still tangled from yesterday's foray into the forest. "How did you know what to do when Jane and I were out of our depth completely?"

"I once trained as a medic. When I was young and without poetry."

How odd there is another part of Percy I do not know. Are there other mysteries to be discovered? The notion is very appealing, and I am easily seduced by men with secret depths.

I dare not speak such thoughts at this inappropriate time, here outside the window of my suffering sister. Instead, I speak of another hopeful possibility. "Perhaps your nightmares were foretelling Mary's miscarriage. Perhaps now that we are safely past that tragedy, all will be well. Your nightmares will end, and our summer will be as idyllic as our long-ago summer at Albion House."

"Perhaps," he says, yet when he turns to me, his eyes are a sad shade of blue. Navy rather than sunrise periwinkle. A recognition that another Albion-like summer filled with poems and music and laughing friends and children will never come again.

Mary remains as weak and pale as a clam shell, and the running of Casa Magni is left to me and Jane. Mostly Jane, who has a better sense of order. She herds her children, Medwin and baby Dina, and I tend to little Percy. Three woman and three children living in such close quarters tears at our patience. Mary bravely rises from her sickbed to deal with the bickering servants and inevitably ends up bickering with Jane instead.

"The kitchen girl has misplaced the wash basin," Jane complains.

"The basin is in my room, and there it will remain." Mary's weak condition hones her voice to a sharp point.

When Mary returns to her bed, I take little Percy into the forest, where it is cool and dim. "Your papa cannot return soon enough," I tell him.

"Papa." He smiles his toothless smile.

Percy has been gone a week. Off in the newly re-vamped boat with Edward and their sailor boy to meet the Hunts, at long last arrived in Leghorn and being shown the good life by Albee. A week is a long time to be in our cramped house of competing women, and Mary fears Percy might return with the multiple Hunts in tow. Smart literary set or not, she has had enough company. "Tell them to stay with Albee in Pisa," she warned Percy before he left. "The Palazzo Lanfranchi has more rooms than people to inhabit them." She forgets about Albee's menagerie of birds and dogs and monkeys that likely adorn every surface.

"It is also said to be haunted." Percy laughed. "Poor Fletcher refuses to sleep in his own room. Not that I will let that slip in front of the Hunts."

"Tomorrow," I promise little Percy. "Tomorrow, your Papa will return, and the house will be filled with laughter and tall tales of the sea."

The next day dawns heavy and hot. The air fills with moisture and there is no shore breeze to bring relief. Mary lies abed to save her strength for Percy's return, and in the kitchen, Jane surrenders her plan to cook for her seafaring men. "I fear a storm," Mary says when I bring fresh water to her bedside. "I hate to think of Percy sailing into a storm."

"Percy has the advice of wise seamen to guide him from Leghorn," I remind her. "Including Teddy the Pirate and Captain Roberts, the boat-builder himself. They will insist he not set out in a storm."

"He longs to return to me, Claire. He will not let a storm deter his plans."

Percy knows precisely what awaits him here in this cramped house in the dreary woods: Mary bemoaning her health and Jane bemoaning Mary and me bemoaning the complete lack of civilization. "When, dear Percy, can we experience more than the fishing village of Lerici?" I ask more than I should.

No, given the choice of staying in Leghorn with his literary comrades and sailing through a storm to keep peace among the women who love him, he will stay. Edward, on the other hand, might want to free himself from the company of intellectual men who play at being sailors.

The storm blows through in the late afternoon and sends us scrambling to close doors and windows. "Percy loves the sound of storms in this house, and the way the wind vibrates every wall," Mary says. "What a shame he is missing this one."

"No hope of sailing today," Jane says as rain and sea spray lash the house, seeping in around the edges and puddling on the floor. "They will set out at first light."

We wait for three days in our damp little abode. Mary stays in her bed, and Jane worries aloud. "I see Percy, Claire. I look out at the terrace, and there he stands, staring into the distance. I come out of the bedroom, and he is here, sitting at this table. What can that mean?"

"That he is thinking of us. That he, too, is worried about being away so long." I do not tell her that I hear him calling to me throughout the house. *Clarabella*, he sings to me when I wake. *What a glorious morning.*

A boat bringing supplies from Leghorn reports Percy and Edward did indeed sail before Monday's storm, yet we dismiss such news as unreliable. On Friday, a letter from Hunt to Percy arrives. *How was your homeward journey, dear Shelley?* Hunt wrote.

Mary collapses into a chair, and the letter falls to the floor. "They have been at sea for five days, Jane. Whatever shall we do?"

Against my sage advice that I go in Mary's place, Jane and Mary and one of the servant boys row away to Lerici village to catch the post boat to Pisa, and I am left to manage the children with Caterina. Even in their distress, even with Mary barely strong enough to walk to the rowboat, my sister and Jane are determined to keep me from Albee's presence. I find their protection of Lord Byron to be foolish. How weak a man do they imagine him to be?

I wave to them from the terrace, their two bonnets bobbing like corks against the blue-black horizon of open water. This journey can reap no good reward. If Percy and Edward are adrift at sea or safely wedged into a small crevice of the coastline as Jane and Mary hope, these women can do little more than bring harm to themselves. If the men are lost . . .

Oh, I cannot think of that possibility.

I am well used to being the one left behind with the children, well-used to children growing cross without their mothers to coddle them, yet I can be childlike myself, and that flaw serves me well now. I sing when I put baby Dina down for her naps. I serve Medwin and little Percy tea under the willows, which they find pleasingly fairy-like when I tell them stories about elves and fairies who live in the forest. When at last they fall asleep for the night, I sit on the balcony, my eyes riveted toward the slap of the water for the lantern lights of an approaching vessel. Any vessel. When I retire to my bed, I listen for the sound of an approaching carriage. A single horse. Footsteps. Anything to ease my dread.

On Saturday morning, I begin again, cheerfully ushering children through a long, long day. By naptime, I catch sight of a boat with bobbing bonnets and rush to the shore just as Teddy carries Mary ashore. "Any word, Claire?" He calls to me in his booming pirate's voice.

"No, no word here." I grasp Mary's arm when he sets her down. "You look like death," I say without thinking. "Let me fetch you some brandy."

"Oh, Claire, I am weary. I am wild with fear."

"We are weary of looking at the sea," Jane says. "Our eyes burn from the salt water and squinting into the horizon."

"Captain Roberts has assured us all is well," Mary says. "Yet in Valreggio, we learned the Don Juan's dinghy and water keg washed ashore."

Under ordinary circumstances, my sister would never refer to Percy's boat as the Don Juan.

"The dinghy could have been set free from the boat," Jane offers.

"I saw crosses." Mary says with grim calm. "When I looked into the water at Valreggio, I saw two crosses of light beneath the sea."

The days drag on, and our suffering is exacerbated by a local feast day. There on the San Terenzo beach, the villagers dance and sing long into the night. As if our desolation is a cause for celebration. Teddy's large presence is our only distraction. He tells his tales of fighting wars and pirates, of building boats and fording streams. His loud voice drowns out the festival and provides a contrast to Percy's high-pitched exclamations which we imagine echoing around the house at night. Teddy sleeps on the bottom floor, there on the earthen surface amidst the barrels and ropes and ladders left behind by Casa Magni's owner, and I take comfort in hearing his snores drift upward through our windows and doors.

"I loved Percy Shelley like a brother," he announces one morning. "He was a great man and a great poet, and I intend to find him." With that, he departs, promising to search every inlet and stream between here and Leghorn. He, too, it seems, has given up hope of ever finding Percy alive.

While buying eggs from a neighbor, I encounter a post carriage, and the driver hands me a letter addressed to Teddy from Captain Roberts.

Under the next olive tree, I stop to read the thin parchment. *Two bodies*, Captain Roberts reports, *have washed ashore in Valreggio.*

At one time, not so very long ago, I would have clung to what the letter does not say: only two of the three missing men are dead. Perhaps Percy is yet alive! Alas, I have grown hopeless since Allegra's death. I have lost my faith in miracles. I lack faith that Percy could survive what Edward and the sailor boy could not.

All the same, I cannot bear to bring Mary and Jane such tragic news. I cannot be the one to diminish their hope. I wait for Teddy himself to bring sad tidings.

"I shall take this burden from you, Mary." Teddy cries as he speaks, tears rolling unchecked over his sandy cheeks. He has spent days searching for Percy. Along every dank waterway and shoreline. "I shall grant Percy's last wishes. His death will be as brilliant as his life."

Mary, not yet recovered from her miscarriage and as pale as wax, is too weak to question someone so commanding. To ask, *precisely what were Percy's last wishes, Teddy?*

Instead she insists on seeing Percy's body. "I shall go to him." She rises with effort and reaches for her bonnet.

"Oh, dear sister, he has been in the water for days. You were the one to suggest I not see Allegra," I remind her. "It is a kindness that I now remember her as she was."

Teddy shakes his mammoth head. "You would regret seeing such a great man in his present state. I identified him by the Keats in one pocket and Sophocles in the other."

"You are certain it is Percy?" Mary asks.

"I am. Positive." Teddy takes her hand and swallows it up between his own. "I shall take charge of him now, Mary. Leave him to my tender ministrations."

So she does. We are relieved not to think about a funeral. The days of waiting have exhausted us, sickened us, and we must now find a way to go on living without Percy. The idea is too great for our souls to bear. Without Percy, we, too, will likely perish.

As details about Teddy's funeral plans come to light, I grow weak with worry. According to our pirate commander, Percy wanted a send-off in the style of the Vikings. It sounds very much like something Percy might have said in one brief flash of time when he was out on the water with the Corsair crew. When the sea and the moonlight and his drunken companions glistened with the aura of an ancient conquering tribe. Mary is likely imagining stately orations, with the smart literary set holding forth on Percy's virtues amongst marble columns of the Roman Coliseum.

Instead, Teddy declares Percy's funeral is to be a small intimate gathering of men, Albee and Hunt and himself, around a blazing funeral pyre on the very beach where Percy and Edward washed ashore. Too gruesome for women to either witness or contemplate, too gruesome in the end for either Hunt, who hides in the carriage, or Albee, who swims toward the sun until he himself is burnt and blistered.

"It was majestic, Claire," Teddy tells me afterwards. "The fire burned blue as the glory of Percy's soul flew into the heavens. For as long as I live, until my own dying day, I shall never regret honoring my best friend's last request. Nor snatching his heart from the flames."

"Kindly do not speak of this again. Not to me, and certainly not to Mary. If it were not for Jane's interference in the matter, Hunt would have kept Percy's heart for himself." I shudder at the thought of where poor Percy's heart rests now, although I suspect it is secreted in Mary's writing desk. "Please, Teddy, grant us some peace of mind."

When Mary requests that Percy's ashes be buried next to Willmouse's grave, Teddy is eager to take on that task as well. When he returns to us from Rome, we learn he failed to find Willmouse's grave and instead followed his instincts by burying Percy in the Protestant Cemetery. "I loved that man, Mary. Rather than leave him alone in death, I bought the plot beside his for myself."

Mary is appalled. She now claims she never cared for Teddy, so darkly handsome and flamboyant compared to her fair, daydreaming Percy. "He is the antithesis of Percy," she says with scorn. "He is impossible."

Perhaps he is. For now, I welcome his attention to our practical needs. He packs up Edward's belongings and sends Jane and her children back to England. He closes up the Casa Magni and transports what is left of us into Pisa. He is likely also now responsible for keeping me a safe distance from Albee. I welcome his hulking presence, and I worry what will befall us two remaining sisters without him to bolster us up and move us forward.

Mary is calm, I will say that much for her. Then again, Mary is well used to tragic death. When I think of Allegra, which I do constantly, I imagine her laughing and spinning about with Percy and Fanny and Harriet and all of Mary's dead babies. Despite Percy's disbelief in Paradise, I imagine he lives on. His soul is too immense to reduce to the ashes of a bonfire.

"Now that we are settled here along the Lung'Arno, I will do whatever will give you peace of mind," I say to Mary.

We stand on the terrace facing the river, and Mary shades her eyes with a trembling hand. "The sun is lower in the sky, and Summer is on the wane. I want to have Percy's work in order before Winter is upon us. It seems an impossible task."

"I have done this work for Albee. I can certainly do the same for you and the memory of our dear Percy."

"He was not your Percy."

Even in death, Percy's reputation troubles Mary. To keep peace between us, I do not speak of Percy the man, only Percy the poet. On his poetry, at least, Mary and I can agree. Most of the time. We ready the poems Percy completed and send them to his editor, and, although she is likely tempted, Mary does not alter those stanzas that are less than kind towards her. The Cold Mary poems, I think of them. When she moves on to tidy up Percy's personal history, I speak up. "Percy *was* an atheist, Mary. You cannot disclaim such a well-known fact."

"He was a schoolboy striving to create a stir when he wrote about atheism. Those tracts were nothing more than a lark to him."

I allow the issue to slide. Any student of Percy Bysshe Shelley can uncover the truth for himself. Or herself.

The days grow shorter. We light the lamps earlier each evening and listen to Teddy hammering crates together like he is building coffins. Our time in bella Italia is drawing to a close and neither of us knows where she will go. "We cannot afford to live together, Claire," Mary reminds me almost daily. "I cannot bear the thought of us existing in some cramped bedsit for the sake of maintaining sisterhood."

"Of course not," I say, although living with Mary and little Percy is precisely what I most desire. Surely even a pathetic flat like the one we shared on Church Terrace would be superior to living alone without kith or kin. Even though neither of us has the means to support herself.

Of course there is always Teddy. "Marry me, Claire," he roars in his wild, exaggerated style. "Marry me or you shall die alone!"

In these days of sorting papers and deciding what to do, I come across another page of discrepancies about the truth of Percy's life. "Mary." My voice shakes with outrage, and she looks up from her desk, the desk that likely holds poor Percy's heart. "You claim you were not with Percy until after Harriet's death? That you were a sweet young maiden right up until your marriage?"

"I wish for Percy to be remembered as a good and decent man."

"Percy was a good and decent man. He was the man to rescue us from Skinner Street and take us throughout the Continent and give you two darling children long before he became a widower. How dare you dismiss the most romantic part of your life? How can you be so callous to the memories of little Clara and Willmouse and their father? Think of your own mother's cause!"

In an instant, Mary, my long ago sister of Skinner Street, rises before me. *You are coming with us?* She asked on the eve of our running away. *Did Percy say why we should trouble ourselves with you?* Right now she could be that same indignant sixteen-year-old girl. "I am the widow, Claire, not you. It is my right to protect my husband's legacy."

Every hope for our restored sisterhood plummets like a shooting star.

"Percy wanted his poetry to be his legacy, and he would never disavow his own flesh and blood. You are the one concerned with being good and decent, Mary."

24. Hindsight

At age eighty, I am ancient. I should be dead. Yet here I am living in lovely Florence with my doting niece Pauline. "You will remember my blue shawl, Plin," I remind her. "When the day comes to bury me, you will wrap me in the shawl Percy gave me."

"There will be no burial today, Auntie." She is so like my brother Charles, so rosy in coloring and spirit. "Besides, you will need your shawl today." She takes it off the back of the chair and drapes it across my lap, a balm to my aching knees. "Especially with your suitor coming to call."

"No longer a suitor, my dear. The man has more wives than he can count." I watch her tidy the parlor. Straightening books and papers. Arranging my pens and ink on the desk. "Do you think he and I are too evil to die? Or is living this long a punishment for our sins?"

"You have no sins." Plin dusts off the mantel clock with quick, sure motions. "And if you ever sinned, it no longer matters as you are now a devout Catholic. Your long life is a blessing."

"Then memory is a curse." I start to say more about sad memories and poor vision and creaking joints when a knock on the door sends Plin scurrying. I grasp Percy's shawl and wait for her to return with a man who is more ancient than I. Ah yes, his flowing dark hair is completely grey and a bit thin on top. His luxurious beard is a mass of white curls. He could, I suppose, pass for Father Christmas. His eyes, deep and dark as his soul, look up from under white caterpillar-like eyebrows, and then he smiles. "What a glorious vision of loveliness."

Stiffly bent over, yet exuding the big bold spirit he always carried, he takes two strides and steals my hand, bringing it to his be-whiskered mouth. His kiss on my skin is quite rough, and, oh, so alive. "How divine to see you again, Teddy."

"Same here, my dear Claire." He sits heavily in the nearest chair, his body overflowing its narrow perimeters. "I was certain you were dead."

"For a while I was, but no longer. I am the last sister standing."

"We are the last of the young romantics. The end of a story."

"A story that will live on without me, I'm afraid. Mary conveniently erased me from all written accounts. As a kindness, she claimed."

"Well, by God, I wrote my own story."

I laugh to find him so much like the old boisterous Teddy. Despite his wizened face, he is as mischievous as ever. Evil beings that we are, we laugh together about all those poor dead souls who once regarded us with extreme distaste. The Godwins. Sir Tim and Lady Shelley. The smart literary set. Jane Williams. "I was not a bit sad to send that one back to England," Teddy says. "Jane liked having all the attention. Telling everyone in London that Mary was distant with Shelley in his final days. That she herself was his muse. That he loved her more than Mary. Bah."

"Jane went directly back to London to marry Thomas Jefferson Hogg and spite my sister. Surely she knew Hogg loved Mary. Jane simply wanted to get to him first."

"Precisely." Teddy accepts the tea Plin pours for him, and I notice he favors his left hand. Too many gunshots in the right arm, as I recall. "You know I went with Byron to fight with the Greeks, Claire? Not that I was ever disloyal to you." Tea sloshes into his saucer. "Given some time, you two might have made your peace."

"Oh please. You are not going to spin a tale of the great Lord Byron in some epic battle, are you?" Teddy's tales, true or not, are quite convincing.

"The poor bastard never saw a battle. He rented a house at the edge of a swamp, caught a fever, and was bled to death by too many doctors."

"And thus Albee died young and famous and became a hero and a saint. Does that strike you as fair?"

"I did not care much for the man when we spent time together in Pisa, but I admired his passion to fight for the Greek cause. When I learned about his death, I went to Missolonghi to pay my respects, and his manservant Fletcher let me view the corpse. I saw his tragically deformed foot, Claire." Teddy shakes his woolly head. "Byron had a difficult life, a tragic childhood not all that different from my own, but I *was* the man he only wrote about. I believe my adventures made him ill-at-ease."

"I was in Moscow when Albee died. There he was considered a depraved example of British aristocracy. When my employers realized I was the Miss Clairmont who was once Byron's lover, I was threatened with dismissal."

"I begged you not to go to St. Petersburg, my dear woman. Such a romantic you were, Claire, so determined to vanish into the hinterland. *I shall be governess for the Countess Zoloff, Teddy, not working in a labor camp.* I knew Russia was brutal."

"I thought I would die. I was always cold, always poor, always sick. I believed I would never see Italy again. Perhaps I wanted to die."

"Yet, here you are, and the others are dead."

"I think of them always. Always. And I remember how kind you were to me and Mary after Percy died. How you cared for us."

"I believe I asked you to marry then, did I not?"

"What a disaster that would have been. Mary and I were penniless. We were women completely without means, and you were a man who hungered for adventure, not domesticity."

Quietly Plin slips in and out of the parlor, refilling our teacups and offering us plates of cake without saying a word. "Byron gave you nothing?" Teddy stuffs a date cake into his mouth and chews loudly.

"He gave us some piecemeal work. Out of pity. Or maybe guilt." I shake crumbs from my shawl. "I translated Goethe and was never paid, despite Mrs. Mason's attempt to shame Albee into it. Mary edited his memoirs, only to have Hobhouse and others of the smart literary set burn them as soon as Albee died. Truly, he left us nothing."

Teddy leans forward. "Had Shelley lived, would he be with you now?" Because Teddy is a man shaped from wild imaginings and brutal honesty, I attempt the same stance. "Percy desired me from the time I was a young schoolgirl. He would have stayed with Mary and found a way to keep me, too." I recognize the truth even as I speak. "Why are poets such depraved souls?"

"I have little knowledge of Byron, but I would say Shelley needed both you and your sister. Mary was the Mind, and you were the Spirit." Teddy nods. "Indeed, your sister was a fine woman. Yet she had no sense of humor. 'Tis ironic, is it not, that you and I were the ones to live the lives Mary Wollstonecraft and Percy Shelley championed?"

Mary rises from my memory. Widowed at twenty-four and the mother of three dead babies, she sailed off for England with little more than her one remaining child, Percy's charred heart, and a lock of Albee's hair. My poor sister. While Death turned our poets into saints, Mary and I were left with their sins. "It is ironic," I say, "that even as a proper widow, Mary was known as the immoral woman who came between the romantic Shelley and the tragic Harriet, while I remained the young, conniving girl who ran away with Percy and had a child by Byron. No wonder my sister wanted to re-write history."

"I count it a blessing to be born a man." Teddy runs his palsied hand over his beard. "A woman has no say in her destiny."

"The Shelleys determined my destiny. Percy took my innocence and ruined my reputation, and yet he left a legacy to me and Allegra long before she was born. When Sir Tim died, that inheritance finally came to me. I ceased my wanderings and returned here to this beautiful place where I once despaired. *Era il mio destino.*"

"*Era il destino.* It was fate. A hard-earned fate, my dear." Teddy grasps the chair arms to help himself to his feet. "I must be going, I'm afraid. I have a new wife awaiting me." He looks down at me from his mighty height. "Did I ever tell you what Fletcher said? That Byron mentioned you on his death bed?"

His words stab, quick and sharp. ""I don't believe Fletcher. Or you -- whichever one of you is trying to give me peace."

"You seem peaceful enough, I would say." He takes my hand for a parting kiss. A tender caress of my bony fingers. "I wish you well, dear heart."

I am not so old nor so frail that I cannot walk Teddy to the door and bid him adieu with a wave of my lace-edged handkerchief. Yet when he is gone, I am bone weary. "I shall have a lie-down now," I tell Plin. "Thank you kindly for the tea."

Sunlight falls across my bed, as welcoming as a warm bath, and I lie here in this pool of light, next to darling Allegra's tattered miniature, to rest my racing mind. Teddy the Pirate has stirred up old truths, and I pick through them one-by-one, like beads on my rosary:

Percy and Albee were flawed and vain and quick to use women to suit their needs. Extremely young women, in Percy's case.

Mary was brilliant and Fanny was tenderhearted, and I was impulsive, and when the poet Percy Shelley came to call on us in Skinner Street, we wooed him as only determined sisters can. We knew about Harriet and Percy's feverish, passionate nature, and we used that knowledge to our advantage.

Fanny and Mary were never bold enough to run away with Percy by themselves, yet I would have gone without either of them. Percy was my destiny. Always.

Albee truly loved Allegra. His fatherly pride, his grief, his anguish are spelled out in the letters left by his late sister Augusta. Whatever evil drove Albee to place our daughter in that orphanage and then ignore her was no greater evil than led me to give Allegra to him in the first place. We were irresponsible, self-absorbed parents.

Today before he departed, Teddy turned to kiss my cheek, to whisper in my ear. "Do you have regrets, my love?"

"Oh Teddy, my regrets are greater than a sky full of stars." I did not bother to add that given the chance, I would run away with Percy Shelley and seduce Lord Byron all over again. Surely it is better to be part of a living, beating force than no force at all.

My patch of sunshine fades and cools, and I fall towards sleep or perhaps towards the grave. I always imagined that Death comes for us wearing a top hat and a black satin cape. As if he were on his way to the Opera. Now I realize Death is quite personal. My Death wears a long, rather rumpled, brown coat. A leaf is caught in his tousled brown hair. "Clarabella," he calls out in joy. "Come along with me and be my love." He takes my hand and kisses my cheek and tugs me from my bed. "Our happiness awaits." When he pulls me through the door, I find we are in that summertime garden at Albion House, and I understand that Paradise is the place where one was happiest.

How surprised Percy our Atheist must be to watch us gather here in the garden filled with blossom and birdsong. All of us. The old lovers and jilted wives, the poets and merrymakers and literary hangers-on. Fanny and Mary and our dear, innocent babes. My darling Allegra, who runs into my arms with a joyful cry. *Mama.* Oh, here we are, filled with laughter and verse, conversation and motion.

I take it all in. Yes, here we are, young and beautiful and radiantly in love with one other. The incarnation of Percy's great commune. I turn toward his blue, blue gaze to chide him. "Your belief is disproved, my love."

"How so, Claire?"

"Paradise exists." I sweep my arm outward in a theatrical imitation of Percy. "Love conquers Death."

"Ah yes." He pretends to be surprised. "Love was always stronger than Death. Surely we knew that once, did we not?" He throws back his head in delight, and his laughter trills, rising like a trumpet's call through my dreams of eternity.

Acknowledgements

I first discovered Claire Claremont among the women listed as Lord Byron's lovers in Edna O'Brien's *Byron in Love: A Short Daring Life* (W.W. Norton & Company, 2009). Claire, a teenager at the mercy of literary greats, became a fixation that sent me scouring through biographies of Byron, Mary Shelley, and Percy Shelley for more details. In earlier publications, Claire is there, usually hovering in the background and identified as stepsister to Mary. In more recent biographies, Claire captures the spotlight in sudden bright bursts before missing journal entries from all involved parties wrap her in mystery once again. *Where is Claire now*, we readers wonder, *and could Percy be with her?* It was those gaps, those missing pages, that led to the creation of *Our Hands Are Pale as Milk*, my fictional account of what may have occurred.

For further reading on the Shelleys, Lord Byron, Claire, and Fanny, I highly recommend the following:

--Daisy Hay's *Young Romantics: The Shelleys, Byron and Other Tangled Lives*, Farrar, Straus and Giroux, 2010

--Miranda Seymour's *Mary Shelley*, Grove Press, 2000

--Janet Todd's *Death and the Maiden: The Death of Fanny Wollstonecraft*, Counterpoint, 2007

There is also Claire's own record of her life, edited by Marion Kingston Stocking and published by Harvard University Press in 1968 as *The Journals of Claire Clairmont, 1814-1827*.

THE AUTHOR

A native of Western Pennsylvania, **Sara Kay Rupnik** now lives in Brunswick, Georgia, and Concord, New Hampshire. Her short fiction was nominated for the Pushcart Prize and short-listed for the Sean O'Faolain Short Story Prize. Her story collection, *Women Longing to Fly* (Mayapple Press, 2015) was a finalist for Georgia Author of the Year Award. She holds an MFA in Writing from Vermont College and teaches Creative Writing for the Jekyll Island Arts Association and GoodLife in Concord. www.sarakayrupnik.com

www.ingramcontent.com/pod-product-compliance
Lightning Source LLC
Chambersburg PA
CBHW061803190726
48289CB00007B/2055